WITCH OF ALL WITCHES

TALES OF XEST #4

DONNA AUGUSTINE

1

_____

14 Years Ago

The needle had pierced the skin on the back of my neck so many times that it felt like surely the skin would be a lump of mutilated flesh. "It hurts, Mommy. Can we stop yet?"

She stabbed again with her needle, and I wriggled forward in my seat. She dug her fingers into my shoulder, pulling me back.

"Stop it, Tippi. You know it's for your own good." She leaned forward, grabbing my chin, her dark hair wild around her shoulders. "You have evil inside of you, and if I don't do this, that evil can spread to the rest of the world. Do you want everyone to know what you are? Do you know what happens then? The bad people come and get you."

"But I don't do anything bad," I said.

She let go of my chin, and I turned my gaze away from her. She'd had that look since this morning, the one where I never knew what she was going to do, and I didn't want to find out.

The needle was pushed deeper into the flesh of the back of my neck. I shouldn't have spoken. If I'd sat silently, maybe she would be done by now.

"You don't have to do bad things. It's what you are, what you were made from. You were born from evil." She turned, fiddling with the ink on the table beside her. She paused, letting out a sigh as her movements slowed.

Maybe by tonight, she'd be calm again. She usually was afterward, but it was hard to know how long this part would last.

She turned to me, needle in hand but pausing, as if unsure whether to stop.

"Mommy, I *want* to be good." If she knew how much I wanted it, maybe she'd stop.

"You can't be. It's who you are. I'm your mother, so I will fix you as much as I can, but you must always be guarded because you aren't normal, do you understand?" She dipped her needle again, her movements growing jerky.

"Yes." I sniffed, trying not to cry. She hated when I cried.

"Move your hair. If I have to tell you again, you won't be getting any lunch."

I pulled my hair over my shoulder and clenched my fists together in front of me, trying not to shift. Mommy didn't eat breakfast, and there was never much food in the apartment. If I didn't get to share lunch, my stomach would hurt.

She pressed her needle deeper, and I forced myself to sit still. *Don't think of the stinging. Anything but the stinging.*

A burst of yelling and laughter drifted through the open window, and then the familiar sound of metal squealing against metal as the kids at the playground hopped on the swing set. All the kids in the complex played there, even me. Sometimes when Mommy drank her medicine and got tired, I would sneak out and swing too. I didn't talk to the other kids, but sometimes I'd wave to one or two of them.

"Don't let me catch you playing with them. You know you're not allowed. Do you want them to discover who you are? Do you want them to drive us out of our home after they figure out that you're evil?"

"I won't."

She put down her needle and stared at the ink again. I didn't speak this time.

She cleaned the needle and then covered the small container of ink with the lid, talking as she did. "I'm the only one who will ever accept you. Don't you forget it. Only a mother could love something like you. I'm the only one you'll ever have, and be grateful that I didn't let them kill you at birth."

I watched her move about the room. "I know, Mommy."

She grabbed her medicine off the counter, unscrewed the cap, and sipped from the bottle. "Even your father wouldn't stay, because he knew what you were. He wanted to be with me, but you were just too much to handle. I don't have a husband because someone had to stay with you. I gave up my life for you, so you'd better not complain about anything. I'm the only reason you weren't killed."

I nodded, knowing that she'd take her medicine and fall asleep on the couch soon. I hoped the medicine worked fast this time and that she was better when she woke up. I didn't like it when she was sick.

Sometimes, when she was better, we'd go for walks or color in my books. Sometimes she'd get us popcorn and a movie. She taught me how to play checkers last week, and we played for a couple of hours. She told me how things were going to be like this forever because she wasn't sick anymore. She was going to make more money because she could do things other normal people couldn't do. She was going to buy me all sorts of toys and games, and we'd always have plenty of food. I believed her, but then she got sick again. She *always* got sick again.

I didn't move from the chair, not wanting to draw attention to myself, even when I had to pee, even when I got thirsty, not even to go get Allison, my doll. I didn't dare move until a long while later, when Mommy's soft breathing turned into an ugly snore that meant she wouldn't be stirring.

I got up, stretched my cramped legs, and went to the bathroom. Her head was turned, drool on the side of her face when I came back and laid a blanket on her. I closed her medicine bottle so it didn't spill, knowing it was the only thing that brought peace when she got sick. Then I went in the kitchen and found a can of chicken broth, because Mommy wouldn't be getting us lunch today.

2

Present-Day Xest

A mother walked down the road in front of me, holding her daughter's hand. The two smiled at each other as if they shared some secret. The girl beamed as she looked at the woman, as if she were the sun, the stars, and everything good in the world.

Had I ever felt that way about anyone? What would it be like to trust someone that completely? Never fear that they would hurt you or betray you in any way? That they'd sacrifice their life so that you might survive?

"Did you hear me?" Bibbi asked.

I dragged my gaze away from the scene up ahead, having no idea what she'd said but hearing the urgency in her tone. "Sorry, what was that you were saying?"

"I think we're being followed." There was a sharp edge to her voice, displaying the steel beneath the coiled curls of hair and the frilly skirt with layers of lace she was wearing. In the past month, she'd bought out every frilly frock Bewitching carried. She was a walking conflict, soft and fuzzy on the outside but rock solid with pointy fangs beneath the surface. She'd come a long way from the timid, unassuming girl I'd first met.

"Yeah, I noticed." The group of six witches and warlocks had been following us for about ten minutes already, and my pulse had yet to break its rhythm. The only thing soft left about me was my rainbow-streaked hair, and even that was tugged back into a severe-looking ponytail. My wardrobe didn't have a frill in sight. My boots were steel-toed, better to kick my enemies with. My pants and tops were well fitted, and not in a vain attempt to showcase my lean form, but to avoid giving an enemy an easy place to grab. My jackets shrugged off with ease for the same reason.

Once upon a time, I'd been soft. That was way before I'd been abducted to Xest and dumped in a wish factory for forced labor. I'd been nearly killed by an invisible evil monster, a dragon, and a gigantic bat, and those were just a few of the fun times I'd had since living here.

Turned out that was the easy part of living in Xest. I'd even thought I was turning a corner, getting ready to settle into some calm, boring day-to-day stuff up until about a month ago. That was when a demon and an angel told me I possessed too much magic to be allowed to live. Too much of *their* magic, to be precise, the very seed magic that had helped Xest come to be. Before that, I'd stressed over the little things in life: would I be homeless; would I get kicked out of the broker building again; would Helen, the Helexorgomay machine, decide a black cloud would be the best thing for me?

Those days were over. Something had broken in me after that last visit and looming threat, or perhaps something had been fixed. All the soft spots left in me had melted away, leaving nothing but hard-angled surfaces. There was only one weakness I had left, and it had zero to do with a marauding group of witches and warlocks who hadn't had their mettle tested the way I had.

"Let's duck into the alley." I motioned to the infamous place of one of the worst beat-downs I'd ever received in my life. A normal person would never set foot in there again.

Normal wasn't even a word in my vocabulary, and I was doing my damnedest to evict the word fear as well. In my opinion, this was the best spot to avenge my previous history, the weakness I'd displayed, and leave a better memory in its wake.

"Why are we turning in here? Am I supposed to run? I'm not running this time. That was a bad plan. You looked like hell after that. It was surprising you even lived. And I thought we were done with that anyway?"

I turned into the alley as Bibbi continued to fuss, knowing she'd follow me in spite of her reservations.

"I'm not going to ask you to run anywhere," I said as she joined me. "I think this is a better place to deliver a beating, is all. I don't want to scare off any more of the witches and warlocks in Xest who still might be friendly." It was bad enough that a lot of them crossed the street when they saw me, like I wanted to eat them for dinner or something.

I shrugged out of my jacket as my words sank in.

"Really?" Her face lit up like she'd seen a rainbow for the first time after living in a pitch-black cave for a decade.

Nothing made Bibbi happier than a good meal of chilled revenge.

"Yes. I'm kicking their asses. If you want to hang out and watch, be my guest. But could you do me a favor and hold my jacket? I just bought it, and I really don't want to throw it on the ground or stain it with blood. I've yet to find a spell that removes those stains for good."

She held it up. "I don't blame you. This is a really cute jacket."

There was rustling at the end of the alley.

"Thanks. If you could stand back a bit, too? I don't want to worry about splatter."

"Have I told you how impressive you are these days?" she asked. She folded the jacket over her arm and took a step back. "I'll be right here if you need me." She gave me a thumbs-up. Bibbi was near bouncing with her blood lust, little sicko that she'd become. She was still the best roommate I'd ever had.

"Thanks." She'd told me the same thing at least ten times in the last few weeks. I probably should be flattered, but I was finding that the farther along I got in not giving a shit, the less flattery seemed to affect me, because, well, I just didn't give a shit. After that last incident with Lou and Xazier, I only had two states of being: kill or be killed. Everything else had been muted.

I cracked my knuckles, waiting to see if today would be a killing day. A head popped around the corner and then disappeared.

The alley opening was empty again. What the hell? I didn't have all day for this crap. I had a client coming into the broker office in a couple of hours, and, even more pressing, I needed to have a tea or two first. I hadn't slept that well and couldn't stop yawning.

Maybe I'd bug Mertie to go get me a cocoa at the Sweet Shop. Ever since Gillian had decided to move out *again*, anybody associated with the broker building or the broker himself were cut off from cocoa. *Except* for Mertie, that was, because no one had the nerve to turn down a retired demon.

Although if I managed to time my visit to the Sweet Shop during Gillian's break, her employees were too scared to turn me away. If these losers didn't hurry things up, I wouldn't manage a cocoa or a tea before my appointment. I yawned again, getting more annoyed by the second.

I glanced back at Bibbi. "We should send Mertie for some cocoa after we're done here."

She waved a hand toward the end of the alley. "Which will be when? A year from now?"

I shook my head, sharing her disgust.

"I know you're there. We doing this thing or don't you have the stones?" I called loud enough for my voice to carry past them and to the other side of the street. If I had to wait to kick their asses, I was going to make it that much worse and humiliate them in the process.

The fifth wind was only making me more annoyed. They said you got used to the bone-chilling cold of Xest, but my body must be a slow learner. It'd been months and I still felt the burn on my skin like two hot pokers every time the wind kicked up, which it was doing right now.

I turned toward Bibbi. "They get two more minutes, then I'm leaving. I really don't have time for this."

Bibbi's smile melted. "Really? But they're right there. I can hear them shuffling about." She pointed, as if I couldn't hear their oafish movements.

I understood her need for vengeance on my behalf,

even if these might not be the same group who'd beaten me to a pulp in this very same spot, but it really was getting quite chilly.

A hand slowly poked out and waved. "Miss Tippi?"

Miss Tippi? Bit of an odd way to start a bloody battle, but, I guess, why not be polite about it? If I thought about it for more than a passing moment, I could respect that.

"Yes? Did you want to discuss something first?"

The top of a shaggy head of hair was followed by a big-eyed face and some lean shoulders, but he didn't go as far as revealing his entire torso, as if the partial building in front of him would save him from my wrath. If he had any idea of the weird things happening around me lately, he'd know it didn't stand a chance.

"We were just hoping to have a word with you?" His question ended on an awkwardly high note, the vocal equivalent of showing me his belly.

Was this a trap? Did he think he was going to trick me somehow?

Was a word going to turn into a spell kind of word? A word before we fought? I glanced at Bibbi again, to see if she had a better read on the situation, being a Xest native. Was there some sort of fighting etiquette I'd been unaware of until now?

All I got was a shrug and a pinched face.

I shook my head. This was not the fun I'd expected.

"You're going to have to come closer for that word." My tone revealed my lack of patience.

The person disappeared for a few seconds, and I walked closer to Bibbi.

"I know this is going to be a disappointment, but if this doesn't pick up soon, we're going to have to leave. I was fine for a fight, but I don't feel like standing here and having a damned tea party while I wait for it."

She crossed her arms, shaking her head. "They should get kicked out of Xest completely for behavior like this. This is just embarrassing, if you ask me. This is worse than getting your ass kicked."

"Look, maybe it'll work out and they follow us down the street. I'll beat them up in a different alley." I wasn't optimistic, though.

"Stop trying to make me feel better. They're never going to do it." She held out my jacket to me. "If it's not going to work, I'd rather just go."

She took a few heavy steps before we both stopped and looked at the entrance to the alley.

There were five witches and warlocks making their way toward me, very slowly. I would've sworn there had been six, but clearly one didn't have the guts to make it into the arena.

I stretched my arms, and then my neck, loosening up because it seemed the appropriate thing to do, according to the action movies I'd seen.

The only thing I accomplished was a crick and to slow the group to a complete halt. I let out a sigh, shooting Bibbi another commiserating look. They really weren't worth the aggravation.

I looked at where they'd stopped and shook my head again. "If you want to fight, you're going to have to get a little closer. If you think you can stand back there and use your magic on me, it's not going to work. I'm a lot stronger than I look."

I was definitely stronger than I'd ever imagined I was. If someone had laid out the challenges that would be before me back when I lived in Salem, I wouldn't have left my apartment ever again.

A year ago, I hadn't known what I was made of. I'd never been tested the way I had been this past year. That was the one beauty about tests: pass or fail, at least you knew what kind of raw material you were dealing with. I'd kept surviving, sometimes in spite of myself. If this ragtag crew in front of me thought they could take me down, they'd find out as well.

The lean kid with the slender shoulders began waving his hands, and not in a hocus-pocus kind of way. This was white-flag behavior. Maybe that ridiculously high tone was legit?

"Oh, no! That's not it at all! We aren't looking to fight you," Lanky said.

"No, definitely not," a short little redhead added, peeking her head out from behind him.

"Spells, then? I really don't see that working out for you, to be honest. Not to judge, but none of you appear to be very strong." When I first got to Xest, what seemed like an eternity ago, I hadn't known what magic was. Back then, everyone seemed mystical and awe-inspiring. Now? I could pretty much pick out the minor threats from the little annoyances. It might've been the way they held themselves or it was this weird sixth sense I got. Either way, I'd come to rely heavily upon my first gut reaction.

"No! Not that either. Actually, we were hoping you'd sign something for us?" He reached into his back pocket and held out a book. *Black Unicorns and Other Unexpected Anomalies That Shape Our World.*

Was I an *Unexpected Anomaly*? I'd been called a lot of things, good and bad, but that was a new one.

There was a very loud sigh behind me. "All that buildup and for nothing," Bibbi grumbled.

A few of the witches and warlocks glanced her way with confused expressions.

"Yeah, sure." I held out my hand for the book, and four more appeared.

The grumbles behind me grew louder.

3

Mertie's hoofs sounded through the office on her way to the back room.

Zab tossed his book on the table as Oscar dumped his tea in the sink. Bertha and Musso took a seat at the table. Even Dusty, the rare and elusive dust bunny, became visible.

Mertie walked into the back room with a tray of cocoas that she placed down on the table.

"I'm not sure how I got stuck doing all the bitch work around here, but here's your damn cocoas."

No one blinked an eye at her salty tone. Who would've ever imagined she'd still be here, *and* would be a better fit than Gillian? In fact, Mertie was such a good fit that she'd even started taking on some freelance jobs, doing especially well with anything causing misery.

She'd moved in when things started going downhill in Xest and never left. I didn't blame her, either. The broker building was about the best place to live in Xest. It was the oddest place I never could've imagined. Close to the center of town but far enough away that the street traffic wasn't that bad. The interior was where it got really interesting. It was a weird blend of an old English library and a witches' lair, buried in a bunch of antiquities you'd find in some archeologist's office. And one could never forget to mention Helen's machinery, which took up over an entire wall with gears and wheels and rivets, always humming, whirling, and whistling.

The fireplace in the back room was big enough to stand in, which was good, since Xest was cold enough to freeze you alive. The only thing the building didn't have was good cocoa, but luckily, we still had Mertie.

"Mertie, you have to go because you're the only one Gillian will let in the Sweet Shop," Zab said, handing out the cocoas.

"And why is that? I live here, same as you all do. Why am I not cut off?" Mertie took a seat and kicked her hoofs up onto the chair next to her.

"Don't take it personally. She assumes you hate us. If you told her you liked us, I'm sure you'd get cut off as well." I grabbed my cocoa, and a puff of dust exploded by my feet. "I didn't forget you." I turned back to the table, knowing we'd be living in the dust bowl if there wasn't cocoa for Dusty. He had a two-a-day habit.

Mertie huffed. "As if she'd ever believe I like you people." She reached down, scooping up Dusty.

"That's unfortunately why you'll have to continue getting the cocoas," I said, watching as she let Dusty drink from her cocoa.

Bibbi was sitting silently at the table, not offering a comment.

Zab placed a cocoa in front of her, and we all watched. She hadn't taken a sip of the stuff in months on some sort of principle. It was nicer to say that than that she hated Gillian too much to drink her cocoa. But the way she'd been staring when the cocoas arrived lately, we were all waiting for her to crack. It was going to happen soon. You could practically hear her saliva glands firing as the aroma filled the room.

Bibbi reached for the cocoa, and we all froze. Then she placed it away from her, and we all sighed. Today would not be the day Bibbi cracked.

"Mertie, I appreciate you picking it up for me, but I find Gillian's cocoa has a bitter taste I'm not drawn to."

Musso groaned as he drank his. Bertha, who'd been on the end of many of Gillian's jibes, smirked quietly in the corner.

Mertie tapped the cocoa cup with a long black fingernail attached to blood-red skin. "As much as I appreciate your ability to hold on to hate, which is really quite impressive, and this is coming from someone with vast experience in the field, you do realize you're an idiot, right? That this is just cocoa and not some sort of master war you're waging? That Gillian doesn't give a shit or know if you're drinking it?"

Bibbi raised her chin. "Just the same, I'll pass. I find it to be inferior."

Bertha actually let out a small giggle.

Hawk walked in, the light of the fireplace harshening the angles of his face in a way that shouldn't have made him more alluring but did anyway. A glint of steel that had nothing to do with the color flickered in his deep-set eyes. Had he always been this hard, or did I see him clearer now from a wider vantage point? Strange how your perceptions were colored by the life you'd lived. It felt like I'd seen everything in muted shades of grey. Now I saw every color of the rainbow and some I didn't know existed.

No matter how hard and cold he seemed, I'd felt the heat that raged underneath that exterior, and it was scorching. As hardened as I'd become myself, his heat was the one thing that could melt me on the spot. I wasn't sure if that was an asset or a hindrance, but it definitely felt like my soft underbelly was showing, and it made me want to growl as much as roll over.

I lifted my head, glancing in his direction as I nodded. His gaze met mine, a frisson running between us that felt like it lit the room with a charge. I sipped a little slower, my taste for cocoa shifting into something much more carnal.

I didn't fixate on the way he moved across the room, or the woodsy, fresh scent that made me feel like I was part feral deep down inside. Or the tingle of awareness that spread across my skin and down my spine as his gaze remained on me, even as I shifted my focus elsewhere.

Oscar tipped his head in his direction. "Any word?"

I didn't have to ask what he was referring to. Hawk had been checking with his sources on a regular basis about my angel and demon problem.

The room went quiet, as everyone in the room was aware of the situation. It tended to have a sobering effect on most.

"Tippi, you're quite calm about everything, you know, considering you have an angel and a devil, not on each shoulder per se, but standing behind you, aiming their little arrows and pitchforks." Oscar let out a half laugh, enjoying his description of my situation. He was never one to let an opportunity for amusement go to waste.

It didn't bother me in the least. I'd take a laugh wherever I could get it, especially from someone who'd proven themselves loyal.

Hawk shot Oscar a glance that said he didn't find it overly amusing as he grabbed a seat at the table, a chair buffer between us. When he looked my way, the few feet meant nothing. I would've needed a few football fields to chill the heat in his eyes.

"I don't see what you people are fretting about. There's an obvious answer to all of this, Dread, the imbalance, the demon and the angel." Mertie waved her hand in the air as if it were all so obvious to her.

"Which is?" I asked, wondering what brilliance she'd figured out that the rest of us were too stupid to see.

"Take down Lou, trap him in the hill somehow, and that'll offset the imbalance of Dread. Xazier likes you for some unknown reason, so he won't put up much of a fuss. All good." She sipped her cocoa as if that were the end of it.

"Even if it were that simple, I still have too much magic. That's one of their issues," I reminded her.

"I bet if you take care of Lou, Xazier will be more willing to negotiate," Mertie said with a smirk.

She was right. Xazier would be. And even if she was wrong, it wasn't a bad idea. Although I might've been alone in thinking that. The rest of the room listened without comment, except Hawk, who was now making his distaste known with a glare in her direction.

I didn't care if Hawk hated the idea and everyone else thought it was stupid. I was open to giving anything a try.

"If one were to give this a go, any idea on how to get Lou in the hill?" I asked.

"I can't be the idea girl, the logistics, the executor of said plan, and the one that has to get the cocoa several times a day. You people have to do some of the work too, you know." Mertie huffed, and a small puff of smoke came out of her nose as she crossed her hooves. She stopped suddenly, looking at her left hoof. "Oh, well, that's *great*. Now I chipped a hoof. I just painted them and they're *ruined*." She got up and stormed out of the room, stomping and complaining the whole time.

"It doesn't matter who wants to kill her. Tippi can live through anything. She's tough," Bibbi said.

Oh no. Oooooh no. How could I have forgotten?

"You should've seen her luring a group into the alley so she could kick their teeth in without an audience," Bibbi continued.

Hawk looked over at Bibbi. "Really? That sounds like an interesting day," he said.

By the avid attention around the table, it was clear there would be no one saving me with an interruption. Bibbi was better than Zab was with a secret, but only if you made sure to instruct her that it *was* a secret. That was what I got for being distracted by cocoa. There were no freebies in life. That cocoa was going to cost me an earful later.

How many times had Hawk said in the last few weeks to keep my guard up? That anything could be a setup? I'd lost count, as I'd gone deaf to all the warnings after a while, but the count was way up there, all the way up with goodies like "make sure you floss" and "wash your hands after you go to the bathroom."

Hawk's attention appeared to be solely on Bibbi as she told the tale with great fanfare, and, of course, embellishing where needed to make it more entertaining. This would lead to one of the things I'd been avoiding the most in the last few weeks, and that wasn't a demon or an angel or a fight. I could do all three of those things standing on my head while simultaneously playing the bongos. What I couldn't handle was the man sitting a couple of chairs over who was going to want to *discuss* things with me.

He was my kryptonite, the one thing left that could slay me emotionally and mentally, and I hadn't quite figured out how to defend myself against him yet.

Although I had some time, as Bibbi laid out all the sordid details of my bravado, knowing I'd single-handedly be paying a fee for the entertainment after the show was over.

4

I'd dodged a bullet. Right after dinner, Oscar pulled Hawk away to some unknown location before he could start questioning me directly. That didn't mean I wasn't going to catch some shrapnel, though.

Bertha and Musso made their way over to me. When they came as a duo, it wasn't usually that pleasant. Then again, it wasn't altogether bothersome, either. They'd say their piece. I'd act remorseful because I felt too bad ignoring them, and then they'd move on, feeling like they'd put the situation to rights or, at the very least, done their best.

Musso cleared his throat, taking the lead this time. "Tippi, you're taking an awful lot of risks."

I'd noticed that they tended to alternate who was the heavy. They might be keeping track, or maybe they had a natural balance in their relationship.

Another weird thing I'd noticed was that I was "kid" when Musso was solo but "Tippi" when he and Bertha felt like I needed a talking to. If they thought using my given name was going to fix me, there really was no hope. Still, I couldn't have them going to sleep thinking that they hadn't done their part in saving me.

I sat a little straighter and nodded. "I know you two are upset and concerned by my actions, but Bibbi made it sound a lot worse than it was. I wasn't in any danger. I knew that group was only looking to talk. They'd been smiling and laughing. I played it up because Bibbi gets a kick out of a little drama."

Musso hummed. I could tell by the slight twitch of his mouth that he wasn't buying my story, but he was staying quiet, waiting for Bertha's verdict. Bertha was fidgeting with a bracelet she always wore. It had been a gift from Musso decades back, and it was better than a mood ring.

"If you say that's how it happened, all right," Bertha said, not looking sold either. "But I'll have your promise to be careful in the future."

"I'll do whatever is needed." I smiled, letting them fill in the blanks however *they* needed.

"Okay then. We'll see you in the morning." Bertha and Musso left, looking content with themselves.

Bibbi came and dropped onto the couch beside me. Zab took the seat opposite.

"Really?" Bibbi said. "You know your voice carried out into the office, right? *I* needed drama?"

Zab was laughing so hard that his eyes were tearing.

Bibbi threw her knotted-up knitting at Zab. She'd been working on it for months, and it had only gotten worse. It was unlikely the toss had done any more damage to it.

"If you hadn't told everyone, I wouldn't have had to use you. You know you have to throw them a sacrifice or they never stop."

"You didn't tell me *not* to. It was a very entertaining story, so of course I'd repeat it. How was I to know?" Bibbi asked before pulling out the latest gossip rag she'd gotten imported from Rest.

A client had left one in the office and she'd been hooked ever since, striking deals to get a steady supply.

"Holy smokes. Did you see this?" She pointed to a picture of an actor I'd never been a huge fan of but who was widely popular back in Rest.

"They're saying he had an affair with someone who was housekeeping," she said. "Can you imagine? How is that even possible? They're so small. He must have killed it."

Zab started laughing again. I gave him an elbow as I explained, "The cleaning crews there aren't tiny fairies. They're other humans."

She went silent, her mouth forming an O before she nodded. "That makes a lot more sense."

"Why do you like those?" I asked.

"I don't know exactly, but I can't seem to stop reading them. They suck me in."

The back door opened and Hawk and Oscar walked in, heading over to where we were sitting. That meant it was time for me to go to bed.

I got up to make tea to take with me, not paying attention to the rest of the room, and when I turned around, Hawk and I were the only ones left.

His eyes were focused on me. I swallowed hard, feeling like something small and furry with an urge to dash across a field. In the space of a few minutes, I'd gone from the badass, ready to take on both heaven and hell and an alley full of witches, to a creature of prey who might have a heart attack if the lights didn't move away.

Something hadn't just changed with him—it had changed between us, and I couldn't quite say what that thing was, except it was different. *Very* different.

Bibbi had sworn he'd declared for me, and now I was beginning to wonder what exactly that entailed. I felt a little like I'd been entered into another contract but no one noticed I hadn't signed on the dotted line.

At each turn, it seemed he was making his interest clear. The clearer it became, the more unsure I grew.

Living in Xest was akin to developing sea legs. It had taken me a long while to feel like the ground was steady beneath my feet when a rogue wave would hit and knock me on my ass again.

I pushed away the feeling of being prey as I finished brewing my tea, trying to pretend I didn't feel his stare, his intensity filling the room until it stole the air from my chest. Being near him was like standing next to a live current, the sizzle of electricity coursing all around, impossible to ignore. The closer he got, the higher the voltage.

His steps sounded behind me, and then his hands landed on either side of the counter, his front brushing my back as his arms caged me in. His woodsy scent and heat worked together to melt every cell in my body to instant mush as a thrill shot straight to my heart, throwing its beat from a fast fluttering to the thundering hooves of a racehorse.

He dipped his head down, his jaw brushing the side of my cheek. The ever-present shadow that clung to his jaw grazed my flesh as he spoke close enough to my ear for his breath to send a shiver through me.

"I know you think you're invincible, but you need to

show a smidge of caution. You never know if you're walking into a trap."

I spun, putting a little space in between us with my movement.

"I had it under control." Weird things had been happening around me lately, things I didn't like to think about, or talk about, or even believe. But I wasn't the girl I used to be. I could handle things better now, even if that meant hurting someone.

"I know that things have been different, but that doesn't mean you can always handle things."

He leaned closer still. He stared in that way that made me feel like not only could he read my mind, but hear the rapid beating of my heart, which only seemed to join the races when he was there.

I attempted to hold his stare and, at the same time, not look at his lips. That was hard, considering they might be the most perfect shape ever created, with enough fullness to look soft, but not so full that they clashed with the hard angles of his face. Sometimes all I had to do was look at him and I went breathless. If he wasn't so basely carnal, being close wouldn't be an issue.

"You'll have to trust that I can handle myself," I said, before clearing my throat, trying to rid it of the raspy sound that had nothing to do with him.

That day on the hill, when I'd sapped nearly every ounce of magic I had to trap Dread, something weird happened. When I was thrown off, I'd gotten a little surge on my way out, a gift of sorts to keep me going so that I could survive the ordeal and live to fight another day.

Something had shifted in me, and I couldn't quite say what or how, but I felt it. Magic was a very personal thing, and everyone had their own recipe of sorts, their own taste. If I'd been banana bread before the hill, now I was spicy banana bread with walnuts. Still a dessert, and by all definitions the same dessert, as long as you looked past the kick of spice and the extra crunch. Somehow, nearly dying on that hill had made me *more*. More of what exactly was yet to be determined.

He dipped his head closer, and I looked down, afraid of what I might do if he pressed me farther.

"You had no idea what they wanted when they followed you, and you went into that alley anyway. Yet you keep trying to dodge me? I'd start to wonder why you didn't want me, except that I can feel your reaction when I touch you." He ran his hand along the column of my neck.

That beginning tingle of worry that this was about to go exactly where I'd been avoiding turned into a blaring alarm. I was about to jump on top of him if I didn't throw a wrench into the situation, pronto.

"Actually, I'm glad we have a moment. I think Mertie is onto something. I'm going to call Xazier for a meeting."

"I don't think that's a good idea." He straightened, dropping his hand.

His jaw shifted, and I knew I'd achieved my target. His heat had turned from passion into pure anger. Now he only wanted to kill someone. I'd done a good job, since he probably wouldn't kill me, and even if he did, it would be an easier death than a slow one from the emotional devastation he might reap.

I was about to slink away when he said, "Oh no, I'm not letting you use that trick again."

Oh shit. He'd caught on to that trick?

He grabbed my waist and hoisted me onto the counter in front of him, where I was forced to look at him.

"Why is it that you can lure a group of witches that

might want to kill you into an alley but you run from me like I'm the one who might hurt you?"

Now that was a good question. Why did I? Was it because I'd already started falling for this man more than once and gotten burned? No one liked a burned banana loaf, all bitter with an ashy aftertaste, especially not me.

Maybe it was because I was so unsure of who I was that it was hard to know how I fit with anyone else. Or if I did let this escalate, to whatever that place might be, who would I end up being? I didn't even know which question needed answering—or maybe it was all of them. What was blazingly obvious was that every time he managed to nail me down to one spot, the way he was now, there was an overwhelming surge of feelings that I couldn't begin to sort out.

He shifted his hands from my waist to my hips, squeezing slightly. I didn't think he realized what he was doing, but every part of me sang in awareness.

"I'm not using any tricks and I'm not avoiding you. I thought we were going to be more open and discuss things? Isn't that the talk we had?"

Had we had that talk? It sounded familiar, but he had this sneaky way of distracting me with carnal thoughts while he was discussing other matters.

"The only reason you decided to discuss it with me was because you needed a way to deflect."

As much as Hawk's intelligence drew me to him, it simultaneously made me want to wrap my hands around his neck and choke the life out of him. That was unlikely to happen, as I couldn't even muster up the strength to walk away from him if I wanted, evidenced by me now sitting in front of him on the counter and not putting up a fight. When he was close, I was a jumbled-up mass of emotions, not knowing which way I wanted to turn.

He shifted his hands to my legs, the ones he'd stepped in between. Did he realize his palms were splayed on the tops of my thighs? That they were inching up slowly and I was painfully aware of every tiny move they made?

"Are you feeling okay? Your breathing sounds a little erratic."

"I'm fine." My breathiness was back twofold.

The back door opened, drawing both our gazes as Oscar walked in. He took one look at us and rolled his eyes. If he found it unsettling, it wasn't enough for him to leave. No, he headed for the couch instead.

Hawk met Oscar's stare. Oscar shrugged and then gave a slight nod.

Clearly something was afoot here, and I was out of the loop. On a normal day, I might care. On this day, in this moment, being on the outside of this circle was a godsend.

"Looks like you have other business to attend to," I said, hopping off the counter.

"Oh yes, he does," Oscar added from across the room while he grabbed a handful of Bertha's sprinkled rounds and tossed them in his mouth one after another. Oscar was like watching a ten-year-old, always seeking out amusement of some sort and usually finding it.

"We will be finishing this," Hawk said.

I knew he wasn't talking about the discussion.

5

"**D**o you love it? I just *had* to have it."

Bibbi spun around, her face lighting up as the skirt of her new dress swirled.

As I watched her, it hit home how I'd never been that girl. Never, not even as a child. I'd gone from terrified and hiding, to running, to what I was now. And what I was now? It was miles away from who Bibbi was. A streak of red-hot jealousy bit me in the ass. I wondered what it would feel like to get joy from something as simple as a new skirt twirling in the breeze.

Two Middling witches from around town passed us, looking down their noses at Bibbi's antics, as if they were so above such a simple act of pleasure. As if they weren't as jealous as I was over being able to get joy out of something as simple as a pretty dress.

They continued on their way, keeping their distance.

"What's wrong? Why do you have that face?" Bibbi asked, looking up from her skirt.

"No reason. I thought I recognized one of them from the factory, but I don't think it was who I thought."

I watched as they continued away from us. One of them took a last glance over her shoulder at Bibbi, who was back to half twirls.

The Middling witch said something to her friend, who threw her head back and laughed. Assholes. I wished they'd hit a patch of ice and fall on their asses. See how funny that was.

Oh no. I hadn't just thought that. Nooooo!

It was okay. I didn't hear any screams. Nothing had happened. It was good.

Bibbi stopped twirling. "Why do you look like you just swallowed an egg or something? Did you know those witches?"

"My stomach felt weird for a minute. It had nothing to do with them." I waved my hand as if to shoo the idea away, refusing to turn around and look at them again.

A yelp was followed immediately by another.

Oh no. Not again. It hadn't been a full flick of the wrist, and I hadn't even waved at them.

There were more yelps, and they had Bibbi's full attention.

"What's wrong with them? It's like they don't know how to use their feet or something," Bibbi said.

As much as I didn't want to look, I had to. Plus, the damage was done.

The Middling witches were both on the ground. They got to their feet and fell again.

After the witches fell yet again, they both began crawling away from the spot, but they slid back. It was as if they were on an incline that couldn't be seen.

"Maybe we should go help them," Bibbi said.

"Nah, I think they've got it under control." I took a few steps backward in the direction of the broker building.

It was getting so I couldn't go out anymore. When I was ready for a fight, I got asked for autographs. When I was trying to keep things calm, stuff like this happened.

"They don't look like they're doing too hot." Bibbi was still watching.

I continued to put distance between me and my latest victims. Getting closer would not fix the issue. It might only make it worse. They might end up with... Oh no, I wouldn't even think about it. If this was like some of the other times things went screwy around me, it would wear off once I was farther away—hopefully.

"They're fine." I reached over, grabbing the fabric of her jacket to get her moving. "Come on, I'm dying for cocoa."

"Are you going to get Mertie to scare some cocoas out of Gillian? Mertie won't do it for anyone else. Zab asked her, like, five times the other day, and she kept pretending she couldn't hear him," she said, completely oblivious to the two witches still falling all over themselves.

"Yeah." I would've said anything to get her away from this spot. Too many people were noticing the floundering witches. My proximity to the odd events would eventually be noticed.

I FLIPPED THROUGH ANOTHER BOOK, looking for an explanation on how I might've caused those witches to get stuck on the ice, without having said a spell or with any real intention to hurt them. Certain things could be done with a flick of a wrist, but so far that seemed to be limited to lighting a fire and trivial things.

I couldn't find anything that would explain today. Or what happened last week, when I saw that warlock who sneered at me. He was walking along like normal and then his hat slipped over his eyes and he fell. And then he couldn't seem to get his hat off his head. A couple of days prior, I happened to see Gillian as she was walking into her shop, her arms full of chocolate-making supplies. The door, which typically opened inward, opened the other way, as if trying to hit her intentionally. It wasn't a violent slam. It was as if the door was poking her antagonistically, until she dropped the items in her arms and her face was covered in cocoa. She'd turned my way, as if I'd done it. I'd been iffy on my guilt at the time. Not quite so uncertain anymore.

Hawk walked in the back. I closed the book, tucked it under the throw blanket, and grabbed Bibbi's gossip magazine. I should've taken the book upstairs, but after the fifth dead end, I'd settled onto the couch to scan them. Plus, I'd begun to think Hawk wasn't coming back tonight.

Now he was settling onto the couch opposite me. It would've been better if he sat on the same couch, because then he'd at least be looking in a different direction, instead of my way.

Just like that, I was the furry little creature in the open field. Only difference was that I wanted to get attacked. The room seemed extremely quiet, but it wasn't because he'd muted anything, as I could hear the distant wind blowing and the creaking of people moving overhead. I could also hear myself swallow, my heart pound, and my breathing go nonexistent as I tried to pretend I didn't want to gulp down air.

There was the slightest lift to the corner of his mouth and a knowing gleam in his eye. Suddenly I had tunnel vision. That was all it took, and I couldn't seem to pry my eyes from him.

"What?" I said, taking the offense before he could shift this into more dangerous territory.

He unfolded himself from his couch and moved to mine. I was wrong. Across from me had been much better.

He pulled the book out from under the throw. "*Minimalist Magic*. Interesting."

"Just trying to catch up on all the stuff I missed growing up in Rest."

"Do you need help?" The testosterone pouring off him seemed to be offering more than magical tutoring.

"No. Did you want something in particular?" I asked, forcing my attention to the magazine, anywhere to not look at him.

"I heard an interesting story today about some witches getting stuck on ice. Seemed they couldn't get up for a good hour, even with help."

"Bad luck, I guess. Just a fluke accident, I'd imagine." An hour? He had to be exaggerating. Or whoever he'd heard it from had been. People loved to make things bigger. It had only been a little ice patch. How could they not be able to get up from an ice patch just because of a little unintentional magic? It couldn't have been *all* me. I hadn't used a spell. I didn't know a spell for that. I'd pored over every book in this place—and that was quite a collection—and not once did one mention anything about spells that didn't actually *use* spells. I couldn't have just thought that into existence.

"Very. That's what everyone else was saying. A few people thought maybe it was a leftover patch of darkness left from Dread." He nodded, not looking at all convinced.

"Oh, yeah, that sounds plausible." Dread? Something I

was doing was being linked with that evil? I had gotten that surge after I got him trapped in the hill. Could it be that I had some of his magic in me now? If Hawk didn't have his eyes trained on me, I would've gotten up and vomited in the alley.

"If something is wrong, you can come to me."

Yes, and tell him that I was walking around unintentionally hurting people? That I might have some piece of evil in me? Not likely. I'd figure out how to get rid of it myself.

"Thanks, but I'm good. I'm really tired. See you tomorrow." I got out of there before this conversation turned into something completely different, and I lost control in an altogether different way.

~

I WAITED until the building had gone quiet before I padded barefoot downstairs. I grabbed a chair and swung it around, sitting cross-legged in front of the mammoth machine that was something much more than metal and gears. It was infused with magic and some sort of sentient being.

Helen's machinery churned, whirling and picking up speed, as if to signal she'd been waiting for me, as if she knew I'd been waiting all night to talk to her. Whatever she was, I didn't doubt her knowledge.

"I'm guessing you know about the weird stuff that has been happening lately." I rested my arms on the back of the chair and dropped my chin on them.

Her whirling sped up and then dwindled.

"I know. There's always something weird going on

with me." I talked to Helen so often that I was starting to discern what her noises meant, or imagined I did. If I guessed wrong, she wasn't shooting out a slip and telling me so.

She made a short squeaking noise, trying to hurry me along with my story.

"Sorry. So, I saw some witches not far from the square, and they were laughing at Bibbi and really making my blood boil. I didn't do anything, or say anything, but they ran into some problems with an ice patch. It was one of those weird things that keeps happening lately."

She replied with a short burst of grinding.

"Yeah, just like the other times, but I was so careful. I tried not to focus on them, and I didn't intentionally motion toward them."

She whistled and then churned a bit.

"You're right. Maybe it wasn't a big deal, or wouldn't be for someone else, but my magic never used to hurt anyone. Ever." Even when it was inconvenient, there had been a comfort in knowing it wouldn't harm anyone. As frustrated as I got at times, there'd been a safe feeling in knowing that, deep down, my magic was good. Now it wasn't. Had I gotten some evil magic in me, or had I somehow twisted it because of something I was?

Helen gave me a sound that could only mean one thing: *Screw 'em. They deserved it.*

Had the punishment fit the crime? Who was I to dole out punishment, anyway? Someone who'd been catty herself on occasion. Either way, it wasn't as if I could browbeat Helen into saying I was guilty if she didn't want to. I wasn't sure I could browbeat her into doing anything at all. My conscience was looking for a guilty verdict, but I wouldn't get it here.

"What if I do something really bad without meaning to?"

She whistled high and then low.

"I know you don't think I will, but what if you're wrong?" Before I'd even finished the question, I knew what she was going to say. I held up my hand. "I know. You're Helen. You don't make mistakes." I got up and laid a hand on her machinery. "Thanks for listening again."

I really hoped she was right. If she was wrong? I didn't want to think about it.

6

I had my feet kicked up on my desk, ignoring all the comings and goings around me. Business was booming these days, and I wished they'd all go home. I needed mental clarity, and my mind was being cluttered with all the nonsense and gossip these people couldn't stop chattering about.

Finnary, the witch in front of me, had signed a contract fifteen minutes ago and was still sitting at my desk. She was getting paid very well to make sure some ditz got a job over in Rest, but instead of taking her pay and leaving, all she did was talk about so and so being snubbed by some Miss Hooty Tooty at Zark's last night. I nodded, making uh-huh noises as I deemed appropriate, since one of the keys to this job was keeping a steady supply of talent coming in.

This job required a niche, and I wasn't sure what mine was. Zab's situation was easy. He was liked universally because he was...I don't know, just lovable? Musso was a completely different animal. At some point, long ago, it must've become the thing to get a grunt and an eye roll from him, since it seemed to be almost coveted. Hawk never dealt with anyone directly, for obvious reasons. As for me? I was still figuring out my place.

"Tippi, are you listening? Don't you think that's the craziest thing *ever*?" Finnary asked.

"Oh, most definitely," I replied, with only a vague clue of what she'd been saying a second ago. I might have to find a different niche. The friend—gossip companion—was not going to work out for me. I'd been personally run over by the gossip train so many times that it had burned out my taste for it completely. It was like eating chicken the day after you'd gotten food poisoning. It was a hard swallow.

Finnary was huffing as she stood up, and I belatedly realized she'd said something else. She shot me an annoyed look on her way out. I might have to be the broker who negotiated really good deals from now on. Maybe that could be my niche?

I got up, heading into the back where it was quiet enough to complete a thought. It was the same thought I'd been dwelling on all day, and nothing seemed to be clicking. Something was different about me, had been ever since I'd lured Dread into that hill. What if I did have too much magic? What if Xazier and Lou were onto something? What if I was unsafe now? What if I did something really awful? Was feeling Xazier out, as Mertie suggested, really such a bad idea? If there was something wrong with me, maybe I'd be able to pick up some sign from him. If not, an alliance against Lou wasn't the worst outcome.

I waved a hand at the fireplace, looking to take the chill out of the back room as I sank into a chair in front of it.

I curled my legs up and used my fist to prop up my chin, staring at the flames. The relative quiet of the back room wasn't helping me get my head together.

The back door opened, and I sensed Hawk's magic as soon as he entered. That was another weird thing that had been happening lately. I used to sense him on some deep level, feel his stare, smell that scent that gave me a heady, blissful feeling. Now? I could feel the tingles of his magic before anything else.

He walked over and leaned an arm on the mantel, staring down at me. Hawk was impossible to ignore, no matter how hard I tried. How long was he going to stand there and stare at me like that? As if he had the key to all my thoughts. Well, he didn't. He might think he was clever, but he wasn't psychic.

"Don't." That was all he said. Nothing else because nothing else was needed. I knew immediately what he meant and because it was the only thing I was thinking of.

The single word sounded like a command and grated on every nerve. Although it might not have been meant that way.

I narrowed my eyes, giving him a look that said I'd do what I wanted, whether he agreed or not.

He raised a brow, as if to challenge me.

Why had I bothered to give him the benefit of the doubt? Of course it had been a command. I'd simply set him up to fail thinking it could be anything else.

"There aren't a lot of options. We need him. Divide and conquer." I uncurled my legs, just in case I needed to make a hasty exit. His style of manipulation these days was scarier than a sucker punch, and much more effective.

His eyes zeroed in on my movement, and I thought I

saw the tiniest beginnings of a smirk, as if he knew he'd already won the battle.

I shot out of the chair and went over to the counter, feigning the need for tea. We'd see who'd win this round.

He didn't follow me, but that meant nothing. He could move faster than any person I'd ever seen. I couldn't let my guard down. He might be giving me the illusion of distance, but every action he did needed to be analyzed for ulterior purposes.

"If that is the plan you're set on, why Xazier? Why not try Lou first?" He straightened, as if he were going to cross the distance, and then leaned again, as if simply getting more comfortable, as if he were screwing with me.

"Because we both know Xazier is the easier target."

"Because Xazier might've had a personal interest in you?" The muscle in his jaw flexed as he crossed his arms, the sinew of his forearms on full display as his t-shirt stretched over his broad shoulders.

He might be the only person in Xest who could walk around in a t-shirt and not freeze to death, besides Bautere, who didn't count. I still wasn't sure if Bautere was more polar bear or man, but either way, that had to do something for your coldness tolerance.

"Xazier has no interest in me, other than how much he can use me. I'm not delusional. But yes, any kind of interest might help." If anyone should be upset about having to interact with Xazier, it should be me. Every cell in my body recoiled at the idea of playing nice with him. "Nice" might be pushing it. I'd see how civil went. Or businesslike. That should be enough.

"It's not a good idea. Do you really want to call upon someone from hell and open up some sort of negotiation?" Hawk asked, as if I couldn't possibly say yes. That if

I said yes, the mere word would proclaim my intelligence as so low that I wouldn't even make it onto the standard deviation. I'd be hanging off the chart somewhere, floating in the abyss of too stupid to live.

He could think whatever he wanted. He might not understand it, but it was a plan of sorts, which was something he'd yet to offer up. All he did was run around and disappear with Oscar.

"It's not what I want to do. If we're going to get picky about it, I haven't wanted to do most of the things I've done. I didn't want to fight a giant bat or kill people, but it happened. Now, this needs to happen." I leaned against the counter, shrugging a shoulder as I gave the best *it is what it is* vibe I could muster. I buried my own distaste at the idea so as not to fuel his already raging inferno of contempt.

I walked toward the back door.

He stood silently.

He could glare all he wanted. It had to be done. We didn't have a plethora of other options available.

I was a few feet from the door.

Hawk took a few steps toward me, and I knew what was coming next.

I opened the back door, taking a small step outside, and said, "Xazier," knowing the fifth wind would deliver the call.

Hawk growled from across the room as soon as the name left my lips. Seemed we were destined to be on opposite ends of every argument.

"Did you do that because you wanted to call him or because you wanted to avoid me? Is there anything you wouldn't do to avoid intimacy?" he asked.

"I don't know what you're talking about."

"Why are you so scared?" he asked, staring at me. "Why do you keep running so hard and fast?"

I dropped my gaze. Maybe because he'd never been so determined. Before, Hawk was some hot and unattainable man that was always a few feet too far away. Now he was hot, wanted me, and might still be unattainable even as he stood right in front of me. What if he had me one night and never wanted me again? Then what? It wasn't like I'd had a successful relationship in my life. Then would I be stuck here with him as he eventually moved on? And he would. I knew it in my gut. He wouldn't want to stay. I was meant to be alone in this world.

"I have absolutely no idea what you're talking about."

"Really? No idea?" His brows rose.

"No," I said, shivering slightly as a gust of fifth wind did its worst at my back and sides, the door still gaping open behind me. That was the worst thing about the fifth wind. There was no way to turn away from it. The only way to avoid it was inside, and Hawk was standing in the doorway.

He reached out, grabbed my arm, and tugged me inside. He reached past me and shut the door at my back before planting a hand on the frame on either side as he leaned close.

"No problem with proximity at all?" he asked, knowing he had me trapped and wondering if I'd chew off my own paw in order to escape, which had yet to be seen.

"None." I plastered myself against the door with that same mixture of emotions that always boiled up when he was close. I couldn't tell if my heart was doing laps around my chest because of fear, exhilaration, or some strange combination of the two.

I dragged my gaze to his. "I think it's time we did

something about that little magical pact that keeps me working here. We haven't talked about it, but it's a loose end that should get cleaned up, don't you think?"

"The one that saved you?" he asked. "When this is finally finished, it won't be needed. As for now, I disagree, and I think you know that too." He laid his hand on the base of my neck. "An insecure man might think you weren't interested, but this"—he trailed his fingers over the column of my throat, my vein pulsing against his touch—"this tells me otherwise."

"I'm being practical. And if my heart is racing, it's because of the cold."

If Hawk had any defects in his personality, insecurity was not among them. The gleam in his eye, the way he was staring at my lips, made it clear he knew my heart was pounding because of him. That I felt like I couldn't get enough air because all I wanted to do was breathe him in. As he raised his hand, lifting it to circle around the back of my neck, my back arched and my lips parted.

All rational parts of my brain shut down as soon as he came close. I wasn't a logical being near him but some carnal creature I didn't recognize, filled with an intense hunger.

"So you're impartial to me? Is that what you're implying?" His voice was deep and rough.

"Yes. Completely."

"Maybe we should test that."

He feathered his lips over mine, taunting me, teasing, forcing me to be the one to come to him. I resented the urges that drove me to do just that. I hated that he knew I would, that he seemed to read my every weakness. I resented that he was right about all of it, mostly that I would close the gap between us.

I leaned in, and he seized the opportunity like a warrior who'd declared himself the victor on the battle-field, his lips crashing over mine, his tongue delving and demanding even more from my surrender. He pressed his body against me from hip to chest, and instead of feeling suffocated, I wanted more contact. Instead of stiff-ening, I molded to him as his leg shifted in between mine as he grabbed my ass, pulling me up against his leg.

In that moment, it didn't matter what he did, or how he touched me, as long as he kept doing it. When our flesh met, there was a short circuit that happened to the logical part of my brain, and I immediately knew why I always wanted to run when he came close. I turned into someone who couldn't form a clear thought. Words fled. Logic didn't exist. The only thing left was a burning desire to be with him. The cost didn't matter. Nothing mattered because I couldn't think that far ahead.

Hawk broke contact and turned his head. "What?"

I instantly realized we weren't alone. He'd noticed we had company, but I'd been in la la land.

I pulled back, straightening myself while I was still concealed by Hawk.

"Did someone summon up a demon? Because the red dude is hanging out in the front," Zab said.

Hawk tensed in front of me, then his jaw shifted and I could see the cords in his neck strain. A speck of black shimmered on his skin, just like the skin of the creature he shifted into, right before disappearing.

"We'll be out in a few minutes. Just leave him there."

"Okay. Sorry to interrupt," Zab said, right before ducking back out of the room.

I wasn't. If Zab hadn't, there was a very good chance

Hawk and I would've ended up banging on the couch, and that was the optimistic view.

Hawk turned his full attention back to me. I was fully composed again, mental armor back in place, already reminding myself how this shouldn't happen again.

"United front," he said, locking eyes with me.

"Agreed." For this, we'd be united. And it would be the only way we'd be united.

Xazier was meandering around outside the front of the broker building, red-skinned, two horns, and as conspicuous as could be with his back to us. He tipped his hat to a group of passing witches, who quickly crossed the street in spite of his smile, or maybe because of it.

As if sensing us, he turned with his smile still in place and pointed at the door, as if asking if we wanted him to come in, as if I hadn't called him. That was the first sign that he was going to make every little bit of this meeting as annoying as possible. He figured I'd called him, and he had the upper hand. He was going to play it for all it was worth until the last bet was made. Problem was? He was most likely holding a royal flush. I was pretty sure I only had pocket deuces, but damned if I wouldn't play them like aces.

"So lovely to see you all again. Seems like it's been an awfully long spell." Xazier looked around and let out a sigh someone might make when getting home after a voyage.

Musso was still sorting things out at his desk and didn't bother to hide his groan.

Bibbi was watching intently from her table. Oscar was leaning against the wall, clearly on high alert and waiting to see if he'd be needed.

It was clear from before Xazier entered that he was

going to put on a show, but the Pollyanna vibe was taking it so beyond the stretch of imagination that it was going to be hard to carry out a conversation with him if he continued this way.

Every muscle in Hawk's body was tense, as if he were physically restraining himself from battering Xazier.

"Care to join us in the back?" I asked, afraid that if I didn't take the lead, Hawk would shift and bad things might happen.

"That would be lovely," Xazier said, and then walked past us.

Hawk turned to me, glaring his thoughts as clear as day. *You thought this was a good idea?*

"It *might* be."

7

Xazier settled on the couch, in the same spot he'd sat last time. He crossed his legs and glanced at the two of us as we followed him in.

"A tea would be wonderful if you have some," he said, as if we'd offered.

Hawk raised a brow as he glanced at me, doubling down on his silent comment a moment ago. It was clear the world would burn down around him before he served Xazier tea.

Wanting one myself, I wasn't as dug in about the situation. First off, it wouldn't start off negotiations well to pour one for myself and not him. Second, I had a big ask coming, and if a warm brew warmed up his...whatever it was that resided in his chest, then I'd serve him an entire pot if needed.

Playing it safe, I brought over the whole teapot setup. It was Bertha's and had intricate, small flowers all over it. She had a thing for making tea into a whole *production* in the afternoon. I'd internally mocked her when I first witnessed it, and then I partook one day after she insisted. I had to say, the tea seemed to taste better after she'd made a fuss over it.

I settled the set on the table in between us and served, really doing a deep dive into the Pollyanna theme, if that was what worked for him. When I silently offered a cup to Hawk, he shrugged and raised a hand, as if he'd had his fill of this show. That was fine. A few minutes later, Xazier and I were drinking tea together quite civilly.

"What can I do for you?" He made a point of glancing toward the empty seat where Lou had sat last time we had a meeting, before turning his gaze back to us.

"We have a possible solution to the issue at hand."

"The issue being hogging all the founding magic in Xest? This should be interesting." He never lost his smile or pleasant tone. He sipped his tea, waiting for me to continue.

I wasn't sure if this request was dead in the water already, but I was committed.

"What about replacing the magic in the hill with Lou's?" I smiled, as if that statement didn't amount to declaring an intention to kill an angel. If this request went badly, it wouldn't be a simple faux pas, it might mean all-out war, but I was already on the brink of that anyway, so what was there really to lose? If I'd read the chemistry right, Xazier didn't like Lou any more than I did. Would he really care if I offed the angel? The main purpose of this meeting was to find out if going after Lou would cause me to fight a war on two fronts.

Xazier continued to take sips of his tea before placing the cup on the table in front of him. He ran two fingers along the crease of his pants. The longer he took answering, the more hope I had.

"You think you're going to be able to trap Lou in the hill? Trap his magic there to balance out Dread?" Xazier raised a skeptical brow.

Seemed it was the day to be doubted, but I'd gone in expecting that. Planning on getting the best of an angel? It was a tall order.

"I'm not sure, but I'm going to try. Your help would be welcome if you care to get on board?" It was a tough sell to be sure. I felt like I was pushing shares in a business that had a ninety-nine percent failure rate. When it probably did fail, he'd be shouldering some hefty fines on top, just for the perk of investing. He'd be crazy to say yes.

As for me, if I could succeed in trapping Lou, I didn't know what would happen. I might end up in a worse position, because there had to be some sort of fallout for killing Lou. I didn't think God would say, "Oh, you took out an angel of mine? No biggie." Everything was a gamble, but it was the only bet available.

Xazier finally took a deep breath and sighed. "I can't help you, but I won't hinder you. Do what you must in that regard, but we still have the other issue of you having too much of our magic at this point. What do you plan on doing about that? It will need to be rectified no matter what happens with Lou."

I glanced at Hawk, waiting to see if he was going to jump in on this at some point. He was sitting quietly, waiting to see what I'd say as well. Guess I was on my own with this one.

"I'm working on it, but I'll have to get back to you on that." It was a line we used with clients all the time and the only thing that came to mind.

"As a friendly warning, you're treading in dangerous territory," Xazier said.

I swallowed, saying nothing.

Hawk didn't have the same lack of words. "Is that a threat?"

"Not from me," Xazier answered, before shifting his gaze back to me. "I'd much prefer you as an ally, but I think you know that."

"I think we're done here," Hawk said, bristling beside me.

Xazier nodded and rose. He walked out of the room, and I hadn't asked the one question that truly terrified me: did his bosses know about me? Was I looking at a whole new set of problems soon?

I rubbed my palms over my pants, trying to look like I wasn't agitated. Hawk probably knew anyway. He had some predatory skills that made me wonder how long ago his kind had started walking upright.

"Could've gone worse," I said with a shrug as I eyed up Hawk. His lack of words during the meeting, and now, wasn't giving me a lot to go on.

"Could've gone better," he said flatly.

"Obviously he could've offered to help, but he's not blocking us, either." That was a positive, right? It was more than I'd had ten minutes ago. At least this would be a single-front war. Maybe... It was hard to count how many fronts you'd be fighting on when you didn't know how deep into the fray you were.

"I wouldn't trust anything that came out of Xazier's mouth," Hawk said, leaning back as he eyed me up.

"I've never been accused of being too optimistic before."

"First for everything." Hawk shrugged.

"Yeah, taking anything that one says at face value is insane," Mertie said, collapsing on the couch in the same spot Xazier had vacated. Clearly there was no shame in her game when it came to eavesdropping.

"How well do you know Xazier, exactly? Or know of him?" I asked. "What do you know of their weaknesses? Do you know of any way that we could lure Lou into that hill?"

Once upon a time, Mertie had, for all intents and purposes, ruled the roost at the wish factory. Before I started to warm to her, I'd disliked her from our very first interaction. But between the cocoa trips and her possible knowledge of heaven and hell, I'd tackle her to the ground if she tried to leave here.

"I said I wasn't doing everything. You remember that, right?" Mertie asked with her predictable grumble.

Her hand was moving over something invisible in a petting motion. Even Dusty had warmed to her.

"I do, but if you know something useful, I need to be pointed in the right direction," I said, not at all deterred. Mertie might *say* she liked her space, *say* she didn't want to help, complain about every one of us from dawn to dusk, but she was the only person who never missed dinner. Was always lingering nearby, waiting to get pulled into the group. The girl clearly had some commitment and intimacy issues. Sitting in a glass house as I was, the only thing I'd be slinging her way was a foam ball.

Hawk leaned forward in Mertie's direction, his forearms resting on his knees, his voice deep as he said, "Let me put this bluntly. If they try to kill her, I *will* kill them. There will be a very long, bloody war that follows, and this place may or may not remain standing. Do you have other options I'm unaware of? Because the way I'm seeing it, you're either with us or homeless."

No way would that happen. I couldn't believe he was

trying this ploy with Mertie, of all people. The man might want me, might like me, even, but it was like the way people wanted a piece of cake, or how I wanted Bertha's old food back. No one in their right mind started a war with heaven and hell for some chick they hadn't even banged. She'd never fall for it. She was born sniffing out better-smelling bullshit than this.

A little stream of smoke left Mertie's nose as she glared at him. "You always have to make things epic, don't you, Hawk?" Mertie said, huffing a bit.

"I'll take that as a yes," Hawk said, without any gloating, like he'd closed a business deal.

"Fine. That's a yes."

She probably thought he'd kick her out if she didn't agree, but he wouldn't. Hawk, like the rest of us, was secretly fond of Mertie.

"Then you're going to help?" I asked, wanting to nail her down before she figured out she'd been conned.

"I'll help, but don't get your hopes up. I'm not sure what I can do. I might go there and instantly know what's going on, or I might have to call in some favors. I might not have anyone that *can* help. But I'm a demon of my word. I said I'd try, and I will."

"That's all I can ask for," I said, wanting to hug the cranky demon across from me.

She must have sensed it, because she leaned back, as if I'd reached for her.

"Don't get all weird about it. This isn't because I like it here. I just have nowhere else to go. After all the shit you two did, you muddied my good name by association. If we're doing this, I want to go see the hill tomorrow. I like to get unpleasant favors over as fast as possible." She stood up, and I noticed the way she was cupping her arm.

She was taking Dusty with her. He seemed to like the plan, because there weren't any clouds of dust kicking up in their wake.

Hawk stood, and I glanced up at him as he made his way to the back door. He wasn't going to try to take up where we'd left off? I'd mentally lined up all sorts of excuses to get out of there and he was leaving me? Had it already started? Had our last kiss already turned him off?

"Where are you going?" I asked before I thought better of it. "Not that I care. Just curious, is all."

"I've got some things to do," he said, smirking, as if he knew he was beating me to the escape. "Figured this was about when you like to have some time to yourself."

He smiled as he walked out.

8

Hawk walked around the area, kneeling every so often, putting his hand to the ground and staying like that, as if trying to read the magic. Oscar was surveying the areas that Hawk hadn't gotten to yet, but he had more of a hovering technique. Bibbi wasn't doing anything as subtle as either of them. Hands fisted, she was stalking the perimeter, as if ready to take on some invisible monster. She had a ten-inch dagger strapped to her pink, velvet-clad leg. She'd opted for a sparkly sheath so as to not completely wreck her outfit. It was quite endearing how she tried to coordinate her weapons.

All I was doing was standing still, trying to keep my breathing calm, afraid to make a move one way or another. I had a good excuse for it, as everyone in our small group seemed to have the same plan: keep me at a safe distance away from the hill. They'd obviously had a chat about it before we came, judging by the way they all seemed to block me the second we got here. I was surprised I'd been allowed along in the first place and they hadn't locked me up in the office, while Bertha tried to stuff me with healthy fare just for fun.

I wasn't sure what they thought might happen, but something was definitely strange. Even standing back here, it didn't matter. I could feel a strange draw, pulling at me, pulsing in the air. Last time I was here, I'd been luring Dread into a trap, bleeding magic out of a self-inflicted wound over my chest. Maybe I'd been too foggy or distracted to remember correctly, but something seemed different about this place, or different about me. I didn't know which, and it could easily be either.

I hadn't felt quite the same since I'd been thrown from the hill. That day, the hill had tinkered with me somehow. It wasn't like I could get an X-ray of my magic and find a broken, pointy finger throwing things out of whack. I didn't even know if it was bad or good. I just knew something was *different*. Or maybe it was the hill that was different now that it had the magic that comprised Dread trapped within it. That would make anything different. Except would that increase the lure of the hill? I'd think it would decrease it, repel me a bit.

I took another look around, trying to size up everyone else's reactions, visually chasing down all moving targets. If this place was different, wouldn't one of them sense it too? Maybe they did feel it and that was why it was taking them so long to walk the place?

Hanging back was both a blessing and a curse. The only other person standing still was Mertie beside me, as if she had all the information she needed already. Could she feel it the way I did? The magic that was seeded here was partially from her realm. If someone would recognize it, or sense something wrong with it, it would be her, right?

"Not much of a hill," Mertie said, looking over the grounds. "I guess they didn't want to plant a flag on it, but still, I would think they could've risked something a little bit more majestic. Shit, even a big boulder or something. Even a nice, grand tree in the center might've been a good touch. I don't know how you people even call it a hill. It's more like a mound, and not much of that."

All very valid points. Considering what it was, the heart of all the magic in Xest, it was a bit lackluster and anticlimactic.

"You think we'll be able to figure something out? Any suggestions on what we were talking about?" I asked Mertie vaguely, hoping she'd have an answer and maybe shed a little light on the weird vibe I was picking up.

"On my own? Definitely not. What I'm feeling, the level of magic here, is beyond my capabilities to alter in any way. I'd never be able to do what you want to the person in question, and it's beyond my knowledge base." She scanned the area, shaking her head as she did. "Considering the last trap you set was based on information he laid out for you, it's not like you can use that trick again. Although he wouldn't fall for that anyway. Something elemental like Dread, all magic and raw emotion, it makes sense it would work, but not the other. He's too smart. No, I'm going to have to call in some favors, see what tricks they might know, and we'll see how well this goes. We need to find out the things *he* doesn't know about."

"Are your friends discreet?" I asked.

"Sure," she said, shrugging, her tone not very inspiring of confidence. "As long as you threaten them, which is what I plan on doing."

"So you've never been up here before?" I asked, trying to draw out the subject.

"No. I don't typically wander around in the forest for no reason." She raised a brow, as if she wondered how I'd come up with such a stupid question.

"It's plausible that you heard what went down here and got curious," I said. The only reason I asked was to find out if she'd sensed a change, but that was impossible, since she was clearly the least curious person in Xest.

"Why would I care to visit the place that had Dread trapped? If I did get some stupid desire to freeze my ass off, this is not the place I'd come. You humans are so weird." She crossed her arms, as if even now the cold was getting to her.

Bibbi bopped around, circling back toward us. "I think the place is clear," she said, still trying to find something —anything—she could justify punching.

"You don't feel anything strange?" I asked.

Mertie's gaze shifted to me, suspicion growing in her eyes.

"Then same as always?" I added, trying to sound nonchalant. Mertie was technically on our team at this point, but even within our team, there were little teams. The only person definitely on my little team was Bibbi. Zab was a switch hitter. I never knew who he was going to bat for. Oscar was always Team Hawk, even when he didn't appear to be. Musso and Bertha were their own little team, but more likely to fall on the side of Hawk than me. As far as Mertie, she was still a wild card. She might be on my team for one second and then switch directions as fast as the fifth wind.

"All good as far, as I can tell," Bibbi said.

As much as I wanted that to mean something, as much as Bibbi impressed me in so many ways I hadn't expected, if there was something wrong with the hill, she might be the last person to pick up on it.

Mertie, on the other hand, was staring hard in my direction. "Are *you* feeling anything strange?" Her chin tilted up as she looked me over. The only thing she was missing was a small magnifier as she scanned me.

"I wasn't myself the last time I was here, so I'm not a good judge, which is why I'm curious." If she didn't pick up on the hint to go sniff around for her mystery somewhere else, my tone of voice spelled it out.

Mertie continued looking for only a few more seconds before relenting and shifting her attention to Hawk and Oscar, who appeared to be finishing up as well.

Hawk walked toward us, with Oscar not far behind.

"Let's talk back at the office," he said.

I FLICKED a hand toward the fireplace in the back room, and it was instantly roaring before I dropped onto the couch.

"You're getting really good at that," Bibbi said.

"Thanks." Unfortunately, that wasn't the only thing I was getting good at. "Well? Any idea about how to suck Lou into that hill?" I asked, looking about the room. Everyone fell silent, no one offering up anything.

"Mertie?" Hawk asked, knowing she'd have to be prompted. He glared at her from where he was leaning an arm on the mantel.

She huffed, shaking her head. "I told you, I'm an idea person. I can't do everything. I don't have all the answers."

"What do you think?" Hawk asked.

"If you pulled in Dread, it should be equally able to absorb Lou, hence your balance would be back."

"But how to trap him is the question," Oscar said, and then shot a hesitant glance over at Mertie, not quite as comfortable bullying the demon.

"I'm not sure you people realize this, although you'd have to be slow not to, but I'm from the other side of the tracks. I don't know what would make someone like Lou tick, other than annoying someone like me." She shrugged and sat there for a few seconds in silence.

We all let her, having come to know Mertie's ways. First, she huffed, then sometimes you got silence, and then...

"I'll check around, though. I might know some people who know some people who might have answers, but I'm not making any promises."

A few more minutes went by before Bibbi said, "I'm going to go help Zab and Musso. Those two shouldn't be on their own all day. My piles are going to be a mess."

Oscar followed her out, but not before Mertie cut him off, announcing she was going for cocoa for herself.

I moved to leave and found Hawk's hand wrapped around my wrist, tugging me back.

"How did the hill feel to you?"

I suddenly knew I was being tested but didn't know the right answer. I went with my gut. Evade.

I glanced around as if I needed to think about my answer and take in the setting. All I was really doing was evading his intensity. When his focus was fixed on me, the way it was now, that was enough to string up my nerves nice and tight. Add the strange hangover I got from the hill and it was going to be hard to play this one cool and make it believable.

"Who could know? I wasn't quite right last time I was there."

He nodded, his stare still on me. He lifted a hand to my neck, and I didn't shirk away, didn't want to do anything that would raise his antenna. He wouldn't understand that I had some strange connection to that place. Even if I swore that there was something good there, something that might want to help me, he wouldn't trust it.

"I don't want you going back there alone," he said, his voice soft, as if that disguised his high-handedness.

"Wasn't planning on it."

He seemed to take my acceptance of his statement as his due. Maybe he thought he'd finally gotten me under control. He should've realized my easy agreement was the biggest red flag going. The fact that he hadn't seen past my lie was near amazing. I'd mastered quite a few things in these last few months, but I never thought I'd pull that feat off.

9

"I know I said we were having the honeydew darling stew, but I've made some real strides with this new dish. I know you'll all love it." Bertha placed a big pot in the center of the table with a smile so wide she could've been putting the Hope Diamond in front of us.

It wasn't Bertha's normal fare that we all craved. She'd been thinking of reopening her meal delivery business, but instead of Hearty Brews on Brooms, she had a new angle. This time she wanted to supply meals for the health-conscious witch and warlock. Her new business was going to be called Healthy Brews on Brooms. Switching over from hearty to healthy wasn't going so smoothly, especially with her lower-calorie subcategory. Although that was my name for it. No one around here referred to calories. I wasn't sure if people in Xest knew what a calorie was. They referred to how much you ate as watts, and if you didn't burn enough, that wattage was going to add up.

Everyone was so quiet that I could nearly hear the steam coming off the bowl.

"That's great. I'm sure it's going to be just..." My words died off as I caught a whiff of an odd smell. Or maybe the odd smell killed them.

"Great?" Oscar asked.

"Yes, exactly," I said. "Everything Bertha makes is always great," I added, kicking Zab, who was sitting beside me.

"Yeah, can't want to dig in," he said, his voice unnaturally high.

There were a couple of other mumbled encouragements, but my attention had shifted to Mertie, who was sitting on my other side. She was muttering under her breath. Even though it was hard to make out the words, the sentiment was clear.

"Mertie, are you feeling ill?" I asked, nailing her with my best *cut the shit* stare.

She glanced at me, scrunched up her face as she came to terms with dinner getting ruined, and then forced the frown from her brow.

"A little, but I'll make it," she replied in a tone that made it painfully clear that all the niceness and pleasantries were a struggle beyond words.

There was another pause as no one made a move to grab the ladle. Finally, a low sigh escaped Musso as he took the lead. He dipped the ladle, taking only half a spoonful.

Before he could get his share, Bertha cleared her throat. "No need for half portions. I've got more of it," she said, watching expectantly.

Musso feigned a smile and filled it to the top.

The smell kicked up as the brew was agitated. It was

going to be a battle to get this stuff down, but if I filled my plate with buttered buns, I could make it.

"Pass the buttered buns?" I said to Mertie, who had already taken one.

She took a deep breath before she lifted the plate to me, a warning in her eyes.

I'd planned on taking two, but looking at the bun on her plate with one small nibble, I downsized. Had Bertha gotten to the buttered buns as well? Was there nothing safe to eat anymore?

The second I felt the roll's bricklike surface, it was clear we'd lost the only saving grace of this meal. Still, it had been heavily buttered. That had to help somewhat.

I nearly chipped a tooth with my first bite, and whatever the stuff on it was, it bore no relation to butter.

"How's the buttered bun? It's a new recipe I'm trying out," Bertha asked.

"It's good."

She smiled but eyed up the bun sitting on my plate.

"I'm waiting for some of the stew. My favorite part is dipping them." Hopefully it would soften it up some as well.

I felt Dusty brush my ankles, looking for his share. I was damned if I did and damned if I didn't. I broke off a small piece, leaning down and letting him take it from my hand, knowing he'd set off a dust bomb in the middle if I didn't.

His invisible tongue lapped it off my palm and then there were tiny gagging noises, followed by some weird chirping I'd never heard. The finale was clouds of dust as he hopped away.

The table looked at me, all with similar expressions:

Did you have to make this night even worse? We really needed a dust cloud, too?

Hawk walked in the back door, the only one who was late for dinner.

Oscar got up abruptly. "Hawk, pressing matter we need to discuss," he said.

The only thing pressing Oscar was the cinder block against his stomach if he got any more of that bun down. I wanted to fling a cinder block at his head, but only because I hadn't thought of that excuse first. I needed to be more resourceful and faster going forward.

The ladle was handed to me. There had to be a way to get rid of this food. I'd gotten witches stuck on ice for hours, coated Gillian's face with cocoa, slayed dragons, but I was helpless against a plate of food? I was so transfixed on my dilemma that I was oblivious to all other things until I heard Bibbi gasp.

My attention sprang back to the room, and I was ready to use the ladle to bludgeon something or someone to death.

It didn't take long to find the problem. Words were floating in the air, glowing white, as if a skyscraper had written something in bolts of lightning on a dark evening sky.

Relinquish your magic or we will be forced to take further action.

The message hovered in the air for a few more seconds before crackling out, like one of those handheld sparklers.

No signature, no name. No deadline. None of it was needed. Everyone in the room knew what this was about. We'd all been waiting for something. This wasn't Lou or Xazier. They wouldn't have been able to pull something like this off within the boundaries of the broker building. The problem had reached upper management.

Further action. The looming threat of the unknown was even worse than having it spelled out. It made me think of the worst possible outcomes, like not only my death and destruction but everyone around me, as well.

The only sound in the room was the crackling fire and a few audible swallows.

"Relinquish your magic? Do they mean all of it? How are you supposed to... Do they mean..." Bibbi shook her head. "You'd have to go back to Rest, or that would..." Her words ran dry as she looked at me, and then to Hawk and Oscar, who were standing next to me.

"Kill me. Yes," I replied when no one else had the heart to say it.

Hawk stepped forward, laying a hand on my shoulder. "She's not relinquishing anything," he said.

No one spoke. No one knew what to say, and I didn't blame them. I didn't have the right words either. Further action might be taken against me, and it might include everyone in this room. It might even mean against Xest and everyone in it.

If it weren't Hawk standing beside me, daring someone to say differently, there might've been further discussion. I saw all the questions they had unspoken in their eyes, but no one said a word.

"Well, we shouldn't let this little bit of messy news ruin dinner," Bertha said, filling in the gaping silence.

Mertie groaned beside me, and I didn't have the energy to shoot her a look. I felt the same. The only thing that had been good about the poorly received message was that it interrupted dinner.

⟳

I WAS SLUMPED on the couch. By the time dinner was done, I'd felt like I'd gone twenty rounds with Ali between the stress and the food.

Bibbi came over and sat beside me.

"I hope you know I would never think you should... Well, you know," Bibbi said in a near whisper.

"You are the last person I know that would ever tell me to roll over, and I know that." It didn't mean that she shouldn't. If I were her, what would I be thinking? This girl shows up in Xest, somehow ends up with even more magic, and now they have to pay the price for it? I wouldn't blame any of them if they told me to give it all back and go to Rest. Not that I knew how that could be done.

Mertie was sitting on the opposite couch, watching and giving me a knowing look. "There's more to this, isn't there? What are you holding back? Why do you look guilty of something, of which I'm sure you aren't, because you're too nice to do anything bad?"

If she knew some of the things happening lately, she might change her mind. I'd done plenty of bad things in the last few weeks. Maybe that was the problem? Maybe that was why they wanted all the magic back? They were onto me.

Hawk, the only other person left downstairs, was leaning on the wall, not saying much of anything.

"They were upset with the amount of magic I had, but

I think that last go-around, when I caught Dread but then got thrown off the hill? I might've gotten a little more on the way out." I took a deep breath, waiting to see what they'd say.

"More?" Bibbi asked, gasping.

"I don't know for sure, but I think maybe." No. Definitely. I'd suspected right after, but there was no doubt anymore.

"Can't you just give the extra back? No harm done?" Bibbi asked.

"I'm not sure that's an option anymore," Mertie said, getting up, probably to go to bed. She never said goodnight, so you couldn't be sure.

Bibbi looked at me, silently asking if that was true. I nodded.

Oscar walked in the back room. "Why are you two looking so glum? It'll get worked out," he said, taking a seat on the couch.

Bibbi nodded. "Yeah, I'm sure it will. I'll see you guys in the morning. I'm wiped out from all the *drama* today." She unwound herself from the couch, making a production of stretching as she made her way out of the room.

Oscar was staring at her as she left, and there was a little too much heat there for my liking. When had he started wanting Bibbi? Not that he shouldn't. She was hot, funny, balls bigger than some of the boulders on the east side of Xest. But when had *he* started noticing?

"What's that look?" I asked him.

"Hmm?" He turned my way, nearly oblivious to how he'd stared.

"You were eyeing up Bibbi like she was a roast you wanted to sink your teeth into."

He let out a short laugh and smiled. "She does have a

really good..." His hands, which were making curving motions, dropped as he got a good look at my expression.

"Don't go there," I said.

"Why? What's wrong with me?"

I might be a newcomer to Xest, but I'd been here long enough to know the class system. It might not be a thing in the broker building and our crew, but would someone of Oscar's rank date a Whimsy? When had Oscar seriously dated anyone, for that matter?

"There's nothing wrong with you. I just don't want you hurting her. She's not the kind of girl that I think you'd be compatible with." For measured words, they still didn't sound very good.

"What kind of girl is that?" There was a challenge in his question.

"The kind that disappears before you fall asleep and has no problem never speaking to you again." Bibbi might be a lot tougher than she looked, but not where it counted. Deep in the middle of her chest was a soft spot. I wouldn't have anyone taking advantage of it or stripping her of the only softness she might possess.

"I'm not saying I'm going to pursue her, but I might be capable of being more than what you're assuming." He shrugged, not looking overly offended.

"Maybe you are, but have you been capable of more in the past?"

"No, but neither has Hawk."

The only thing his argument did was expand on why I shouldn't be involved with Hawk. Good work, Oscar. I'd needed that reminder.

10

I wasn't giving up but couldn't drag them down with me. I hadn't come this far to lose everything I'd worked for, but taking this place down? Not an option. I didn't have the right.

My door opened. Hawk walked in and closed it behind him. All the normal sounds, creaks, and humming of the building disappeared.

I scooted up in bed, knowing this wasn't going to be a lying down kind of conversation. When Hawk sought me out, it never was.

"You didn't say much downstairs." He stood at the foot of my bed with his battle face on. It was a simple statement, but it came out more like a declaration of the war he was gearing up to wage, this one against me.

"I didn't have much to say. I'm still taking it in and thinking it over. I'm trying to not be reactive." It sounded good, logical, calm, and thought out. It was exactly what I was doing, and there was no reason to tell him where my decision might be leaning.

He crossed his arms, watching me. "You do realize you can't give them what they want?"

I bent my knees, wrapping my arms around them as I tried to wrap my head around what had happened. I'd known something was coming. We all had. I'd been warned by Lou and Xazier, what seemed like ages ago. But the warning had been from lower-level personnel, not upper management. You couldn't fight heaven and hell, could you? Especially when they both wanted the same thing? In this case, *it* being my destruction. The truth was that I had magic to spare. Couldn't I somehow give a bit back? Just enough to calm things down? The hill had given me more somehow. There had to be a way to return some of it.

"What if there is a way to compromise? Can I afford to turn them down?"

"We'll find out when we do." He looked like he was carved from granite.

"This isn't your problem. This is my issue."

He hesitated for just long enough to make it clear he was choosing his words. Hawk always knew exactly what he wanted to say. Perhaps he was trying to figure out a nice way to tell me he'd help me out as much as he could but then I'd be on my own? Was he finally seeing that we couldn't fight this war?

"Not acceptable. You live in my building. You work at my business. Any attack or threat against you is personal. We need to call Lou and Xazier in separately for meetings. I want to know exactly what they know." His tone was all business. Not only didn't he see he might not be able to fight this war, he thought it was winnable.

"If there's a way I can give some of this magic back, maybe it's not worth the battle?"

"The message said *all*." His gaze was laser focused.

"If it comes down to destroying Xest, or the people here, I go back and live like a regular human in Rest. I did it once and survived." And then I'd come here and realized what life could be like. I'd fallen in love with Xest. It was the first real home I'd ever had. That was why I'd never be the cause of its destruction.

"That's not acceptable." His tone was heavy, as if that was truly a fate worse than death.

Were regular humans that unacceptable to him? Was my going back to Rest really worth destroying lives over? Destroying Xest for? I was one witch. There were plenty of others.

"You can get another broker. You'd have a line around the block. And as far—"

"I don't want another witch. Why are you so ready to give up?"

He didn't want another witch? I couldn't let those words go to my head, and they easily could. It wasn't me, exactly. He'd just never had an obstacle in his life. He hadn't won me yet. Or conquered me. Whichever way you wanted to see it. That was what this was about. If I went back to Rest, it would be harder for him.

Still, I got off my bed. It was safer that way.

"Why? If I'm giving up so easily, constantly throwing in the towel or running—"

"Then you're finally admitting it?" He leaned his shoulder on the wall, waiting for me to say the words, as if I'd admitted to a felony.

Even if I were guilty of it, which I wasn't, there would be no admitting anything. How was a sane person supposed to react? He'd spent the majority of the time I'd known him either trying to control me or pushing me out.

If he thought that was the foundation for hopping into bed with him, he was crazy.

"I admit nothing of the sort. I'm merely repeating your complaints. If I'm so difficult, why do you keep trying? Why not move on to someone who'll be easy like Gil..." I stuttered out, unable to form her name. Even the sound of it in my head made me feel like I was sucking on a dirty penny. I tried to avoid walking past the Sweet Shop whenever possible, even if it meant walking several blocks out of the way in the stinging wind.

"You think I should pursue Gillian?" he asked calmly, as if giving it some thought, a small smile teasing the corners of his mouth.

In for a dirty penny, in for a nauseating pound.

"Why not? She's about as easy as it gets. She'll cut your food for you, say whatever she thinks will please you, probably do cartwheels on command if you're so inclined." She'd probably do anything he wanted, whenever, however. My pulse ratcheted up at the mere idea of it, and here he was, smiling like a cat with a bowl of cream. I didn't know if it was because he could sense my heart racing from the fury of the idea or because maybe he was having a change of mind and Gillian seemed like a good idea now.

He shrugged slightly. "What if I don't like easy?"

My heart slowed just enough to be noticeable, which was way more than enough to annoy me. I had no right to be jealous over this man, or relieved he didn't want Gillian. He wasn't mine, and I didn't want him to be. He'd be nothing but a headache.

"Then you're saying this is all about the chase?" I'd known it, but it did my brain good to hear it. This was why my gut kept telling me to stay away from him. Nothing but trouble.

"That's not what I said."

"Sounded like it to me."

He came close enough that when I breathed in, all I could smell was him. There was something about the warm scent of him that made me breathe deeper, made my heart flutter and race, warmed everything in me.

I held my ground but looked at my nails, examining my cuticles, when I couldn't hold his gaze. I wished I was as unaffected as I pretended to be, but I knew where this might lead, and I wasn't too proud to know my weaknesses.

He lifted his hand, threading it through my hair, tugging my head back and forcing me to look at him. My chest rose and fell sharply as I saw the raw need in his eyes. I prayed he wouldn't kiss me at the same time my back arched.

His head dipped down and my eyes fluttered closed.

Instead of his lips meeting mine, they grazed my ear.

"If I wanted you in bed, we'd already be there. This isn't about the chase," he said.

"Really? You think so? You could just get me in bed at any point you want?" It was enough to drive a little steel back into my spine. I pulled away from him, putting a couple of steps in between us.

"Yes," he said. I could hear the smile in his tone.

He didn't follow, but it felt like he was granting me my space, which enraged me more.

"If I'm so easy, why haven't you worked your magic yet? And by magic, I mean your charms that are so outstanding that I'd trip over my own feet in my rush to sleep with you." I took another step back and crossed my arms, all of which he watched and seemed amused by.

"Because if I slept with you now, you'd wake up the next day and push me away harder." He nodded to my current stance, as if I was proving his point right now.

"What does that matter? What if once is enough? Why do you assume there would be more times needed?" I buried my fear that it wouldn't be enough for me. I wasn't sure I'd ever tire of this man if I got a true taste of him. Even this cat-and-mouse game we were playing was becoming addictive. But I needed to hear him admit it. The pretense that this could be anything real, having that lingering out there as if it were a possibility, was almost a drug unto itself.

"It won't be. When I finally do fuck you, I want you to be there with me, one hundred percent, not thinking of what the morning might bring, or the next week."

"You're good. Does this normally work for you?"

He smiled and then dipped his head to my throat slowly. So slowly I could've moved out of the way at any moment, and yet I stood there, daring him to do his worst.

His lips found the column of my throat and slowly moved over my flesh, while he wrapped one arm around my waist, curving me into him, not that I needed help. It was as if my back's normal position became an arch when I was anywhere near him.

Feathering kisses along the column of my throat. His hand running up my back in almost a massage.

I was putty in his hands and I didn't care. My big talk a second ago vanished, leaving nothing but a groan in its wake. I was incapable of having a lucid discussion as the roughness of his shadowed jaw grazed my skin, sending tingles everywhere.

He straightened.

"Good night, Tippi."

He walked out, leaving me standing there angrier than ever, but at myself.

He was right. He could have me at any time he wanted. I barely put up a fight, if you could call those couple of steps a fight. After he'd touched me that last time, I hadn't even bothered *trying* to fight. As soon as contact was made, as soon as his flesh touched mine? I might as well destroy the eject button, because I'd crash and burn just for the thrill of the fiery spiral down. As much as I wanted to fool myself and say it wouldn't happen again, I couldn't delude myself that much. The only chance I had was if he never touched me again, or I avoided seeing him, which was never going to happen.

HAWK HAD LEFT THE BUILDING. I'd watched him as he disappeared into the night. Everyone else was finally asleep. I'd stopped hearing Bertha and Musso moving around upstairs an hour ago.

I walked into the office, staring up at Helen.

"How bad could it get?"

She didn't leave it to guesswork this time and shot out a slip that tumbled into the air, doing a flip in front of me. I snatched the note before it dropped to the ground.

Unknown. Something feels different, but I'm not privy to the workings beyond Xest or Rest.

"Yeah, well, different makes sense. I doubt that this sort of thing happens often. Any advice?"

She let out a long, soft humming noise I'd never heard before.

"Yeah, I'm scared, too." I gave her machinery a pat. "I'll try to keep us all intact."

11

I had my head down as I tried to work, but I knew they were staring at me. Not the clients, who had no idea about what happened last night, but the rest of them. They pretended they weren't, but all their energy was focused on me, as if I were going to snap. The thing no one understood was the more they focused, the more I felt like I *would* snap.

It made me want to tell them I was okay, except we had a room full of clients who would surely eat the gossip up like day-old cake. I'd catch an occasional suspicious glance, as if they knew something felt odd, but that was about it, and I wanted it to stay that way.

It wasn't that I had a problem being the main gossip of Xest. I'd grown used to it. But I didn't know myself how I was going to dig out of this current mess, and I didn't need clients piling in and giving me their two cents with every meeting I had.

I was sipping my fifth cocoa, thanks to Mertie, who

was having a grand old time torturing Gillian today, when an older witch named Tagga cleared her throat.

"You messed it up *again*," she said, pointing at the paperwork as she sat on the other side of my desk. "You wrote Tabatha. That's my daughter."

"Sorry." I took the sheet back, erasing the spot until the paper nearly had a hole.

Hawk strode into the office and stopped in the middle of the room, eyeing everyone in the place, which had been bustling with activity right before he walked in. I leaned back, staring at him as he stared at everyone else, their presence in his building clearly annoying him.

"Everyone out. We're closing early," he said, his voice ringing clear to every corner of the room.

"Here." I held out the form to Tagga. "Look it over and bring it back tomorrow, after you've signed."

She took it, giving me a skeptical look before shoving it in her bag and vacating the area with everyone else.

The place emptied out of clients in under two minutes.

It was a very good thing Hawk wasn't on the front lines of client relations. He'd drive the business into the ground in a matter of days.

Musso stood up from his desk, stretching. "Do you need me, or can I take the night off? Told Bertha we'd go out to dinner tonight."

Zab, Bibbi, and I tensed in unison. If Hawk messed up their dinner plans, we could very well be stuck with Bertha's food tonight, when we didn't need to be. That was a capital offense in my book. That was nearly worse than having heaven and hell wanting to kill me. If I didn't get a break from the healthy new cuisine, I'd be begging for death soon.

"No. I only need Tippi. The rest of you can take an early day," Hawk said.

Zab stood, saying something about heading over to the Watering Hole, his favorite place to get a drink, where a lot of his fellow Middlings hung out.

Bibbi was scowling as she moved around her table in an effort to get closer to Hawk.

Hawk's shoulders dropped a hair as she approached. Hawk liked Bibbi, and was often as impressed with her as I was, but this was an area where she could be a bit much.

She planted herself in front of Hawk, her hands fisted on her hips, ready for battle. "Are you sure you don't need me? Maybe I should stay behind. If there's going to be trouble—"

"It's a few meetings, Bibbi. I've got it under control."

Bibbi stared hard. Hawk turned and walked into the back, making it clear he was finished with the discussion, whether she was or not.

She watched his back, her muscles twitching as she took a half step to go after him but then stopped. She switched her attention to me.

"What's going on? Do I need to be here? If something big is going down..."

"I think he's got Xazier or Lou heading over. I'll fill you in later. I promise. If he does, the meetings will go better off with fewer people anyway." The last thing I wanted to worry about was Bibbi getting angry and somehow getting on their radar. It was bad enough I was on top of their list.

She looked over her shoulder, at the back room, as if it were taking everything she had not to force an invite to the meeting.

"What if you forget something important?" she asked.

"I won't," I said.

Zab was grabbing his jacket across the room, watching us, and I shot him a look.

"Bibbi, you want to come with me and get a drink?" Zab yelled from across the room. "I'll get the first round."

She glanced at the back room one more time, sighing as she accepted she wasn't getting in on this meeting.

"You're buying the first two." She grabbed her jacket but paused by me on her way to the door. "Take notes."

"I will."

The door shut, everyone gone, and I made my way to the back room, where Hawk was leaning a hip on the edge of the sofa, arms crossed, waiting for me.

"Both, or one?" I asked.

"Both. Xazier first, and then Lou."

That, I hadn't expected.

"Why Xazier first?" He hated Xazier more. Hadn't we just had an almost-argument about me contacting Xazier over Lou?

"I think he's less likely to know anything and more likely to be forthcoming if he does."

I let that sink in for two seconds before the hypocrisy was too thick to not remark upon. "It's okay to use his inclinations when it's your decision?"

He looked up, as if actually thinking about it, before he said, "Yes. A little more palatable."

I shook my head, letting it go, mostly because I had bigger fights at the moment.

I moved over to the couch and dropped onto it, afraid of any answers we might get today. If Xazier didn't know anything, nothing gained or lost. If he did know something, it might not matter, as it was over his head and he couldn't do anything about it. The other possibility was that he had full knowledge and at least some negotiating power. That was the outcome that made me want to pace the room the most.

"Maybe I should try to strike a deal," I said, floating the idea to see if it sank or floated, already sensing it would have the buoyancy of a cinder block.

He looked at me over his shoulder, pausing for a minute as if to make sure I was serious before he bothered answering. "We do nothing of the sort. This is strictly for information."

"Unless he puts an offer on the table that I can't turn down," I countered, ignoring his glares.

He turned fully toward me, resting both hands on the couch. "We don't make any deals."

"What if it's amazing and with an immediate response clause? I might not be able to say no."

He was staring at me as if I were insane, but neither of us knew what Xazier would come in here saying. I wasn't taking anything off the table, no matter how many glares Hawk gave me.

"Yes, we can. No deal. We do nothing until we talk to both of them, and even then, we don't rush to action."

The door in the office opened, ending the discussion.

"Hello?" Xazier called out from the other room.

"In the back," Hawk said, giving me a last look.

I gave him one right back.

"You rang?" Xazier asked as he walked in, as if he had no idea what was afoot. I might not have believed it was his call, but clueless? That was the one thing I seriously doubted. Still, I kept my eye rolling to a minimum.

"Let's not drag this out. I'm sure you heard about the message already. What's your part in it?" Hawk asked, not mincing words.

"I have nothing to do with it at all." Xazier put his hands up.

"Is this from your boss?" Hawk asked.

"I'm not privy to his every move, and before you bother to ask, I'm not in a position to question him, especially not right now. The situation here is not being looked at favorably. To be quite honest, I'm keeping my distance from this whole mess as much as I can." Xazier smoothed his hands over his jacket and had yet to sit. He kept looking at the door as if deciding how long he should even stay. The demon really wanted nothing to do with this situation. Whatever was going down, something had shifted in his opinion and he wanted out of the mess.

"Why did you bother to show up for this meeting at all?" I asked.

"Didn't have any other plans for the evening, so I figured, why not? I'm not a fan of completely ignoring invitations. But now I will be off. Good luck to you all." He tilted his head in our direction and then made his exit.

Hawk leaned against the couch. "He knows something more than what he's saying."

"But I don't think he's involved. He was too anxious to leave," I said, not feeling better about the situation. If Xazier didn't want anything to do with it? That was as bad as it got. He liked getting his fingers in everything. That was who he was.

"On this we agree," Hawk said.

"That doesn't make me feel any better." Actually, it made me want to groan aloud, but I wouldn't, not now. I'd wallow later, when I was alone.

Unlike Xazier, Lou walked in like he'd expected to be called and was pleased by the invite. He strode in as if he'd just come off the back nine on a sunny day.

"I'm assuming this is about the message you received? Are you looking for further instruction? If you are, all you need to do is go to the—"

"We're not looking to do anything of the sort, and she's not going to give anything back." Hawk hadn't moved off the back of the couch he was leaning on, hadn't raised his voice, and didn't need to do either to get the message across that this wasn't a meeting to surrender. He had that war tone down to a science.

Instead of hearing what Lou was about to say, Hawk's interruption, which I was sure was timely, in his opinion, left me guessing.

Lou's face immediately shifted away from gracious winner to frustrated brawler. He turned his attention away from Hawk and settled it on me. "Is that what you bothered me for? To tell me you're not interested in negotiations? That's the message you want delivered?"

I had one ally in the room, who I didn't agree with, but I wasn't ready to run a bus over him, either. There was some benefit to showing a united front, even if there was a mile-wide crack right behind it. But could I risk Lou going back and shutting down all negotiations? Hawk might be ready for a war with heaven and hell, but I wasn't.

"We're still thinking—"

"Yes," Hawk said, cutting me off.

I glared at him, ready to hit the gas pedal on that big old bus. I turned back to Lou, hoping Hawk took my silent warning to heart. I didn't want to run over him, but I would do what I had to if he kept at it.

"We haven't decided yet," I said in my calmest negotiation tone. "As you know, I did get a little extra magic recently. I'm not looking to be greedy. We might be able to work something out."

Hawk was bristling in the corner, telling me with his eyes that I wouldn't be giving back one iota if he had anything to do with it. I tried to ignore his energy filling the room, which was extremely hard on a normal day, and focus on Lou.

Lou shifted his head, as if he was on the fence on what he could do. "I'm sure giving *something* back might help, but will it be enough at this point? I'm not sure."

The conversation had the feeling of trying to get a salesman to come down another ten percent when he already knew the bottom-line price but wouldn't tell me until after he'd gotten his pound of flesh.

"There must be some sort of middle ground," I said.

Hawk's energy was filling the room.

Lou tugged at his collar, as if he could use a little air. "As I began to explain, if you go—"

"If there is a formal offer in writing, have it presented. Otherwise, we're done." Hawk stepped forward, putting an end to the discussion.

Lou raised his eyebrows, shaking his head as if that were a colossal mistake. He nodded toward me before leaving without another word.

Hawk and I both held our silence until we heard the other door shut.

"What was that about?" Hawk asked. "What in the world would make you think it was a good idea to have him think you're open to giving anything back?"

I spun on him, fisting my hands on my waist so I didn't punch him. "Because it's *true*. I did take more somehow, and it wouldn't be the end of the world if I gave some back. I'm trying to compromise so we don't end up in a mess."

"You didn't take anything. It was given to you. You did

nothing wrong in any of this."

"That's what you think, but you don't know that. Maybe somehow I did take it?"

"What I do know is I don't trust him."

"He's from heaven. How bad could the deal be? And it's not like I'd be giving it to him. His *boss* wants it back. Do you realize the kind of pressure that is, to have that"— I waved my hands upward—"to want something from you that you're not giving up?"

"You're being too trusting. We don't do anything unless it's delivered directly and carved in stone."

"It's not *we*. It's me, and if something bad happens, that's not on *we* either. It's very hard to do nothing when there might be an easy fix. If things go bad, you aren't the reason." I gave up and devolved to pointing at his chest. I'd be poking it next, which was nearly as bad as punching. Anyone who'd ever been poked could vouch for that.

He stepped closer, looking like he wanted to strangle me. "It *is* we. You're not in this alone."

He could say that all he wanted, but it wasn't the truth. If people got hurt, it wouldn't be because he hogged all the magic. No one would say he should've tried to give it back. His tombstone wouldn't read, *The girl who took it all.* I hadn't asked for it, but if I didn't give it back, was that any better?

"That's what you aren't understanding. This is my problem. Not yours."

Of all the things I could've said, that seemed to punch his buttons worse than anything.

He didn't say another word and walked out of the room.

All you need to do is go to the...

That blank was easy enough to fill in. The hill.

12

Don't negotiate.

Give them nothing.

Easy for Hawk to say when he wasn't the one on the hook for the fate of everyone. He wouldn't listen to logic. He was so sure his way was right that it was impossible to speak to him. He'd lost his mind. Only a person who'd lost it would think they could win a fight against heaven and hell.

I pulled my jacket closer around me as I hiked up the mountain. There was one opinion I trusted that I hadn't heard yet. Bautere was tough, logical, and steady. Most importantly, he wouldn't bullshit me.

A loud sound, like a clap of thunder that was right on top of me, blasted through the air and shook the ground violently. I fell to my knees as an earthquake shook Xest to its core.

And then the ground right beneath me broke open. There was nothing to grab at but snow as I slid into a chasm that grew as wide as a building. I grabbed at anything I could as I slipped along the wall of dirt, finally grabbing on to a tree root, my feet dangling over the abyss.

"Help!" I screamed, my fingers feeling like they were slipping on the muddy root. Every perch my feet found fell away as soon as I tried to put weight on it. I screamed for help as loud as I could as I dangled, hoping someone might be near. I wasn't that far from Bautere's, and there were always people patrolling his area.

"Tippi?" Bautere yelled in the distance.

"I'm here! I'm in the hole!" I yelled.

He was leaning over the newly formed cliff seconds later, taking in my dangling form and my precarious position.

"Hang on! I'm going to get something to drop down to you," Bautere yelled.

"Hurry!" I tried again to find purchase with my feet, but no luck.

A long branch was dropped down, but it was ten feet shy of my grasp.

"I'm going to get something bigger," he said, leaving before I could tell him I wasn't going to make it too much longer.

My fingers were slowly slipping down the root as my grip weakened and my forearms burned with my weight. I was a witch, conceivably the strongest witch in Xest, and I couldn't save myself? This was how I was going to die? I wasn't even trying to use my magic.

I closed my eyes, imagining myself as a feather, floating upward on a draft of air, and felt myself inching up slightly. I opened them and saw I had, and immediately plummeted again, slipping down the root a few more inches.

I closed my eyes. *Focus.* I had to do this or I was dead.

Light as a feather.

My weight grew lighter; the strain on my grip became easier. I was lighter than a feather. I envisioned myself as a speck of dust, carried along by the fifth wind. The wind that would gust upward and carry me higher. Slowly, I could feel myself lifting, my hand now level with my shoulder and slowly dropping lower.

I was nothing but a speck of dust, the nothingness you see floating in a beam of sunlight, drifting with the air.

My hand was now holding me back, pinning me to the spot. I had to let go. I needed to let go and let myself rise.

I'm a speck on a current of air, nearly weightless.

I let my fingers unclench, feeling my body drifting higher, carrying me slowly across the way, out of the depths of the looming chasm to safety.

I'd been floating for a few minutes and I could feel myself moving horizontally now, hopefully away from the chasm.

Nothing was certain until I opened my eyes, which I was afraid to do because I might panic. Panicked people dropped like two-ton weights, or at least that was what happened in my mind.

And I am a weightless speck of nothingness.

"You're flying," Bautere said from somewhere just below me.

I used his voice as an anchor as I pictured my body drifting softly toward him. A few seconds later, my feet made contact with the ground. I took a breath and opened my eyes to see Bautere and a few of his people all gaping at me.

"You flew," he said, staring at me.

"It was more along the lines of floating, but I guess

close enough." I was getting technical, but I didn't have anything else worthy to add.

"How did you do that? I've never seen a witch fly without a broom," he asked, his people looking as intent as he was on the answer.

"I don't know. I guess desperation does some curious things." I looked at the gaping hole in the ground a good ten feet away. "I didn't know Xest had quakes."

"It doesn't," he said, walking closer to it and staring down into the pit that seemed to go on forever.

I stayed where I was, not needing to get anywhere near it again. I'd already seen it too closely.

Xest didn't get quakes. Some people might've said that this was just a coincidence, that it had nothing to do with me. I wasn't one of those people.

The elation of floating was worn away, down to barely a nub, with the realization that I'd received a warning of things to come. Now I knew what would happen if I didn't make things right. The fate of Xest, of the people I cared about, was resting in my hands. I could fix this or we could all end up in a bottomless chasm of hell.

"Were you coming here to see me when this happened?" Bautere asked.

"I just... I wanted to walk," I said. The conversation I'd been planning didn't need to happen anymore. I already had my answer, and nothing was going to change it.

"I'll walk you back to town."

～

"So the ground just cracked open? Just split in half?" Zab asked, staring at me from the other couch.

"Yeah, something like that," I said, trying to figure out what Hawk and Bautere were saying on the other side of the room. Obviously, I was part of that conversation. I would've known it without their many glances in my direction. Still, they could've tried to not be so obvious about it.

"And then you *flew* out of it?" Bibbi said, sitting beside me.

"More like floated. I didn't really steer or anything, and there wasn't any great speed. The fifth wind did most of the work." I shrugged, thinking about the situation. "Honestly, I don't think I did anything at all when I really think about the situation."

Bibbi and Zab were shooting each other looks.

"I really don't," I said, my eyes getting drawn across the room to Hawk and Bautere again, as one or the other of them wouldn't stop looking my way.

Hawk's tendons looked like they were going to snap. That was never a good sign. He was clearly upset about the chasm situation, which was understandable. I was surely going to get the blame for it, too. Somehow my walking would be the issue. He was the one being stubborn about giving back even a drop of magic. He should be mad at himself. That was why there was a big crack in Xest.

"Bautere said Xest never gets quakes?" I asked, knowing that Bautere was a reliable source but needing to hear it again anyway. Everyone made errors at some point.

"Never. Didn't even know they could happen," Zab said, then sipped his tea as if this wasn't ground-shattering. As if it was just a coincidence.

It had to occur to them that this was because of me, right? They couldn't believe this was a coincidence.

"You think it's because of, well, maybe..." It was hard to say the words, because if it was my magic issue, and they weren't being nice, what if they hated me? I shouldn't have brought it up at all. Having Zab and Bibbi angry at me today might be the thing that made me crack.

"Because of you? That's what you were going to say, right? That God and the devil are pissed off you stole all the Xest magic so now they're cracking Xest open like a bad egg?" Bibbi asked.

"Yeah, something like that." I fiddled with the fringe on the blanket.

"Could be, but we don't think any less of you," Bibbi said, smiling. "I'm sure it'll get worked out, and no one goes up to those parts anyways." She shrugged and sipped her tea.

"You'll figure something out. You always do," Zab added.

The two of them were sitting there like this was just another day in Xest. Did they not realize the warning? Where this could lead?

"What if it gets worse?" I asked, looking from one to the other.

"You've got this," Bibbi said.

"You will. We're not worried," Zab said. "You're like the witch of all witches. You just *flew*. You'll work something out."

Hawk and Bautere disappeared out the back door, probably to go talk about me some more. Bibbi and Zab went up to bed, but not before relaying the entire event to Musso, Bertha, Oscar, and Mertie as they all filed in to see the floating witch.

I stayed sitting on the couch through the retelling and then after, wondering how everyone could be okay with what had happened. No one was angry at me or mentioned leaving Xest. They all took it in stride, as if there was no relation to the message from the other night.

No. They were being nice. That was all.

The rest of them might be fine with the chasm, but that didn't mean Hawk wouldn't be ready to give me the boot. If nothing else, this had to wake him up to the real danger Xest was in by me staying and keeping my magic.

Hawk strode in the back door, as if I'd summoned him somehow. At this rate, I wasn't quite sure what I could do.

"Well?" I asked before the door had time to shut behind him.

He took one look at me and said, "Well, what?"

"The chasm."

"Yes." He walked over and sat on the other couch, looking deadly serious.

Here it came. He was going to kick me out. He'd finally decided I wasn't good to have around and this was it. I'd have to start over again, and that was fine, because I wasn't taking everyone down with me. The bottom line: I wasn't meant to be in Xest. I'd fought to be here, but at some point, I had to accept the reality that maybe I was a problem.

"Until this situation is resolved, you're going to have to use more caution. Bautere told me how he found you. If you hadn't figured out how to float, you could've died."

He looked angry enough, but for the wrong reason. Did he not realize what this meant?

"You don't think that maybe it's time I give up some magic and go back to Rest?" I asked, hating the sound of the words. *Give. Up.* Saying those words made my stomach revolt. They turned me into a quitter. I was a lot of things, but that had never been one of them. But did I have the right to keep fighting when I might ruin Xest for all the people I loved?

"What I think is you're going to have to be more careful," he said, as if there had been a way to avoid a chasm that opened up underneath you.

"This wasn't about being careful. *This was a message.*"

"Things happen. Not everything means something," he said, getting up and walking away.

He was never going to see reason. If I listened to him, Xest would end up in flames. I was on my own.

13

Hawk walked over to my desk. "You're sure you don't want to come and see Rabbit?" he asked. He'd approached me this morning when he mentioned he was puddle-jumping over to Rest.

My heart ached at missing the opportunity to see her. She'd been my very first friend in Xest, and if it hadn't been for her depleted magic, she'd still be here. As much as I missed her and wouldn't mind seeing Salem again, I had too many other issues.

I'd gotten maybe an hour of sleep last night, and that might be an overestimation. When I slept, I'd dreamt of standing at the hill as Xest burned around me. If Hawk was going to be out of Xest, and I had my afternoon free, this was the best opportunity I was going to have.

"I can't. I've got an appointment later with a new client I don't want to miss."

His eyes narrowed and a visual interrogation commenced. I sat firm, not budging from my seat, not flinching, not letting my gaze flicker from his. He walked away without too much fuss, but there was a warning in his glance before he did.

I didn't let it bother me as I went about the rest of my day, working, keeping myself busy until an opening to slip away presented itself.

Hawk was gone and Zab had a light day, so the only ones left in the office were Musso, Bibbi and me. It might've been paranoia, but if Hawk was going to leave anyone here with instructions to keep an eye on me, it was Musso. Bibbi was my girl through and through. No way was he turning her, so I had one last hurdle and then I'd be out of there.

"Bibbi, I've got a while before my next client. Want to go grab something to eat?"

Her head snapped up and her pencil hit the desk. "Definitely. I'm starving."

Things had been a bit leaner this past week with Bertha's new business idea.

Bertha had been upstairs experimenting on recipes all day. So when I asked Bibbi if she was hungry, I knew the answer already.

She was already grabbing her jacket when she glanced at Musso. "You want to come with us?" she asked.

"Yeah, want to come?" I added, hoping he'd decline.

"Wish I could, but..." He let out a long sigh, shaking his head. "I have a taste test today."

"Want us to bring something back?" I didn't plan on eating with Bibbi, but I'd make a stop to perk up Musso. This was one sad state of affairs for all involved, but mostly for him. Maybe if we hadn't had it so good for so long, we'd be happy with what Bertha was dishing out lately. But no, it was like every meal we were a bunch of lab rats, waiting to see if the newest meal would torture us, kill us, or both.

"Not worth the fallout," he said.

Bibbi and I exchanged glances. It was hard not to remember last week, when we'd made the mistake of bringing Musso some lunch back. Bertha had walked in with her "healthy" dish for Musso. He'd been in the middle of attacking a roast like he was a starving lion in the Serengeti that had finally caught prey after a week-long fast. She'd dropped her tray when she saw what was going on. The horror displayed on her face, you would've thought she'd caught him banging some chick on his desk.

He'd responded similarly, dropping the half-chewed hank of meat as he stared back in stunned shock, repeating, "I'm sorry," over and over as she ran from the room.

"Well, we'll see you in a few, okay?" I said, taking backward steps toward the exit.

Bibbi was matching my pace, afraid to be left behind.

Musso stared at us as if we were leaving him on an abandoned planet to die a slow death.

Bibbi finally sped up, making a dash for the door. I followed quickly, afraid to be left alone with the guilt.

We didn't speak of it once we got outside. All it would do was remind us of the dinner looming in the future and our own trial by fire.

"I'm going to have a really big lunch," Bibbi said, revealing thoughts in line with mine.

She started walking toward the main square, where all the best restaurants were. My steps slowed. I'd planned on grabbing a bite, but knowing where I was heading killed my appetite as fast as Bertha's new menu did.

"I know I asked you to lunch, but I think I'm going to have to pass."

"Huh? You just told me not five minutes ago you wanted to go get something to eat," Bibbi said, looking ahead toward one of her favorite places, Bits and Pieces. Everything they made looked like some weird variation on pulled pork mixed with other bits and pieces. The servings were huge, heaping affairs that could take a solid hour to eat.

This was *Bibbi*. If I told her my plan, she'd jump right on board. I could've told her we were going to sail across an ocean on a dilapidated sailboat, destined to capsize. She might give me a few questioning looks, but she'd climb on board right behind me. That was who Bibbi was. Solid to the core, ready for anything and loyal to a fault.

That was the problem. This boat *might* capsize, and I wasn't sinking anyone else with me. I could stand the hit. I wasn't so sure she could. As much as I would love a co-captain, this was going to have to be a solo voyage. And a secret one at that.

"I do, but I really need to talk to Bautere. I didn't get a chance to thank him for trying to help me the other day. Why don't you go to the Watering Hole? Zab's gone over there, and they've got some good food on the menu if you haven't tried it yet."

"I don't know. I'm really hungry, and it's a bit of a dive." Bibbi was scowling as if that place couldn't possibly have edible food.

"You wouldn't think the food is good, but it is." I had been drunk when I ate there, but still...

"Okay, I'll try it, but you know how angry I get about bad food, especially since Bertha's cooking went downhill. I don't want Zab to be booted because I'm having a fit. If he gets kicked out, he'll be in the back room with his sad face on, and no one wants the sad face every night."

She was right about that. It would be like living with Eeyore. If it was even a possibility, I'd block her from the place myself. But I knew the Watering Hole too well. They had one priority: keeping people drunk and happy. They'd never give Zab, or her, the boot. They'd just get them both drunk. I'd barely made it home from that place on more than one occasion.

"Trust me, it'll be fine," I said, waving her off in the right direction.

"Okay, but if I end up punching people, you're taking part of the blame. I don't want any lectures about anger management," she said, but started on her way.

"When have I ever lectured you?"

"You haven't, but I see the looks."

"If you have to punch someone, I'll back you up a hundred percent," I yelled as she continued on.

"You better," she yelled back.

With Bibbi on her way, I double-timed it toward the hill. I'd check it out, walk the perimeter, and leave. I didn't have to make any hard and fast decisions. I didn't even know if it was the hill that Lou was going to say. There was no danger in checking it out, right? Since this place was part of the other plan to get Lou stuck, the more familiar I was, the better. In a way, this was due diligence. I was being a team player and going above and beyond.

It took me a while to get there, but the moment I neared it, there was a peaceful, serene feeling that immediately called to me, soothing my nerves, as if it had been waiting for me to come here by myself.

I walked around the place, slightly narrowing my path as I lapped it a second time, and then making an ever-shrinking circle the third. By the fifth lap, there was no denying the call toward *that* spot. It didn't matter that it was covered in mounds of snow. I could feel the exact location I'd joined with it last time, as if it pulled at me. It had never quite felt this intense or well meaning, either. There was no malevolence in this place, in this feeling. It was dying to help me. Maybe this was how I made everything right?

I circled again, not allowing myself to get too close but still feeling its presence. Dread's magic was here too. I couldn't ever forget the battle it had been to trap Dread. It would be crazy to do anything that might make it easier for that magic to break free again.

I circled again and then stopped when the feeling overwhelmed me. This spot—there was nothing but goodness here.

I bent slightly, letting my hands graze over the snow in the place it felt the strongest. A feeling of happiness and bliss tingled up my fingertips.

I knelt, telling myself to only lay my hands on top of the snow, and then digging them deep in, ignoring the burn of the cold against my flesh, until there was solid ground. An instant flood of warmth shot through my system. It felt like comfort and warm buns and cocoa on a cold day. It felt so overwhelmingly good that I knew in my heart it was the right thing. I let the feeling course through me, reveling in it. Letting it seep into every pore of my being.

"Tippi."

Bautere calling my name jerked me out of a haze. I jumped to my feet, wondering how long I'd been kneeling there. The sun was beginning to set, so it had been at least a couple of hours. Time had completely escaped me.

But I hadn't gotten stuck. As soon as I'd gone to move, it hadn't tried to keep me.

"I heard you were about." He looked to the place I'd just stood up from, not saying anything, even as the question was there on his face.

Had his people seen me here? And for how long?

"I actually wanted to thank you for your help the other day," I said, putting some distance between me and the spot, trying to move his attention away from it.

He nodded. That was the most acknowledgment I'd gotten, and it didn't bother me at all. Bautere and his people were a hard sort, not inclined toward frivolities and compliments. They didn't stand around all day patting each other on the back and talking a big game. But when the game was afoot, he'd be there kicking ass without anyone having to ask for his help. In my book, that wiped out the need for fluff and show or whatever other niceties people who lived in cushy little worlds might expect.

"Would you like to come and get warm before you return?" he offered, looking at my hands.

I shoved them in my pockets. "No, I think I better get back. Everyone at the office will wonder where I am." Bautere wasn't much of a gossiper. Not much of a talker at all. Would he tell Hawk I'd been here if he was asked? He wasn't much of a liar either, so probably. Still, there was no reason that Hawk would think to ask.

I turned to leave.

"Tippi."

I turned back to Bautere.

"The magic in this place hasn't been right in a long time. Be wary with whatever you are attempting. You might get something altogether different."

There was a warning in his eyes that chilled my heart. He didn't feel the goodness here.

"Thank you," I said.

~

HAWK WAS in the back room when I walked into the broker building. His gaze ran the length of me, and then his eyes narrowed.

"Where have you been?" It seemed like every muscle on his body stilled as he waited for my response.

The tone wasn't that far off normal, and the question was about as common as oatmeal.

"I went up to see Bautere to thank him for the other day."

He walked over, laying his hand on my neck, feeling for my magic. I hated the way my pulse jumped at the smallest touch from him, how he could sense what his nearness did to me.

When he dropped it, I wanted to grab it and put it back. He hadn't kissed me in forever, and as much as I dodged him, I was becoming obsessed with kissing him again and more.

"You're off."

Had the hill done something to me? Left a trace of something? It was true that I didn't feel bad. In fact, I hadn't felt this relaxed in weeks, maybe months.

"Maybe all the walking wore me out, or maybe I'm catching something. I don't know, but I don't feel sick," I said, moving away from him, knowing not to tempt fate.

14

Bibbi's head was tilted to the side as she stared at me from across the office, chewing on the end of her pencil as she did.

I ignored her as best I could, which wasn't easy, since she was acting like I was a science experiment.

"Sign here." I pointed to the line and handed my client a pen. She was a new Middling who'd become an independent contractor last week. She was young and green but had a real flair with romantic crushes and was a genius with surprise pregnancies. New life forms were pretty tough, and typically not under our scope of influence.

"And you'll supply transportation to Rest until I can work something else out?" she asked.

As good as she was at her niche, she, like me, couldn't puddle-jump worth a damn. I'd come to realize most Middlings could puddle-jump over to Rest, but not all. When they couldn't, they usually teamed up with someone who would escort them for a small fee or cut of the commission. Considering how busy she'd be, there would be a line of witches and warlocks around the corner, willing to work with her. Until she made those arrangements, we made them for her.

"Yes. I'll set you up with someone. If it works out well with them, most people typically negotiate a rate and continue working with each directly."

"How much should I offer them if I like them?"

"For a reliable puddle jumper, with smooth landing and getting you to the right location without being conspicuous?" I looked down at her paperwork and fee. "I wouldn't go over ten percent, not on the rates you're getting. Just make sure they realize the specific niche you're in, and they'll gladly do it."

"Great. Thank you so much, Tippi."

She skimmed down the paperwork to the fee and then shifted the paper closer, as if she wasn't seeing it right. "Wow, I get this much? Is that right?" She held it up, pointing at the number.

"Yes, that's right." Babies and love paid out big. Between the pay and the beneficial exchange rate, this girl was going to do very well for herself and make us a lot of coin in the process.

She stood up, smiling. "I'll do a great job. I promise."

I gave her a wave goodbye as she stood and left, leaving me a clear view of Bibbi, who was still staring at me. "Why do you keep looking at me like that?"

She finally stopped chewing on the pencil, but only so she could use it to point in my direction. "Are you feeling okay?" she asked. "You look a little off, and I can't figure out why."

"I feel fine." I got up and walked into the back to make a tea and get out from underneath her microscope. She was getting as bad as Hawk with the examinations.

"You don't look fine," Bibbi said, because of course she'd followed me into the back room. Bibbi wasn't just your run-of-the-mill dog with a bone, she was a mastiff with a rib eye.

"Bibbi, I'm telling you, I'm fine." I kept my focus on the tea I was brewing, afraid to look at her in case she picked up on something else.

"You can say that, but I know you too well at this point. I've listened to you breathe. I know when you're off, and you're off. Maybe you should go lie down for a bit?" She was twisting her head this way and that, trying to inspect me from different angles.

I went utterly still as what she said sank in. "You've listened to me breathe?"

"You've done some crazy shit. How else was I supposed to make sure you were still alive? The day you came back from the hill, after trapping Dread? You looked like you were half in the grave. If I hadn't put my ear to your face every so often, you might've passed on, and then what?"

If it had been anyone else...

"Okay. I guess, but I'm telling you, I'm fine."

"I don't think so." Bibbi crossed her arms and tapped a foot as she continued studying me.

"Can you stop before someone else hears you and decides to drive me crazy?" I grabbed a mug and placed it on the counter a little harder than I meant to.

"I'm just saying, you look like you could use some sleep, is all."

"I'll go to bed early if you'll stop mothering me."

"Fine, but..." Her gaze shot to Hawk, who'd walked in the back door. At least she'd taken enough pity on me not to make a thing of her observations in front of him. Inquisitions from Bibbi were bad enough. I didn't need it on both ends, and he'd already been suspicious last night.

Bibbi gave me a side glance, as if to say that if she'd noticed, no way he wouldn't, before she left the room.

Hawk scanned me, and I turned back to my tea in an attempt to discourage closer scrutiny.

He walked over, and before he even closed the distance, his attention already seemed fixated on me. Was I putting something out? I thought I was acting perfectly normal, but I must have been doing something.

He stopped right beside me, resting a hip on the counter. "You still look off. What exactly did you do yesterday?" he asked.

Did he already know? Was this a test? I really needed to figure out what was raising a warning flag over my head. Bibbi hadn't even touched me and she'd noticed. Now he clearly saw a good night's sleep hadn't fixed whatever difference he'd noticed last night.

"I told you. I went for a walk up to Bautere's."

He continued to stare. I went back to fixing my tea, because of course there was nothing wrong.

He laid his hand on the side of my neck before I'd realized what he was going to do. I let it rest there for a few seconds before nonchalantly turning to sip my tea, which effectively removed it.

His eyes were narrowed. Obviously even those two seconds of contact were enough for him to pick up on something.

"You're still off. What were you doing today?"

"Working. Why am I being interrogated? I'm allowed to have off days." He was acting like I'd committed some crime. As if I couldn't go for a walk without coming back damaged.

"Why are you so defensive?" he asked, his tone slow and measured.

"Because I didn't realize I was a prisoner only let out on good behavior. I thought I lived here and came and went as I pleased." I tried to match his calm tone.

He tilted his head ever so slightly as his eyes narrowed, as if the more I spoke, the more suspicious he became. He was right. I was being defensive and there wasn't a reason for it. I'd taken a walk and stopped by the hill. So what? I should just tell him. It shouldn't be a secret.

I stirred my tea, ignoring him, or attempting to.

"Not for nothing, but you do look a little shitty today, not that I care," Mertie said, walking over and stopping on the other side of me.

"Thank you. So nice to hear." I was gritting my teeth so bad I might chip a tooth.

"Any word?" Hawk asked, turning his attention to Mertie as she walked in.

"Yes. Was just coming in here to tell you people. I've got someone that might be able to help with luring Lou over to the hill," she said as she helped herself to a cup of my tea and then groaned. "This is almost as bad as Bertha's stuff. No wonder you have me running out for cocoa five times a day."

I didn't care what she said about my tea. The only thing bothering me was: did I want to mess with the hill? I didn't know what happened when I went there, but it felt right. Maybe I was coming to a truce with it, and them, or whoever. It was hard to know, but I did not want to change anything.

"When?" Hawk demanded.

"Any moment now," she said, then sipped on the tea she'd complained about.

"Good," Hawk said, nodding.

Shit. How was this happening so fast?

Bibbi bounced into the back room.

"This...*person* can help?" Bibbi asked, pretty much proving everyone in this building eavesdropped at all available opportunities.

"I have no idea." Mertie shrugged.

I moved to the couch with my tea, trying to figure out what I was going to do. It was now three to one in favor of the meeting. There'd be no stopping it. It wouldn't hurt to hear Mertie's friend out. I might go back to the hill tomorrow and change my mind. Bottom line was that I might feel calmer today, but I still had a looming issue of massive degrees, and this might be a fix.

And why did I feel like my emotions were all over the place today?

"Is the person coming a friend of hers?" Bibbi whispered as she took a seat on the couch near me.

"I don't think she has friends—other than us, that is," I whispered back.

Oscar walked in. "Are we getting company?" he asked.

Hawk nodded him over to the side as Bibbi leaned in and said, "I told Zab. Zab must've called Oscar over. Musso and Zab are stuck with clients. I have to fill them in afterward." Bibbi glanced around, nailing down where everyone in the room was before whispering, "You think they're going to be from *hell*?"

"Mertie didn't say, and I didn't ask. Assuming that was the case was enough for me." My gut said they would be. Those were the circles she'd run in. What had my life become if my best possibility for survival was joining forces with them?

"Do you think he or she will try to steal our souls?" Bibbi asked.

I got stuck on that question for half a minute before replying, "I don't think so."

Mertie was glancing around the room. When her glare landed on Bibbi, she rolled her eyes. "My friend doesn't like crowds."

"You might not realize it, but I'm a very important part of this meeting," Bibbi said, making it clear she wasn't budging.

There was a soft rap at the back door, almost imperceptible.

Mertie shook her head, went to answer it, and cracked the door as she spoke to whoever was in the alley. She was speaking in a language that was unrecognizable but made the hairs on my arms stand. They weren't even quite words. They sounded like strange grunts and noises, and gave me the same feeling I'd get walking through a cemetery at night.

She took a step inside, opening the door wider. I was trying to not be impatient, even as Bibbi was practically leaning in front of me to catch a glimpse of who was here.

Hawk and Oscar had moved closer to the couch but remained standing, leaving the other empty for our guest.

I wasn't sure why I'd assumed whoever was showing would look like Mertie: a bit red and hoofed, but nothing shocking.

A warning would've been nice. I took a deep breath, keeping it together. It would've been better if Bibbi didn't let out a little squeak, but I wasn't going to fault her for it. It was amazing that was all she did.

He walked in, and his skin was red, and he did have hoofs, but that was where the similarities ended. Where Mertie had a human-shaped form, this...man had the legs of a buck. His skin, or what I could see of it poking out from the dark cape he wore, was rough, like a rhinoceros's. His eyes were solid black, not even a fleck of white to be seen, and his mouth had no lips. His nose was long, thin, and pointy, reaching down close to his chin.

"This is Zurdoch. He knows what we're looking for." Mertie gave us all a glare, letting us know we were walking on thin ice with him.

Zurdoch nodded to us, taking in all the occupants in the room.

"We're not all like Mertie, who can blend so easily into society," he said, remaining standing like he was waiting to be rejected and ordered out of the room.

It was like a light switch had been flipped. I went from leery of him to immediately feeling his pain. I'd always been able to hide in plain sight when I lived in Salem, but I'd never fit in, not until I came to Xest. This Zurdoch was a kindred soul with Mertie, but unlike her, he immediately inspired fear when people saw him. There was no softening his appearance.

"Thank you for coming. I greatly appreciate it." While I hadn't made up my mind whether his presence was a good thing, I felt for him on the deepest levels.

Zurdoch inclined his head in acknowledgement, his eyes flickering away from me as if he was not sure how to handle too much kindness.

Hawk nodded to Zurdoch then pointed to Mertie before asking, "Has she explained our problem?"

"I know what you're asking for," Zurdoch answered with a glance in my direction before facing Hawk again.

"Can you do something for us?" Hawk asked.

"Yes. I can't do it myself, but I believe I can get you the information you need in order to know how to trap him. But it's dangerous for me. There's a price for my part in this." Zurdoch leveled his gaze on me and left it there.

"Whatever it is, I'll pay it," Hawk said.

"You can't pay it. She has to." Zurdoch pointed at me.

"What is it you want?" I asked.

"I saw what you did for the immigration witch. If you can do that for her, you're the one I need. I want a spell to look human, and not one that will run out. I'll need to hide after I do this." Zurdoch stood straighter.

I'd known what he was going to ask for before he said it. What he didn't know was that I would've made him this potion even if he did nothing in return. What *he* didn't say was that he would've wanted this potion even if he didn't have to go into hiding. He was dying for any reason to change, just as I had been.

"Is there one that does this?" I glanced at Hawk.

"Yes. It's tricky and needs a lot of magic, but you should be more than capable of making it for him."

I turned back to Zurdoch. "I'll get it done. You have my word on it."

15

I turned on my side. Flopped on my back again. Turned on the other side and then exploded into a coughing fit, choking on a dust plume.

"I'm sorry. I can't sleep," I said between coughs.

Dusty ignored me, hopping off the bed and heading for a more peaceful place. He'd been slipping into Mertie's room more and more often. I was losing my bunny to the reformed demon, and it burned.

I flopped around on the bed for another fifteen minutes before I gave up, got dressed, and threw my boots on.

The streets were quiet, but not because people were scared or worried about going out. It was because it was the middle of the night or early in the morning, depending on your preference. Sane people were sound asleep in their beds. I no longer counted among the sane because of where I was heading.

As I walked alone, heading to the outskirts of Xest, all the reasons to go to the hill seemed silly. I'd checked it out the other day. I'd touched it, connected with it. Other than feeling more relaxed and calmer than ever, there was no reason, right?

Or maybe wrong. What if connecting with it was fixing something? Why else would I feel so good when I did? Something was happening. Could I really tinker with the hill anymore, try to trap Lou in it if I didn't know what was going on? I'd go up one more time and just see what happened. Try to get something concrete with which to know the way forward.

By the time I got there, I was near shaking with impatience to lay my hands on that spot, figure out what was going on.

It had nothing to do with the way it made me feel. Nothing at all. This was a fact-finding mission only. I'd touch it, connect with it, and figure out the best way forward.

I fell to my knees in the snow, not caring how cold it was. Touching my hands to the ground, I let the feeling of the hill course through me, the warmth, the love. I'd never experienced anything like it in my life. It didn't matter what anyone told me. This couldn't be a bad thing.

The passage of time seemed to stop until I noticed the sun lighting the sky. I jerked my hands off the hill, knowing I wasn't going to make it back to the broker building before everyone was up, no matter how hard I tried. But try I did.

I entered through the front, knowing Bertha might be in the back room already, as she tended to rise with the sun.

Hawk had also apparently decided to rise early today, as he was standing in the office when I walked in.

The tendons in his neck were tense and his eyes were hard as he took me in.

"Where were you?" he asked, as if he already suspected.

"I couldn't sleep, so I went for a walk—not that I need to explain." I headed toward the door upstairs, giving him a wide berth. The last thing I needed now was for him to reach out and tell me I was "off" somehow. I didn't have time for it. I was late and not interested in the fight. I was feeling too good from the hill, and he was already ruining that.

He watched me as I walked around him, keeping my distance.

"Worried about something?" he asked.

"Not a thing," I said, escaping upstairs.

The best thing about my black leather pants was how well they hid wetness. I'd barely escaped Hawk's scrutiny as it was. If he'd seen my pants were soaked, it might've gone way worse. The bad thing about them was when they were wet, they were a bitch to peel off. It was like wrestling with a snake that was hugging my legs.

My knees were a shade of blue. How long had I spent on them? Or was it because they'd gotten so cold? Didn't matter. I changed into a fresh pair of pants, and then stalled long enough that I'd miss breakfast and Zab, Musso, and Bibbi would be settling in for work. There was definitely safety in numbers.

The place was buzzing by the time I settled at my desk, clients already in for appointments. Luckily, it was going to be a busy day.

Hawk walked in from the back room, beelining it to my desk. He dropped a book on my desk. "Chapter five has the potion you need for Zurdoch. Shouldn't take you more than a few minutes."

I nodded and moved the book to the side. I'd deal with it later. It wasn't as if I had nothing else to do.

He watched my movements, as if wondering why I hadn't flipped it open immediately.

"I don't have time right now," I said.

If anything, he looked more suspicious after I'd spoken.

"I need to handle some things today. While I'm gone, I wouldn't go for any more walks," he warned me.

The look he gave me made it clear that we would be at war if I crossed him.

He didn't wait for a reply, not that I was offering one up. I stared back silently. That was all that comment deserved. No one was telling me where I could go or when.

He headed over to where Oscar had walked in and was waiting for him. The two of them ducked into the back room, but not before I got one last warning glance.

Don't do it, Hawk's glare said.

I'll do whatever I choose, I silently replied.

His eyes narrowed.

I leaned back and kicked my feet up on the desk. Let him try to stop me. Seriously, I should chase after him and ask where he was off to. See how well that went over. If he thought he was going to micromanage my every movement, he'd lived in Xest with the sycophants for way too long.

Bibbi grabbed a chair and dragged it over to my desk as they disappeared.

"What's going on with you two now? I swear, you go from looking like you're going to fuck to looking like someone is getting stabbed to death faster than anything I've ever seen. I can never figure out what caused the change, either." She started staring at me in that knowing way she had. "You don't look good at all. Are you coming down with something? Maybe we should get a healer to check on you?"

"I didn't sleep well with everything going on."

She leaned back and nodded. "Yeah, that makes sense."

It did? Was that all I had to do? Tell her I slept badly? I wished I'd figured that out a little faster. Bibbi typically latched on to any irregularity like a bloodhound on the stink of a rotten rib eye.

"Want some tea?" she offered.

"Thanks. I'd love some."

She smiled, getting up and heading into the back room just as Zab's latest client was leaving. I made my way to his desk.

"Hey, Zab, if I wanted to get across Xest a little quicker, is there a way? You know, say I needed to get something at a shop across town and it was an especially windy day? Are there brooms or something?" The witch on a broom had to have come from somewhere. After everything I'd discovered, I refused to believe it was completely made up.

He put his papers aside. "Brooms haven't been a thing in a long time. The weather being what it is, it's tough to fly unless there's no other option. Brooms are very outdated. It's like taking a horse and buggy in Rest when you could hop into a coupe. Most people who are capable of flying make a token these days. Easiest way to get around if you've got the capabilities."

"A token?" Oh yes. This was the ticket. Hawk didn't

want me to go for a walk? I wouldn't, or not a long one, anyway.

Zab leaned back, stretching his arms and yawning. "Yeah, like the door Hawk uses? That's technically a token. His is larger, but it has to be, since he uses it regularly to go so many places. Plus, he can bring several people with him. There's easier and smaller versions, say if you only need it to take you to a few different places and you're okay with having less flexibility."

There was only one place I needed to go at the moment, and I didn't need to bring anyone with me.

"That sounds really useful. How would I make one?"

"I've never made one myself, as I don't go that many places, but I'm pretty sure there's a book on the shelves over there that tells you step by step." He got up from his seat. "I think I know right where it is."

Bibbi walked back into the room, two cups of tea in her hands.

"No, sit. I'm not going to read it right now," I said, trying to head him off.

"Read what? Need a book recommendation?" Bibbi asked. She was always reading something or other.

Zab opened his mouth.

I stepped in front of him. "Just some brushing up on magic skills that might be useful. Nothing very interesting." The last thing I needed was for Zab to dump a blood trail for her to pick up on. "Anyone seen Mertie? I could really go for cocoa, too. I like a cocoa chaser," I said, knowing that was the surest way to divert her attention, as she was still standing strong on her cocoa ban.

She handed me the tea. "I prefer just tea," she said, walking to her table.

Helen's gears churned so loud it seemed the very walls of the building shook with her machinery. If she didn't stop, she'd have everyone downstairs and on top of me, asking what I was poking around for, what book was I trying to find, and that was the last thing I needed. According to Zab, the book was here in the office, and it wasn't that easy to get during the day with everyone in and out and watching everything.

I knelt by another section, and Helen grew louder still.

"Are you trying to call everyone in here?" I whispered.

I didn't know why I bothered to ask. She was clearly trying to get me caught. For all her churning and grinding sounding like plain old machinery, I could've sworn I knew exactly what she was saying right now, and she was siding with Hawk and Bibbi and everyone else who liked to butt into my business.

"Stop," I ordered her. "I know what I'm doing."

There was one last spurt of movement and then dead silence. That was it. Not another hum, whistle, or churn.

"Just for the record, I don't care if you give me the silent treatment. This is my choice."

Candle in hand, I skimmed a few more books, looking for one that might have the instructions for tokens, and found a title that had to be it. *The Wandering Witch.*

I shoved it under my sweater in case Helen decided to raise the alarm on my way back to my room.

I flipped open the book. Chapter two was labeled "Tokens."

For the witch with many gifts, or looking for a larger vessel, flip forward to the next chapter, Advanced Tokens; otherwise, continue on.

For short travel between one place and another, and more clandestine trips, a small, indiscriminate object that is easy to travel with works best. A coin, clip, or any such frivolity will suffice for the witch or warlock looking to travel light.

INCONSPICUOUS AND ONE PLACE—THAT was exactly what I needed.

I looked for something small no one would notice. My eyes shot to the necklace Rabbit had given me. If anyone would want to help, it was her. But what if it was ruined somehow? No. It was too precious.

A hair clip? Nah. Too flimsy. A scarf? Awkward. I had a pile of coins on my table, one with an odd dent, like it had gotten partially melted by something. Perfect.

I went back to the book, looking at the spell. Seemed easy enough. I held the coin in my closed hand and then wrapped my other around it, as instructed, before reading the spell.

"Bring me somewhere I need to go. Bring me now while no one knows. Take me back here when I am done. Reverse the path, one for one. Be true and sure, swift and pure. Do this for me now and in yonder year."

A small burst of light flashed in the room, and I felt a burst of heat in my hand.

If it worked, all I needed to do was concentrate on the place as I held the coin.

I was about to try but stopped. The only person that I'd ever seen use a token, or any entrance into this place other than the regular doors, was Hawk, and there was no way that was a coincidence. No. Using this in the building might shoot off a warning flare. The back alley was a much safer place.

I sat down on the bed and grabbed my boots. Dusty jumped onto my lap.

"Not now. I'll pet you when I get back," I said, nudging him off my lap.

He jumped back on.

I picked him up and put him on the floor this time.

"Go find Mertie or Bibbi," I said. "I've got things I need to do."

16

A couple, probably close to my age, walked out of the Sweet Shop in the early-morning hours. They couldn't stop staring at each other and smiling. He broke a piece of chocolate pastry in half and then gave her the larger piece. She took a bite and looked at him as if he were her entire universe.

He reached over and gently wiped a piece of smudged chocolate from her lower lip right before he leaned down and kissed the rest of it away. She leaned into him, as if her body was a magnet for his. He wrapped his arm around her waist, pulling her closer. They stood there, in the middle of the road, kissing, oblivious to the cold or other people or pretty much anything beyond them.

"Why are you staring at them? Are you becoming a weirdo voyeur or some crap?" Mertie asked, holding out a cocoa to me.

"They love each other. You can't fake that kind of adoration." I couldn't stop looking at them, wondering how it must be to feel that adored and cherished.

Mertie looked at the couple with me before mimicking a vomiting noise. "Thank Satan you can't fake that or more people would be doing it." She thrust out my cocoa to me. "Can we go now, because I can't be seen liking this kind of crap."

The couple began walking away anyway. I turned to head back to the broker building with her.

"Don't you think you might want that yourself one day?" I asked.

"If I end up with someone, I would never stoop to that kind of behavior. Screw me in an alleyway, but please don't act like a milksop in front of the world. Total turnoff." She stopped right before she got to the door. "Before I forget, did you do that spell for Zurdoch? Hawk said it would be fast."

"I meant to but I got sidetracked. I'll do it soon." Guilt made me want to squirm under her scrutiny.

Mertie hummed.

"What's that supposed to mean?"

"None of my business," she said, walking in the office.

HAWK STOPPED beside my desk about an hour prior to closing. I kept my head bent, reading over the many things I suddenly had to do. Many, many things that left no time for him.

"Where's the potion?" he asked, not moving from his spot in spite of my clear *I'm so busy* attitude.

I sighed loudly, glancing up as I kept my pencil hovering over my paperwork.

"Upstairs. I'm going to give it to Mertie as soon as she comes in." She was over in Rest right now and would be there until late tonight if I was lucky. I might not see her until tomorrow, even.

"You made it?" He sounded so skeptical that he might as well have called me a liar outright.

It was a touch insulting, even if it were true. And insulted was the way I'd have to play this out, or he'd never buy my bullshit.

I leaned back in my chair, making a show of putting my pencil down.

"Yes, I did." I dared him to call me a liar.

He didn't flinch. He gave me a short nod, which somehow still seemed accusatory, and walked away.

He'd be checking in later with Mertie. There was no doubt about it. As much as I wanted to help Zurdoch, I knew where it was going to lead. I should've told Hawk I wasn't sure I wanted to do anything to the hill, except how could I backtrack now? There was no way without coming up with some other lie. It was easier to embrace the current one. Giving Zurdoch the spell didn't do anything but give us information, which didn't have to be acted upon. And I really did want to help Zurdoch.

I waited until Hawk walked out of the office and Zab walked into the back.

Musso glanced up from his desk, watching me. He shook his head but didn't say a word as I stalked Zab.

"Zab, do you have a cauldron I can borrow?"

He laughed softly. "I knew you were full of it. You're still a really bad liar. You do know that, right?"

"Is that a yes or a no?" I didn't bother refuting that my abilities had improved, at least slightly. I occasionally managed to pull a lie or two off.

"You know it's a yes. I've got that rusty old one here if you need it. Just go grab it out of my room."

"Do you know how awesome you are?" I sagged against the counter. Things were looking up. I'd make the spell, give it to Mertie, and then figure things out tomorrow or the next day.

"Do you know who's going to coerce Mertie into getting cocoa all next week?" he said, brewing himself a cup of tea.

"Twice a day. You deserve it," I said, before shooting up to his room.

The cauldron was thrown in a corner, right where he said it would be. I shot over to my room and waved a hand at the wood stove, needing it fast and hot so I could knock out this potion. It started, but it was mediocre at best. To anyone else, it might've seemed normal, but no one else knew how much energy I'd just put into that wave and thought. A week ago, a mere flick of my fingers and the room would be boiling like the infernos of hell in minutes.

I was getting weaker. The hill was taking some of my magic back. But why did it feel so good? Because this was what they wanted. I was giving the magic back. I was saving Xest. I was doing the right thing, and if there were consequences, I'd deal with them.

The potion was fairly simple, and after a couple of trips around the building, I was able to gather up everything I needed. The only tricky ingredient was virgin tears, but Bertha had a vial stashed in her upstairs kitchen.

I dumped it all in the cauldron, wincing slightly as some of the shavings from a thousand-year-old corpse dropped on my stove. It could've been worse. I might've spilled the urine from a demonic goat.

I stirred it, chanting and trying to be patient as it took its time coming to a boil.

"What are you doing?"

I jumped at the sound of Bibbi's voice. "Come in and shut the door," I said.

"You missed dinner again," she said. "Are you okay?"

"Just had to get this done."

I didn't add that it was also convenient to miss that meal. And breakfast. It wasn't that I didn't want to see anyone. I didn't want to hear questions. It seemed as if everyone was looking at me oddly lately. Even if they didn't say anything, they said it silently with their eyes. It was as if no one had anything else to do with their time but watch me and try to figure out what was wrong with me.

Truth was that there was nothing wrong. It was them, and if they were more open-minded, maybe I'd tell them what I was doing.

She crossed the room and looked in the cauldron at the potion just beginning to simmer. "Is that the potion you said you made already?"

Her face wrinkled up like a pug's. I wasn't sure if it was my potion or the rusty cauldron. Both were questionable looking, but at least with the pot, it was clear what was wrong. The potion, on the other hand...

"It is. What do you think?" I asked. Although this type of potion would be beyond the skills and abilities of most Whimsy witches, I'd learned to never underestimate this particular witch.

She leaned closer, giving it a long sniff. "I'm not sure what it's supposed to smell like, but my senses tell me this isn't it." She waved a finger over the brew. "I think you need to give it another go."

I couldn't. I was wiped out just from chanting over this one, not that I'd tell her.

I didn't know where Hawk was, but he'd surely be back and question Mertie sometime tonight, because that was just who he was. If Mertie didn't have the potion, I knew how things would go. It would start with a lot of questions and end with him harassing me about the hill. And logical or not, I was going back to the hill. Nothing that felt that right could be the wrong thing to do. He wasn't stopping me, and I wouldn't fight about it.

"I don't have time. This will have to do," I said, grabbing the ladle and pouring the potion into a glass flask.

"I've never been good at potions anyway, so maybe I'm wrong." She shrugged, but the way she was staring at the potion made her feelings obvious.

"Was Hawk downstairs?"

"No," she said.

"Was Mertie?"

"She's in the back room."

"Good." I grabbed my flask and ran downstairs, leaving Bibbi in my room.

I caught Mertie right before she was about to walk out the back door.

"Here, give this to Zurdoch. It's his payment." I held out the flask, glad it was corked so she couldn't catch a whiff of the off smell.

She held it up, tilting it and watching the way the fluids were separating. If she realized something was wrong, she didn't say anything as she tucked it into her inside pocket.

"And also, if you could do me a solid and—"

"Another solid? How many solids do you need? I get any more solid and I won't be able to walk due to the denseness of my being." She was getting riled up, as Mertie tended to do.

"I need a few extra cocoa runs a day," I said, knowing it wasn't really a solid at all. Everyone thought Mertie was doing us a favor by handling all the cocoa runs, since the rest of us couldn't get served in the Sweet Shop if we stood on our heads and juggled with one hand. I was the only one that suspected the truth. She liked going. It gave her an excuse to annoy Gillian, who she definitely didn't like.

Her posture softened. "Oh, well, I guess I can do that if you really need me to. It's a burden, but I can manage. I mean, I *am* a team player."

She walked out, smiling as she probably dreamt of harassing Gillian.

I turned and found Oscar walking in. "Been trying to catch you alone, but it's been pretty tough, as you've been disappearing a lot."

"Catch me? I'm hardly evading anyone," I said, my back immediately stiffening with the implication. He might like being stared at like a zoo animal, and it wasn't my cup of tea, but that didn't mean I was hiding.

I made my way to the counter, intent on having some tea in spite of his presence in the room, however irritating it might be.

His gaze stalked my movements. "I don't know what's going on with you, but I don't like it," he said.

"I don't remember asking for opinions on my life, but thank you anyway. And if we are offering up opinions, I don't like this version of you either." This Oscar was nothing like the man who made all sorts of idiotic and lowbrow jokes that I'd found oddly endearing. This Oscar I could do without.

He followed me to the counter where I was brewing tea.

"I'm telling you as a friend, I don't know what you're up to, but you're not right. You need to stop it," he said.

This Oscar, along with not being very funny, didn't take a hint well.

"Let me spell this out for you. If I want you to tell me how to live my life, I will come and ask you. Otherwise, it's none of your business."

"You're with my friend. It's my business."

"I'm not with him, not that any of this is your concern."

"You're with him. *You* just haven't figured it out yet."

"I think I would know." I was ready to throw my cup of tea at his head if he didn't shut up soon.

"And yet you don't."

"Oscar, last time I'm going to tell you to stay out of my business."

He pushed off the counter, giving me hope he was going to leave. After his "disappearing" comment, I'd be damned if I left first.

Instead of walking toward the door, he leaned in my direction. Oscar wasn't someone I'd put on my menacing list, but tonight's darker version was a bit more threatening than I was used to. Still, he wouldn't hurt me. Hawk wouldn't let him, but I wasn't quite as at ease as usual.

"You want to keep doing what you're doing? Fine. But keep Bibbi out of it."

These were fighting words if I'd ever heard any. I spun toward him. There was still a few-feet gap in between us, but that would narrow really fast if he didn't back off.

"I would *never* do anything that would hurt Bibbi, and I resent you implying I would."

"You wouldn't intentionally, but you don't know what you're getting into."

Yeah, another person telling me I was too stupid to have a clue about what I was doing in life. I'd had it up to my ears with people trying to tell me how I should be living. Now I was supposed to listen to him on who to talk to and be around.

"And when did Bibbi become your business?" One day he was staring at her and now he thought he was closer to her than I was? Who was he to say anything about our relationship? She was my friend. I didn't know if she had any relationship worth a damn with him.

"When I saw a threat to her."

"You're her protector now?"

"If need be, yes."

I snorted and shook my head in only partially feigned disgust. "And who's going to protect her from you? That's what I'd like to know."

"I would never hurt her," he shot back.

"I guess we'll see."

His chest rose and fell as I waited to hear how he'd defend himself. We all knew he was a womanizer. As wonderful as Bibbi was, I doubted anyone would change Oscar's ways.

I must've struck a nerve, because he walked away.

17

Four hours more and I could sneak out to the hill. It felt like an eternity spreading out before me, but it wasn't. It was nothing. The fact that I couldn't wait to get back there, that I felt so good after I did, had to mean this was the right thing. Could something bad feel this right?

I leaned back, taking long, deep breaths and wondered if I could sneak out a little early without anyone noticing.

Zab had customers and Bibbi was deep in slips. Musso appeared to be concentrating on his paperwork. Mertie was hovering by the door to the back room, watching everyone, but especially me. She hovered for a few more minutes before she jerked her head toward the back and then disappeared.

I followed immediately. Mertie didn't typically call me over for secret meetings. This was one of two things: Zurdoch had information on the hill, which Mertie needed to share secretly, or something had gone wrong with the potion. Right now, it was a coin toss either way.

"What's wrong?"

"That potion you gave me? The one that was going to be payment? It didn't work." Mertie fisted her hands on her hips.

Looked like the coin fell on tails, if that was the bad side. I never really did know if there was a good side.

She was staring at me, expecting some response that I didn't have.

"Maybe he's lying? He doesn't want to pay up now that he got his end? Or he can't because he couldn't find the information he promised in the first place?" All plausible but a stretch. I'd suspected something off with the potion myself.

"No. If he said it didn't work, it didn't work." She was shaking her head. "Ever heard of the saying honor among thieves? They've got nothing on demons. We don't bullshit each other. We don't even try because we can't. We've got a thing."

Did this mean I couldn't even do a potion adequately anymore? No. That was extreme. I hadn't ever done that one. Made sense it might have a glitch or two on the first go-around. What was a *thing*? Whatever it was, how reliable was it?

"A thing?" I asked.

She let out a sigh and rolled her eyes. "Yes, it's sort of an occupational gift. Point is, you can't bullshit a demon. Even a retired demon can still see through the bullshit, which is why if I were you, I'd try a different angle you think is more plausible." She crossed her arms and angled her head.

Okay, there was a *thing*.

"Oh, God." My potion really hadn't worked. I'd

screwed things up before, but lack of magic had never been an issue.

She started shaking her head again. "God has nothing at all to do with this. I mean, I guess we could put out some feelers in that department, but—"

I waved a hand to stop her. "I didn't mean that literally. It's a Rest saying."

"Oh, yeah. Gotcha." Mertie nodded.

"So he's not doing it?" Sounding disappointed when I was relieved was a lot tougher than I'd imagined.

Her brows lifted almost to her hairline, as if she doubted my current intelligence. "No. Of course not."

My magic might've taken a hit, but this wasn't all bad. I wasn't sure I'd wanted to mess with the hill anyway. Now I wouldn't have to. If whatever was happening during my visits was fixing things, I wouldn't need to do anything to the hill at all. I'd make all sides happy, and I still had some magic left. It wasn't as if I were depleted. It wouldn't take it all, would it? I was still a long way off from that happening.

There was only one problem right now: Hawk. He wouldn't take my word that what I was doing was the right thing. The man didn't know the word compromise. He'd want to start a war when there didn't need to be.

"Are you going to tell Hawk? I mean, I know you will, but when were you planning on it?" I sucked in my lower lip, chewing on the edge.

"I'll tell Hawk he's not going to make it and try to stall to buy you some time, but eventually it's going to be an issue. Hawk is going to press for answers on why my friend isn't doing a job he was supposedly paid for, and I'm not throwing him under the bus because you don't have the mojo anymore. Something is going on with you. We all see it. I think you need some help or...*something*."

I crossed my arms, matching her stance. "I have plenty of mojo, thank you. I don't have a problem."

Instead of getting her back up, she dropped her arms and looked deflated. "Look, I don't care what you do. I don't rule anyone's life. But if you can't do magic, something isn't working. That's all I'm saying. Do with that what you will."

~

"What do you mean he's not coming for a while?" Hawk said.

When Mertie offered to buy me a little time, I selfishly assumed she'd break it to Hawk when I wasn't around. The only reason I'd come for dinner was that I hadn't been able to shake Bibbi, and all the absences had been making suspicions worse. If I'd known this was coming, I would've bailed anyway.

"He had an appointment that couldn't be put off," Mertie said, toying with the food on her plate. It wasn't nerves that affected her appetite but Bertha's latest meal. Mertie was one of the few people in existence that didn't mind taking on Hawk.

"When does he plan on coming, then?" Hawk asked.

"He said he would reschedule for next week, maybe the week after." She scanned the table, clearly appraising it for something edible.

"Not acceptable. He was paid. He comes soon or we're going to have a problem," Hawk said.

That was the tone he used when he was getting ready to declare war. I'd heard it myself more than once, right before the battle ensued. Mertie had given it a valiant effort, but this ship was sinking.

I opened my mouth, and Mertie shot me a look, signaling she had it under control. She might've thought she did, but one look at Hawk said she definitely did not. The longer this went on, the worse it would get.

"He doesn't want to come, and it's not his fault," I said.

Hawk turned to me and locked in with laser focus. "What do you know about this?"

The entire room's attention locked on me. They were all like family to me, and maybe that was why it was even harder to say I'd failed. I'd be more comfortable with strangers thinking poorly of me than these people. But it was done now. They'd all hear eventually, and everyone probably screwed up a potion here and there.

"He wasn't paid. My potion didn't work for some reason. I'll have to make him a new one." Which might also not work, but there was no reason to add that bit in. I was sure everyone would wonder anyway.

I braced myself for the barrage of questions. After that was done, Hawk would launch into some other warning or argument, telling me what I should or shouldn't do.

I took a deep breath, wondering how to stall him until later, and then put that off until never.

I leaned back in my seat, waiting for the questions that didn't come. They all seemed to be too interested in their food tonight, which left more time for Hawk.

He didn't speak for a minute. Then he said, "Fine."

That was it. No explosive fight? No yelling or arguing? Just fine? Worked for me.

I made it through a few more bites, right until Oscar

called Hawk away. A minute later, I had my jacket on and an excuse about needing some air. With the token in my pocket, ready to go, I was gone.

I was at the hill a second later, and all the tension was eased in minutes.

18

The back room was empty when I walked in, just as I'd hoped. At this time of night, most everyone would be sleeping, but there was never a guarantee when it came to Hawk. No matter how I tried, nailing down his schedule was impossible, and I'd been taking notes lately.

I wasn't alone for long. Hawk stepped into the room, his gaze burning on mine.

He stepped closer. "Where were you?"

"Took a walk. I didn't realize I was supposed to log my comings and goings for your approval." The warm, calm feeling I'd had a moment ago was fading fast.

"Bautere said you've been going by the hill. Why?"

"Like I said, I took a walk." So much for not telling tales.

I walked over to hang up my jacket, and he wrapped his hand around my wrist.

"What are you doing?" I asked, trying to pull back from him. He crowded me against the wall, reaching up and feeling my neck, ignoring my tug on his wrist.

So what if I was a little off? A little weaker? The last thing I needed was to hear it from yet another person. Everyone around here acted as if you had to be good all the time. You were supposed to be perfect, top of your game.

"You feel drained," he said, his hand still resting at the base of my neck, feeling the fluttering of my heart that I couldn't stop whenever he was around, no matter how much I wanted to. I could be encased in a cement jacket and my heart would flutter as he neared.

"I feel fine. I think I'd know."

His eyes narrowed but he dropped his hand. I moved away, trying to put distance between me and his close perusal.

"Stop going to the hill. It's doing something to you," he said, letting me move away.

"You mean relaxing me? Soothing me? I didn't realize that was illegal."

"More like sucking the life from you," he said.

"You don't understand the connection I have to that place. You just don't want me to have something you don't." No one did. You'd think I was murdering people on that hill the way he made me feel like I had to hide it.

"Do you hear yourself? You're not thinking clearly." He ran a restless hand along his jaw.

I'd never seen him anything but in complete control, even when he was angry. His visible agitation was making me feel edgy myself, like it was a contagious condition.

"Yes, you're the one who always thinks clearly, right? Knows what he's doing all the time and always gets what he wants. Isn't that right?"

"If that were true, we wouldn't be standing here arguing," he said, his voice getting gravelly.

The deep vibration of his voice settled over and around me, triggering a counterpart inside of myself. It didn't seem to matter if we were at peace or at each other's throats—there was something that happened when I got too close to Hawk, and it wasn't getting easier with exposure. It was growing.

His eyes met mine, and we locked gazes. It was as if I couldn't turn away from him this time. Couldn't shake off the cravings I'd been shutting out. Maybe he was right and the hill was doing something to me, because I was losing the strength to fight this. I couldn't even remember why I'd fought it in the first place.

The heat swelled around me until I felt as if I were boiling from within. My chest rose and fell as something shifted, like the boiling anger was pulling all sorts of other feelings to the surface in a crescendo that was impossible to fight. Standing there with him so close and resisting felt like I was being battered by waves in a storm that would eventually take me under.

He reached toward my neck. I thought he was going to feel my magic again, but he shifted his hands, running them through my hair at the base of my head.

We'd kissed; we'd touched; we'd had our stolen moments. But this, right now, was something different. Every cell of my body felt it as my hair stood on end, and goosebumps spread down my arms. The way he was staring at me, it was as if I was the only person alive, the only thing that mattered, the only thing he wanted.

It was a feeling I reflected right back at him. My lips parted, my tongue wetting them as my gaze shifted from his eyes to his mouth.

It was the last straw as he crashed into me. He gripped the back of my head, holding me still while he devoured me. I was drowned by a wave of arousal so fierce that it was as if I'd never been touched before, never been with a man. His tongue danced with mine, demanding I answer.

He didn't have to demand anything. I was beyond holding back, matching every move. Months of daydreaming what it might be like to sleep with him were demanding an answer in the flesh. We'd barely begun and my body was already aching, wanting more.

He wrapped his arm around my waist, lifting me easily. I wrapped myself around him as he walked us over to the couch, dropped me onto it, and followed me down.

I let my hands drift over his shoulders, his midsection, his back, everywhere I could reach, my hands greedy for the feel of his hard body.

My shirt was yanked off. His fingers curled into the waist of my pants, and I raised my hips, letting him tug them down. He leaned back to finish the job, and his eyes went to the dark bruises on my knees. I'd been so in the moment that I'd forgotten they were there until he was sitting back on his haunches, looking at them.

It was as if someone had doused us, or at least him, with a bucket of cold water. The carnal heat in his eyes had changed into something completely different.

I shifted my legs, trying to angle my knees from view.

He grabbed my ankles, stopping me.

"What's wrong with you? I have some bruises," I said.

He grazed his fingers over one knee, and I could do nothing but watch him.

"How did you get these?" His tone was so steeped in accusation that any desire I had left was now as cold and soggy as a newspaper left out in the rain for days. His gaze shifted from my legs to collide with mine.

"I don't know. I probably tripped or something. Who

keeps track? I don't live in bubble wrap." I really was a miserable liar.

"You know exactly where you got them." His fingers tightened around my ankles.

The moment had soured fast. I wouldn't sit here and be interrogated. I tugged away from him. He released his grip, but his stare was as hard as ever.

"Clearly you can't handle a few bruises, so we should call it a night." I found my sweater and threw it over my head, grateful for the break in eye contact.

I wasn't an idiot. Clearly the marks turned him off. *I* turned him off, and I wasn't begging anyone for anything. I didn't wait for an answer as I located my pants and tugged them on. The only thing I wanted was to get away from him and forget how hard I'd nearly crashed and burned.

I turned my back on him and walked toward the door.

He was sitting on the couch one second and shoving me up against the wall the next, leaning his forearms on either side of my head.

Even before he spoke, I wasn't delusional enough to think he was looking to pick up where we'd left off.

"Don't go there again," he demanded, proving me correct.

His words were soft but didn't disguise the strength behind them. He was drawing a line, and there was no doubt there'd be war if I crossed it.

The heat of him pressed against me made my breathing shallow, as my body still craved something my pride refused to let me have. I'd been tossed aside too many times by this man, slighted more than my soul could take, to pick up where we'd just left off. Even if his eyes were fixed on my lips, the heat in them was taking another turn.

"Are you done? Because I am," I said coolly, as if my heart wasn't beating so hard that it was as if it were trying to escape. Rejecting him was the only salve available to my ego after all the damage he'd done. But even as my words put the final nail in the coffin, I realized I wanted him more than I wanted to keep the last shred of my pride intact.

He leaned back slightly, and the same pride that was burning inside of me and ruining an otherwise entertaining night had him pulling back the reins as well. Neither of us were the type to beg, or bend, for that matter. I just might have to remind myself of that a bit more often. Either way, it was done now.

Maybe it was better this way. Maybe people who were this hardened didn't belong together, because they'd break each other into pieces instead of one molding to the form of the other. Me and Hawk? If we ever did collide, it would be an explosion, the heat scorching but leaving nothing but destruction in its wake. We'd burn like a supernova only to take out the entire system.

He dropped the arms that had been caging me in, his signal clear. Leave if I wanted. He wouldn't chase me again.

It was another slight to an already bruised ego that was a fraction of the size it had once been.

I stepped away, refusing to look at him as I left. He reached out, wrapping his hand around my wrist at the last moment. My heart hitched back up into my throat as I wondered if maybe he was going to apologize for acting so disgusted by my bruises, say he didn't care, and that he was sorry.

"Don't go there again," he said instead, in true Hawk fashion.

How silly I'd been to believe he'd rethought his actions. No. Not him. As I'd already figured out, he didn't bend for anyone. Why would it be different for me?

His words did me one huge favor. They infused steel back into my spine where there had been nothing left but want and desire. He reminded me of exactly who I was dealing with, and it wasn't a man to ever care for how I felt.

"Independent contractor, remember? You're not the boss of me." I grinned in spite of my boiling anger, just to reinforce how little his demands meant to me.

I jerked at my arm, but he didn't relax his grip.

"I won't bend on this," he said with a stare that made his intent frighteningly clear.

Hawk was not a man you wanted to go up against if you didn't have to. Lucky for me, I was too pissed to let his words frighten me out of my own stance. He wanted to do battle? Then so be it. We'd fight to the bloody end if that was the way it had to be.

"When have you ever bent for anyone?" I asked.

"Don't push me on this."

"Then don't push *me*, because I've bent so much there's no give left." I jerked on my arm again. This time he let go.

"Then someone is going to break." The steel in his voice let me know he didn't plan in it being him.

"I guess that's the way it'll have to be." I took a step backward as I gave him a fuck-you shrug, with palms up and a smirk that was more acid than honey.

I exited before he made a move, because he looked as if he were going to tackle me to the ground.

19

I walked upstairs to my bedroom and pulled the coin out of my pocket. If I couldn't get to the alley, I'd try it in the building.

My fingers were firmly wrapped around it, but nothing happened. I'd suspected it wouldn't work inside the broker building, and now I knew.

I took off my jacket and sat. I got up and stood. I sat. I paced.

Then I waited. After an hour, when I didn't hear any more noises, I crept downstairs.

I walked into the back room and stopped short. Oscar was lying on top of Bibbi. One of her legs was wrapped around his waist, his hand grabbing her thigh like it was a thick hank of meat on Thanksgiving. I backed out of the room, but not before Oscar looked up, catching me leaving.

"What's wrong?" Bibbi asked before she spotted me.

"Are you trying to leave?" Oscar asked, untangling himself from Bibbi.

I was being guarded. That crazy man had put Oscar on guard duty? I was speechless. What was there to even say? I walked out of the back room, and he followed me, glancing at the front door.

"I'm going back upstairs, so you can stand down now," I said.

His expression was a cross between wanting to apologize and asking me what I thought was going to happen.

Mine was pure rage. I turned, leaving before this devolved into a fight.

I did exactly as I said I was going to, pacing in my room. I turned and found Bibbi in my door, arms crossed and clearly afraid to come in.

"I didn't know he was watching for you," she said, and then waited for my verdict, as if I'd charge her with the crime.

"I know you wouldn't be a part of that." I waved my hand in the air. We both knew who was responsible.

She took a few steps in, as if hesitant she'd get kicked out.

"I'm not blaming you," I reassured her.

Accepting my word, she walked in and then shut the door.

"Are you okay?" She was watching my hands.

I realized I was wringing them. "I'm fine. Just aggravated." And tense, and strung too tight.

Bibbi's eyes kept scanning me.

"Really, I'm okay." I forced the tension out of my limbs and unclenched my hands, trying to look calmer than I was. "Actually, I'm more interested in you. What's going on with Oscar? It looked pretty intense downstairs."

She leaned back and actually giggled. "It definitely

feels very intense, especially that moment the other night, that's for sure."

I was going to have to spell this out. Should I leave it alone? No. This was Bibbi. The girl had my back at all times, every day, no matter what happened. I knew she wasn't a virgin or anything, but someone like Oscar? I couldn't help but think she was hanging out in the deep end.

"So are you dating?" It was an easier way to ask if this was serious or hit and run, not that she'd definitely know.

She sobered up for a few seconds, and at least seemed to be giving it some real thought. Then she waved her hand.

"I don't have the slightest clue. He hasn't brought it up, and I haven't asked. I'm not sure I care, either. It's only happened one other time, and I'm having way too much fun to ruin it with talk." She dropped onto the edge of my bed, a dreamy look on her face. "When he touches me, it feels like right before a fight, except no one is going to get hurt and everyone gets a prize at the end."

Wow, did I envy her optimism and outlook. If she were messing around with anyone else, I'd trust it a lot more. But Oscar? He was a player. He knew how to reel them in fast, but I wasn't sure if his release technique was so good.

I didn't want to rain all over her parade, but if I was going to be there for her, it was time for the doom and gloom, or at least a hint of storm clouds. Someone had to knock her off her rainbow and get some sense into her.

"What if you get hurt?" I asked, treading as carefully as I could.

"How would I get hurt?" Her face scrunched up as if she couldn't imagine why that would happen.

"What if it doesn't lead anywhere?"

She shrugged. "Then it doesn't, but that doesn't mean I'm not going to do it just in case nothing comes from it. I'm young, with a lot of years ahead of me. If Oscar isn't the one, there'll be more." She was leaning back now, swinging her feet and not the tiniest bit fazed.

"Aren't you afraid?"

She laughed and shook her head. "The only thing that scares me is not having every possible experience in life. When I die, I want to be so thoroughly used up and exhausted that I can't wait to go because there's not a single thing left to do, and even if there is, I'm too wiped out from all the fun I had to care. I want to wring every ounce of excitement I can out of this go-around. I want my tombstone to read, 'She did it all.'

"So does messing around with Oscar scare me? Not in the least. I'm thrilled he's interested enough to give me a whirl, and I can add 'banged a really hot player' to my biography. Had sex in every place, in every position, and did it every way imaginable. And if I fall in love, all the better. If I get my heart broken, well then, I got that experience too. At least I felt something deep and lived life to the fullest."

This wasn't an act. She was completely okay with however things turned out.

I sat speechless on the bed, looking at her, wondering why I thought I knew better, that I had to step up and save her from some peril. At this moment, I was an absolute idiot. Actually, I was an idiot in a lot of moments, but this one really hit home. All I'd wanted to do since I got here was sleep with Hawk, and the only thing I'd done was run from him like a big chicken.

"You know, you're absolutely amazing. You're fearless."

I'd never been so impressed with someone in my entire life.

"Thanks. I might not be the strongest witch, but I've still got it going on." She buffed her nails on her shirt before getting up and making her way to the door.

She paused before she left.

"Tip?"

"Yeah?"

"I know you're probably furious with Hawk right now, but I think he means well.

"Bibbi, I—"

She held up her hand. "I know. I'd be mad too. But he's doing it because he cares. I don't know how Oscar feels about me, but Hawk's feelings about you are as clear as the blue sky on a sunny day. You're it for him. When he sees you, everyone else ceases to exist. There are some gorgeous witches that come into the office, and he doesn't spare them a glance. There's something special there. Don't let fear blind you to it."

I nodded, because it was easier than going into a lengthy spiel about exactly how I was feeling about Hawk at this moment. He was literally holding me hostage in the building, and she thought I was going to think nicely of him?

Luckily, she left before I cracked. Without an audience, I went back to my pacing.

20

The day crawled by. Every time I got up, everyone watched me, as if on high alert I'd make a break for the door. I didn't just have one guard today, but multiple. I couldn't even walk into the back room for tea without an escort showing up.

By midday, I canceled my appointments, claiming illness. It wasn't that far from the truth. I was getting shakier by the minute, my body felt tense, and my skin felt like it was crawling. It was because I was backing out on my end of the deal. I was supposed to be at the hill, and I wasn't. *He* was stopping me.

I won't bend on this. That had been Hawk's words about me going back there. Well, neither would I. He had enough people he could dictate to, and I was not among the crowd. I'd always found my own way and always would.

By dinnertime, Bibbi was knocking on my door. I told her I was sleeping, and then I counted the hours, hoping they'd all have given up and gone to sleep. I hadn't seen

Hawk once today, and without him here driving them, they might not be as diligent.

Once the building grew quiet, and the moon was overhead, I walked downstairs with the token in my hand and made my way to the back room. I'd only taken a few steps inside when I froze. Hawk was sitting on the couch, watching me like I was a kid about to sneak out after curfew. My heart was hitting my ribcage like it was a coked-up drummer in an eighties rock band.

"What are you doing up?" I asked, as if I didn't currently hate him, it was any old night, and I'd just happened upon him.

"Nothing. What about you?" His eyes roamed over my figure, pausing at the boots, then the jacket. Luckily, my hat was still shoved in my pocket, although it was like plucking the cherry off ice cream, but leaving the whipped cream and syrup. Cherry or not, you still knew you were looking at a damned sundae.

"Couldn't sleep. I figured I'd have a tea and maybe read for a bit." I made my way to the counter, ignoring his fixation on my every move. I reached for the kettle and then angled my body so he couldn't see how bad my hands were shaking. There was always a chill in this part of the back room, but Hawk would say it was something more sinister, looking for any excuse to claim my trips to the hill were bad. He didn't get it. It was a good thing, but he couldn't see that.

"You always wear your jacket for tea?"

"Didn't think the fire would be going." I shrugged, my back still to him.

I poured my tea, wrapping both hands around the cup, glancing around and wondering how I could stall for time. The last thing I wanted to do was go and sit on the couch, Hawk staring at me the entire time I drank like I was a criminal. Lying wouldn't get me anywhere. He saw through good liars, let alone mediocre ones, such as myself. I needed to brush up on those skills, but by my calculations, I'd probably need a decade past my death to pull off lying as well as I'd need to convince him of anything.

Forget this. I'd go over and have my tea, and if I was caught, that was fine, because even if I wasn't a good liar, it didn't matter. I was excellent at standing my ground, and I'd done nothing wrong. He might think I needed his approval to breathe, but that didn't make it true. He could think my trips to the hill were bad, but again, it didn't matter.

I settled on the couch. I'd drink my tea, and when I was done, I was going out.

"Were you planning on doing some reading as well?" I asked, meeting his gaze without so much as a blink or flutter of a lid. I was galvanized steel, hardened in combat and re-forged many times since. Nothing would shake me.

"No." He smiled.

I smiled back, taking sips of my tea.

"Not going to read?" he asked, rubbing his jaw.

"Changed my mind." I took another couple of sips, realizing how few there were in a cup. Maybe I needed another?

No. I was steel. Steel didn't drink cup after cup of tea to avoid confrontation. And there might not be any. He might suspect my motives, but he didn't know for sure. I wasn't a prisoner here, and if I was, I'd find somewhere else to live. I didn't know why I'd stayed so long anyway. All the people here stared at me like I was up to no good, and for no reason. I was beginning to hate them all.

That was it. I was making my move. "I'm going to go stretch my legs a bit. I'll see you later if you're still up."

I stood.

Hawk stood.

So this was how it was going to go down? Fine. If he wanted a war, we'd have it. Then I'd go upstairs, pack my bags, and get out of this hellhole.

I took a step to the side, and he matched me.

"Get out of my way."

"Not a chance in hell." He held out his hand. "Give me the token."

How did he know I had one? Must've been Zab. He was too Team Hawk to trust with that knowledge, especially lately. He seemed to have the idea that being on Hawk's team was beneficial to me somehow. Wrong. Wrong in so many ways there needed to be a new and worse word for wrong.

"I don't know what—"

"You're not getting up there and back that quick without a token. Give it to me or I'll take it."

"I don't have to give you anything. It's my token." I walked around him, and he followed me. Would he stop me from leaving? That might be the stupidest question I'd ever thought of. Of course he would. He was Hawk. He did whatever he wanted, anyone else's opinion be damned.

Better question was, could I make it to the door in time? Probably not. Could I fight him off? It hadn't worked in the past but I'd had softer feelings that had interfered back then. Now, I didn't care. I was getting out of here. I went to open the door, and he slammed it shut, planting a hand on it near my head.

I tried to conjure up some sort of magic. It bubbled up but felt like wet wood, all smoke and no fire. It was probably because I needed to get to the hill. I was too anxious to think.

Footsteps sounded in the room.

"Everything okay? We thought we heard..." Oscar trailed off as Hawk looked over my head, his gaze on them hard.

I turned and saw Oscar and Bibbi standing there.

Bibbi took a step toward me.

"Not now," Hawk said to them.

Oscar reached out and grabbed Bibbi's arm, tugging her back. When she resisted, he wrapped an arm around her waist, picked her up, and walked out of the room.

"What are you doing? She's my friend and she might need my help," Bibbi said as she was being hauled off.

"And that's what he's doing, so we need to stay out of it," Oscar said as they disappeared.

I was on my own. No one was going to walk in and back me up, help me get out of here.

Now what? I could get back to my room, pack my bags, and leave for good. It wasn't like I didn't have other things to do with my life. I didn't need this place or these people. They all wanted me to be miserable.

I changed directions, and Hawk planted himself in front of me again.

"You're in my way." I used the haughtiest tone I could muster, learned mostly from the eighties chick flicks where some popular girl bullied a downtrodden newbie from the wrong side of the tracks. It was definitely not a role I was used to, but I might as well stick to the eighties trend I had going on.

"Give me the token." His hand was out, palm up, waiting.

Talk about a sore winner. Couldn't he leave well

enough alone? As far as he knew, he'd won this battle. He had to rub it in as well? It was like he was reading off the same bad movie script I was.

"In case you haven't realized it, I'm not going anywhere, so step out of the way." I gave him my best glare. My glares didn't budge anyone back in Salem, but that seemed like ages ago, when I was afraid of my shadow and content working in a little shop. That girl didn't exist anymore.

He moved close enough that I had to crane my head back to hold his gaze. "Do you think I'm idiot enough to not know you'll be back here in ten minutes?"

"I wasn't coming back in ten minutes." Stupid man. How dumb did he think I was? I was going to wait at least an hour.

"Hand it over." His words were clipped, the hard edges of him all on glorious display. This was the man that people crossed the street for. I would've too, except there was no avoiding this confrontation. There would be no defeat, no handing over a token I'd barely muddled my way through making.

If I couldn't outrun him, I'd out-argue him.

"Why do you think you're in charge? I'd like to know that. Why is this any of your business?" I wouldn't let my life be dictated to me, not by him or anyone else.

"I'm not letting you self-destruct, no matter how intent you are. Hand it over." He didn't budge.

My arguments hadn't even gotten a flinch.

"The token is mine. I made it, and I'm not handing it over." My chest tightened as I said the words that amounted to war. He wasn't going to back down, and neither was I.

"That's your final answer?"

Something about the way he asked set off a flutter through my gut, as if maybe I should reconsider for a second. I had a bad feeling that this wasn't going to go my way.

"It's my token and you're not getting it." I wasn't going to back down. If he wanted this token, he'd have to claw it out of my cold. Dead. Hands. He must've thought a whole lot of himself, or his kisses, if he thought I'd roll over without a war.

"You really think you can stop me?"

He might be the scariest warlock in Xest, but I'd beaten Dread. I'd kicked a dragon's ass. I was far from a slouch myself.

I lifted my chin another fraction of an inch, ready to do battle. "You're not taking anything."

He shook his head and made a soft sound of exasperation as he looked over my head.

See? I was tough. He was afraid to try to take it.

"I thought so," I said, moving to step around him.

He shot his arm out in front of me and then circled my waist, lifting me off my feet as if I weighed nothing. I concentrated as hard as I could, trying to conjure up something that would take him down at the knees. Trip him. Knock him over. Nothing worked.

By the time we hit the hall, I'd given up on magic and used my legs to kick off the walls. Something finally threw him, and he dropped me as he fell. I immediately went to take off, but he had a grip on my leg before I could get far. He used it to flip me around, where I used my other leg to kick him, until he got that ankle too.

We fought our way up the hall as I screamed and kicked, missing him most of the time but making a good impression on the walls, the stairs, anywhere I could.

Zab's head popped out at the top of the stairs. "Are you guys..."

Bertha walked up behind him. "They're fine. They're just working things out."

Zab lifted a hand in my direction. Bertha used her boot to shove him the rest of the way into his room and shut his door before returning to her own, leaving us alone in the hall again.

"Let go of me. You can't have it," I yelled.

Hawk finally let go of both my ankles, and I shot to my feet, belatedly realizing it was a trap the second his shoulder hit my hip. He'd let me stand to make it easier to load me up again. With an arm wrapped tight around my legs, there was no option of kicking, and the blows I was raining down on his back didn't slow him.

He kicked his door shut and continued across the room, dropping me onto the bed. I shot to my feet immediately, not that it made a difference. Hawk wasn't budging, and I was all smoke and no fire.

"Since you've made your own token, I'm assuming you understand the basics of how they won't work? That they won't operate for anyone but the owner?"

He didn't need to spell it out. Once he'd shut that door, I was done. There was no way out of this room without him.

I might only have smoke, but I was going to make a hell of a stink with it.

"You think this is going to stop me from going to the hill? You think you can stop me from doing what I want?" I yelled.

"Yes, that's exactly what I think." He angled his head down.

I'd never realized how much arrogance could be packaged into such a slight movement. It was misplaced. The girl that had been dragged to Xest, the one who ran from her own shadow, wasn't the woman who stood before him now. No one told me what to do.

I planted my hands on my hips. "And what about tomorrow? The day after? You think you're going to lock me up here forever?"

"If that's how long it takes, it can be arranged."

I'd never seen his eyes so hard, unmoving.

"You can't watch me every second of the day. I'm going to get back to the hill." Even as I said the words, I wasn't sure if they were true. Hawk was unmovable.

"Only way you'll get back there is if you kill me," he said, his voice low and soft.

"If that's what it takes."

"Do your best, honey."

He'd never called me honey before, and it didn't sound sweet.

I grabbed the first thing my hand wrapped around and flung it at him. He ducked, the jar smashing against the door, leaving a golden liquid dripping down its surface.

He opened the door, not in a hurry as he smiled back at me, daring me to try to get past him.

I refused to give him the satisfaction.

He walked out. The door shut and I looked for something else to break.

21

I screamed until I had no voice left, and then broke everything I could get my hands on. I tried to break through the walls, the doors, but it was like hammering on the side of a mountain. It hadn't brought Hawk back. He couldn't hear me. No one could with the way he'd set things up.

The bed on its side, I dropped onto the floor, dragging a blanket over myself as a chill set in and the shaking grew worse. I lost track of time as I lay there, beginning to cramp everywhere.

I felt Hawk's presence as he walked in a while later. He came over and knelt next to me. "If there was an easier way to do this, I would." His hand touched my cheek.

"Stop talking to me. I have nothing to say to you." I turned, giving him my back, trying to settle the edginess that was coursing through me. My hands shook, so I gripped the cover, not wanting him to see. He'd just say it proved his case. All it proved was he liked to torture me.

He didn't leave. I listened as he moved about the room, putting the bed together.

He knelt at my side again, his fingers grazing my neck this time. I shivered—even as bad as I felt, as much as I hated him at this moment, my body still craved his touch. I moved away from him on principle. He curved his arms around me, cradling me against his body as he stood.

"Get off," I said. Every movement made my body ache.

He placed me on the bed before I had time to complain again.

"I don't need your help. This is your fault. You're the one torturing me." Instead of sounding forceful, the words came out soft and hoarse.

My head was lifted and a pillow placed underneath it as he ignored me. He draped another blanket over me, tucking me in. I would've shoved it off, but I was too cold. I decided my best course of action was not to talk anymore.

Hawk grabbed a blanket and a pillow and walked across the room. I spied on his movements through my lashes as he dropped down in front of the door and settled against it, just to make sure I was thoroughly trapped.

"I hate you." I pulled the blanket up closer around my head as another chill spread through my body.

"I'm not doing this to torture you. If I was, I'd let you keep going on as you were until you were dead or had to go back to Rest." He spoke calmly, as if my bitterness and anger didn't touch him.

"I think you like being a bastard and making me miserable," I said.

He got up from his spot, walked to the trunk, and pulled out a familiar box. He tossed it onto the bed beside me.

"Touch it. Let me see your magic flare to life. Show me you're fine and you can walk out of here."

He stood there, arms crossed, daring me to prove

him wrong. I froze, and a shiver that had nothing to do with the weird sickness passed over my body as I told myself to grab the stone. If I proved him wrong, he'd have to back off and leave me be. I could still get to the hill.

The struggle I'd had making the potion for Zurdoch had nothing to do with being weak. Nothing at all. It was a magic I'd never used before. Of course it would be a strain.

Just do it. Grab the stone.

"Too scared to be proven wrong?" Hawk didn't move from his spot, waiting, daring me with his eyes to show him otherwise.

My magic had always been blinding, and it would be now. Even if I was stressed out and less brilliant, who'd notice?

I reached for the box and pulled the stone out. A rainbow of light broke out into the room, but it was no longer a blinding light. It was beautiful but easy to keep your eyes on, its intensity less than half of what it had been the last time I touched it.

I tossed the stone to the bed. "Your tricks aren't going to work. You did something to it."

There was no way my magic had gotten *that* weak. I looked at him, expecting to see glee. His lips were pressed together as if he were more worried than I was.

He reached forward and wrapped his hand around my wrist, feeling my magic again, before dropping it.

"So what if the hill took some of my magic back? Maybe it's better that way," I said, giving him my back again.

I'd known it, hadn't I? Seeing it didn't make any differ-ence. Or it shouldn't.

"You might be fine with something draining your magic, but I'm not."

He moved away, neither of us talking.

～

I DOZED ON AND OFF. Each time I woke up, I felt worse. Tremors were running through my body, like I was withdrawing from some sort of drug. My muscles cramped and I was covered in a cold sweat.

As the pain grew worse, my head seemed to be getting clearer. I hadn't realized it was foggy until this moment. What had happened to me? I'd been going to the hill like some kind of addict, looking for a fix, all the while telling myself it was the right thing to do. I had no agreement from anyone. No sign from heaven or hell that this was part of a deal. I'd been willingly letting some unknown force leech magic out of me, and now here I was, a mess.

The sound of voices in the hall drew me further awake. I shifted until I could see Hawk at the door, talking to Bertha and Bibbi in hushed tones. He turned his head slightly, as if he sensed my attention. He nodded at them and then shut the door, but not before I caught the concerned looks on their faces.

I was glad. I couldn't face anyone right now the way I was feeling, both physically or mentally.

The door opened and shut again. His footsteps grew closer. When I opened my eyes, he was staring down at me.

"There's something wrong with me," I said, and we both knew I didn't mean physically, although that was obvious. I slunk down farther under the covers, shivering.

"I know," he said, as if talking to someone who'd

finally figured out the seriousness of their issues, when he'd been aware all along.

A few uncomfortable seconds passed by, and the painfulness of what I'd been doing continued to hit home. I couldn't quite remember everything, but the room was tossed, and that had been my doing. I'd been a raving lunatic, trying to get to the hill. Out of my mind, trying to give away everything I had.

"Do you know what's wrong with me?" I asked.

"No. You're thinking clearer, so that's something." Hawk handed me a steaming cup of broth as he sat beside me on the bed. "I can't fix you, since we don't know what's wrong, but this might make it a little easier."

I nodded, swallowing past the nausea. "Give me whatever you've got."

I shimmied upward, willing to drink anything for a little relief at this point, not caring what it was or where it came from. I took a sip, and then another, before draining the cup. I sank back down, hoping it would help.

After fifteen minutes, I was hopeful. After thirty, skepticism was setting in. After an hour, with my muscles spasming, I realized it might've made things worse.

Sleep wouldn't come. My body was racked with pain. It felt like someone had reached inside me and was twisting my intestines and knotting them together.

Hawk was near me and then gone. Then back yet again. I'd feel his hands hovering over me with soft chanting. There were other hushed voices in the distance as well. Everything was filtered through a haze of pain as I tossed and turned, unable to find any position that offered me comfort.

My eyes were shut as I heard Oscar speaking to Hawk by the door. "Did you try to do it with..."

Their voices grew softer as the door was shut partially.

A few minutes later, Oscar's voice was clearer. "You need to offer her the choice, then."

I could feel Hawk's gaze on me as he hesitated to answer.

"I will if it doesn't let up soon," Hawk said after a minute or so.

"She's been like this for more than a day. How long are you going to wait?" Oscar asked.

"I don't want her to have to make a choice like that in this condition," Hawk replied, growing impatient.

"I'd want the option if it were me," Oscar said.

Curling onto my side toward them, I opened my eyes. "What option? Is there something that can help? Whatever it is, I want it."

Hawk's jaw was locked, muscles twitching.

"Going to have to tell her now," Oscar said.

Hawk shot him a look like Oscar was the one about to get his insides torn apart.

"You'll want to discuss this in private, I'm guessing," Oscar said with a shrug. He gave me a nod, sympathy in his eyes, before he walked away from the door.

Hawk hesitated for a few moments.

"What is it? Why are you holding out on me?" I asked.

He stepped forward but looked awfully stoic for someone who might be able to release me from my pain.

"I'm not holding out. I was hoping it wouldn't be needed," he said. "It's not an easy fix. It's not guaranteed to work, either, since we don't know what's wrong with you."

"I don't care what it is. Just try it." I curled tighter as more spasms stole my breath.

He moved closer, kneeling near the bed. "Because of what I am, things, other magics, they slide off of me.

There's a chance that whatever is affecting you can be drained somewhat onto me, but we'd have to join together."

"Then do it," I said. I lifted my hand toward him so he could join us. If I wasn't in so much pain, I might start raging about how long he was taking and why he was staring at my hand, instead of doing what needed to be done. Fortunately for him, I didn't have the strength to rage against anything. All I could do was lie there, my hand shaking from the exertion of even outstretching it, because all my strength had been sapped by fighting the pain for so long.

"That's not the kind of joining that has to happen."

I looked from my hand to his eyes, making sure I understood fully. The seriousness of his expression told me I was reading it exactly how he'd meant it.

I'd imagined sex with Hawk more times than I'd admit to anyone. In my visions, I'd been clean, wearing a cute outfit that he'd drag off my body in his need to have me. I'd smell sweet and be fresh as newly fallen snow. Not once had I been a disgusting, sweaty mess feeling like I was dying.

"Do you think you could?" I asked, knowing I would be a tough sell to anyone in my current state.

"Tippi, that is not going to be an issue," he said, taking my hand.

"But look at me. I'm a mess." Waking with more awareness of how utterly crazed I'd been was enough to make me want to hide under a rock for a decade. Now this? I wasn't sure if my body was burning with fever or humiliation.

"You're beautiful." He brushed back the hair from my face.

I gritted my teeth as another spasm took hold.

Then he was pulling the blanket down. He was going to do it. I didn't know how he'd stomach touching me, but I wasn't going to argue. I couldn't handle too much more of this.

He slid off my pants, his hand grazing my hip as his eyes took in my form. He didn't look disgusted, but I wasn't sure how he wasn't.

The pain was ebbing as he stood beside the bed, stripping out of his clothes. I'd seen him naked before, seen the way his muscles flexed with each movement, the way the ridges of his abdomen moved as he reached back and yanked his shirt off. He was a well-built man in every department, and he seemed already prepared for what was needed. If he was conjuring up thoughts of other women, I wasn't going to ask. I wouldn't even think about it.

He kneeled on the bed beside me. "I'm not sure how to do this without hurt—"

I grabbed him, pulling him closer to me, as a wave of pain pushed me past any embarrassment.

"Okay, then," he said, getting the hint.

He smoothed his hands up my legs as he eased them apart and settled between my thighs. His arms rested on either side of my shoulders as he stared down into my eyes. I nodded, knowing he was waiting for one last signal from me that this was the route I wanted to take.

He rested on one arm as his hand followed the curve of my waist to my hips, before drifting across my stomach and then lower. He made slow circular motions, and my body jerked and arched. My breathing became panting, and it had nothing to do with pain.

"Hurry," I said, tugging him closer.

"I don't want to add to your pain," he said softly.

"I'm ready. God, I'm ready."

Hawk removed his hand from my center to position himself, the tip of his cock pressed into me only the slightest bit, testing my entrance. Even now, under the worst possible conditions, I was wet for him.

He pressed in further, slowly chanting as he did. The pain immediately eased.

He cradled my face between his hands and watched for a reaction as he chanted.

I couldn't hold his stare and closed my eyes. The darkness behind my lids accentuated the pleasure.

"It's helping," he said with what sounded like a sigh of relief mixed with something more urgent, as he became fully seated within me.

The sudden easing of pain felt like a miracle. I went from unbelievable pain to pleasure in a heartbeat. The only thing painful now was him not moving at all as he stared down at me. I could tell from his tensed shoulders and neck that staying still wasn't all that pleasurable for him either.

"It's helping, but the pain is still there. We should keep going for a bit to be sure." I arched my back, bucking my hips a bit, trying to help him along.

He nodded, his eyes settling on my lips. "The more joined, the better it might work, if there's still some pain."

"Good point," I said, looking at his mouth.

He closed his lips over mine and withdrew slowly, returning with a more forceful thrust.

With every movement, the reason we were joining our bodies became more lost. The hesitancy to touch him completely disappeared as I was taken up into the moment. His lips moved from my mouth to my throat to my breasts, scorching my skin everywhere he touched.

He took my hand and laid it on his neck, the same place he would touch me when testing my magic, and it was as if a door to his soul opened. I could feel his magic's life force swell through my fingers, down my arm, and it felt like we were joined in two places. I'd never felt so connected to another person in my entire existence. I hadn't had that much sex in my life, but if this was what it was supposed to feel like, I wasn't sure if I'd ever had real sex at all.

He brought me to the edge of the only heaven I believed in anymore, and with a final thrust I was more satiated than I'd ever thought possible. I'd gone from the worst agony to riding waves of bliss.

He collapsed beside me, having withdrawn suddenly, his erection still obvious.

"How do you feel?" His voice was rough around the edges.

"Better." Like a miracle had been performed on me.

"Is the pain fully gone?" Hawk asked.

My limbs had gone from feeling like I was strung up on a torture device to Jell-O.

"Mostly," I said, holding back again on full disclosure.

"Did I stop too soon?" He leaned on his side, hovering over my body, his cock throbbing against my leg.

"You might've," I said, even as my body was screaming at me to get his cock back in me. "You might need to finish yourself for it to work."

His hands were already roving over my flesh again as he said, "Don't worry, we're going work at this until you're completely cured."

22

I'd lost count of how long I'd been in Hawk's room by the time I finally woke. I was just as pain-free as I had been right before the second, and then third go-arounds. As I'd said to him, I didn't want to take any chances.

My head felt clearer than it had in weeks. Reality was hitting me as harshly as the bright sun on my face, streaming through the window. Hawk had been right—Zab, Bibbi, all of them—but I hadn't been able to see it.

The door opened and Hawk walked in. I glanced in his direction and ran a hand through my knotted hair. I didn't know when the last time I bathed was, and that was only the tip of the mess I'd been. That he'd slept with me while I was in this condition made me hope a bomb would strike right where I was lying. It was the only thing capable of obliterating the humiliation that was the last few days of my life. Someone could take a blowtorch to my skin and it wouldn't feel any hotter. As far as morning-after awkwardness went, this was one for the record books.

"You look better."

I couldn't discern if there was regret in his tone or if I was just expecting it to be there.

I nodded, still searching for words as the realization of how crazy I'd gotten settled into my now-rational mind.

"I am." Not perfect, but a whole lot closer to human than I had been.

"Might take you a few days to feel completely normal." He walked over and laid his fingers on my neck. I wasn't going to look at him. I didn't want to know what he felt. Not to mention after how he'd had to fix me, it was hard enough to keep my skin a normal shade. People were going to think I was related to Mertie if it didn't stop.

Don't look. Don't. Look.

I looked anyway.

His lips were pressed together and his gaze flickered to mine but moved on. For a change, he was having a hard time holding *my* gaze. It didn't make me feel any better.

Wait, which part of what was going on was his problem? Was he afraid I'd want to sleep with him again and he was no longer interested? That I'd expect something more from him that he wouldn't want? Or was it my magic being a jumbled-up mess?

"You're weaker, but that doesn't mean you'll stay that way." His hand dropped.

Wait. This had nothing to do with sex?

I wasn't sure which was worse: him being disgusted and done with me or that my magic was a mess. I guess it would depend. Was I permanently damaged goods? And not in the old-fashioned way, but in a Xest way, where my magic might not return?

"That sounds like you think I could be permanently diminished."

I'd been an Infinite. It was supposed to come back. I regenerated. That was how it worked. I wasn't a witch who had to worry about budgeting my daily magic use, reclaiming what was left after I started a fire or lit a candle. That had never been a concern for me.

"Is it possible I'll continue to weaken?" Suddenly I had no problem meeting Hawk's gaze. Desperation had kicked embarrassment's ass right out of my mind.

"I don't know. I'm not sure what happened. Even if you do, it's not the end of the world. You still have enough magic to have a long life in Xest."

He leaned against the wall, his expression resigned, as if he'd already thought this all through while I was too busy falling apart.

I hadn't wanted all the magic I'd had. More often than not, it seemed like a burden. Now, I'd lost my mind and a good chunk of my magic, turned into an animal, all to get to that hill, and I couldn't even say why. Everyone had seen me morph into this crazed person, and now they'd see my failure. It would probably be talked about all through Xest. The witch with it all, the witch of all witches, did something stupid and now had to budget lighting a fire.

The worst part was that whatever had happened might happen again. What if whatever was lying in that hill still had a pull on me and I wasn't capable of stopping myself? What if I went back there until I had nothing left to give? I felt like I was on the precipice of falling apart, and I wasn't going to do it here, not again. Hawk had picked up enough pieces of me yesterday and the day before.

"I'm going to go get cleaned up." I walked toward the door, waiting to see if he'd try to stop me. I went slowly, seeing if he'd trust me enough to be on my own, wondering if *I* trusted myself. Would the urges that had been driving me come back?

He moved to the door first, opening it. "I'll tell Bertha you're up. She's been cooking nonstop in preparation for you feeling better."

I groaned.

He stood beside the open door, waiting for me. "She's cooking her normal comfort food. She said too much was going on to cut out all the good stuff right now."

I WAS clean and dressed and feeling a little like the first time I'd walked down the stairs, back when I didn't know anyone but Hawk. This time was way worse. A blank slate would be better than the memory I'd last left them with, clawing and fighting on the staircase as I tried to leave. Then there was the sweaty mess version from Hawk's room. They might also know what Hawk had to do to...

Nope. Not thinking about that one.

I walked into the back room and grabbed a chair at the table, the shame I felt upstairs still riding me like a devil with the flames of hell. Bertha piled up dishes in front of me as if she didn't notice she could cook her vittles on my forehead.

Bibbi was glowing at me, like I hadn't been a wild animal. Zab had a toothy grin going on, and Oscar was unfazed, as usual. Musso was nodding, like I'd done something right somehow. Hawk was reading over something in his books, probably working out how to fix me.

Mertie took a seat beside me and said, "Glad to see you're not still psycho. It wasn't a good look."

"It wasn't her fault. It was a spell. Nothing to be done about that," Bibbi said, glaring in Mertie's direction.

So much for pretending. I might as well lay it all out.

"I just want to say I'm sorry if I wasn't myself lately," I said, hoping that might be the end of it.

"We know. It was the hill," Oscar said, grabbing a bun off one of the many plates piled up in front of me.

Zab leaned closer, whispering, "Now that you're normal you probably won't care, but I told Hawk about the token after I realized what you were up to."

"Thanks." I meant it. Zab might've saved my life. How much magic had that place drained from me? What if I'd kept going? What if I went again? It was all I could think of.

"We think someone planted something at the hill to slowly drain you. That's the running theory right now," Oscar said.

Hawk walked back over, and it seemed like the room grew quieter the closer he got to me.

"Might've been some sort of trap set by Xazier or Lou," he said. "We've all been up there, trying to figure out what's wrong, but no one has been able to pick up anything. We want to go back with you tomorrow if you're up to it."

"Yeah, sure." I'd finally gotten Bertha's good food back, and now I couldn't eat.

I WAS SETTLED on the couch in the back room, realizing how I'd been avoiding this spot. My favorite place in the building, and I'd been afraid to sit here.

Bibbi spotted me on the couch, and her face lit up as

she walked over and joined me, grabbing half of my throw blanket.

"I'm glad you're still hanging out. It was lonely without you," she said.

"Thanks." There were usually other people about, but we'd always had a close bond. Bibbi treated Zab like an annoying brother. Mertie was like the stepsister she never wanted. Bertha and Musso were usually doing their own thing. Then there was Oscar, but I wasn't touching that subject at the moment.

"I know you had some rough days, but you're looking much better."

There was this hope in her eyes that I'd be the same old Tippi. Would she still think that if she knew it all? There might not be any slaying dragons in my future. My days of being a badass might be officially done. I wasn't sure how weak I was. I might be clinging to Whimsy status soon. I'd never wanted to be a hard hitter or some super-powerful witch who couldn't be touched, so telling her shouldn't feel as hard as it did. There was no point in pretending either way.

"There's a chance I might never be the same, or as strong as I was," I said.

She smiled, her eyes soft. "No matter what happens, you're still my peeps. I don't care what you've got going on under the hood."

That was the dichotomy of Bibbi. She was either a raging monster if you were on her bad side, or the kindest person you'd ever meet if you were her friend.

"I never cared how much magic I had. The thing that upsets me is it was taken from me, and I willingly let it be. I was an idiot and walked right into a trap." I was shaking my head, still reeling from the idiot I'd been.

"I feel like a fool almost once a day, so don't let that get you down. But as for the stealing? Yeah, that would burn. I had this bracelet, and one day it disappeared. I knew this girl Rhonda had taken it. We'd been close, and she was the only one who could get in my stuff. It wasn't even a nice bracelet." Her nose crinkled. "Actually, it was a downright ugly bracelet now that I think about it. But having it taken still burns."

"You never tried to get it back?" I asked, knowing that Bibbi wasn't one to roll over.

"Oh, I did. She said she didn't have it, and then she died not long after. It was of suspicious causes, and people had heard us fighting. I thought it best to let it go at that point." She gave a little shrug. "As to your situation, you'll be okay. You're tough. You'll figure out something."

I wasn't so sure. I'd made some really bad choices. My resourcefulness felt like it had run out the back door, skipping and holding hands with my luck as it went.

Bibbi was watching me out of the corner of her eye, a little smirk blooming.

"What?" I asked.

"Oscar said Hawk had to *fix* you." The smirk graduated into a smile.

There was no doubt that Oscar had told her just *how* Hawk had helped me, details and all.

"He did." I was not going to blush.

Shit. Too late. I was already blushing.

"Hmmm." She smiled and nodded. "Well, considering how good you look, he must be a very fine fixer."

Suddenly her attention was off me and at the door, where Oscar was lingering. It didn't take a genius IQ to read his expression as he caught Bibbi's eye.

Bibbi stood, stretching her arms. "Man oh man, I'm tired. I'll see you in the morning, okay?"

"Sure. Hope you get fixed up really well yourself," I said, trying not to laugh and failing.

She turned back to me, her smile eating up the lower half of her face. "Oh, no need to worry there."

23

I topped my tea off and curled up into the chair in front of the fireplace, everyone else having long gone to sleep. No one was watching me outright, but I wouldn't be surprised in the least if Hawk had set up some sort of silent alarm on the door. Not that I minded at the moment. I was more afraid of sneaking out than anyone at this point.

I felt for the token in the pocket of my long sweater, even though it was gone. I'd never use it again, but part of me wanted it back to remind myself of how slippery my existence could be, of how little I knew and how fast I could fall.

The back door opened and Hawk walked in, the warm glow of the fire making the angles of his face harsher. Or had the last couple of days taken a toll on him as well?

"I didn't thank you for helping me." Should I, in essence, thank him for sleeping with me? "You know, because it had to have hurt," I said. Did it, though? Did using his magic to fix mine really cause him pain? What probably really hurt was the gross mess I'd been. That couldn't have been good, not that he'd seemed to struggle with it. Did I say something?

No. Way too awkward.

"You don't have to. Pain doesn't affect me like others," he said.

At least he hadn't thought I was thanking him for the sex.

"Or affected by the cold?" I would've asked almost anything to move the subject along.

He smiled slightly. "Or cold. My kind have been around since nearly the beginning of Xest. Not everything was planned. Some of it happened on its own."

"Like Bautere?" I asked on a hunch.

"Yes." He rested his arm on the mantel, silence growing in between us as we both seemed to be separately brooding on something.

He was staring at me like he could read my every thought. "Nothing will happen tomorrow," he said.

There was a steadiness and determination in his voice that almost made me believe he could shift reality into whatever he wanted.

"I know. I'm not worried." I wasn't, not while I was surrounded by people who would stop me from doing something stupid. But what if it triggered me again? What if it set off that strange driving force that robbed me of all logic until I was a rabid animal running back to the hill? Then what? How close could I get to it before I had a problem?

"Nothing like that will happen ever again because I won't let it. Your story won't end like that."

I nodded, wishing I could trust he was right, but he didn't know me as well as he thought. I could be persistent and stubborn like he'd never seen. Next time I wanted to get there, he might not know I was going. Acid swirled in my stomach as I imagined losing myself, everything I had here.

I got up, not wanting to talk about tomorrow, or think about it. I'd deal with tomorrow when tomorrow was here.

He reached out, wrapping an arm around my waist and tugging me closer.

"What are you doing?" I asked.

"Go ahead, try to get away from me. You don't need to be scared."

I turned my face to the fire. "I understand the point you're making, but you might be underestimating me, you know, when I'm determined."

"Tippi, look at me."

When I didn't turn back to him, he cupped the back of my head, forcing me to.

"I'm telling you, I'll make sure it doesn't happen again." He massaged my scalp in a soothing caress.

I gave up denying a fear he could so clearly read on me.

"If you were capable of stopping me, you would've done it the first time. I can be very resourceful, but it's my problem, and I'll work it out."

"But I did stop you. I just didn't do it fast enough. I saw it happening and didn't do anything about it. You're always saying I'm trying to control everything, so I backed off. I was trying something different, and it clearly didn't work. *That* won't happen again. You want to see determination? This is what it looks like."

Hawk, the same Hawk who tried to tell everyone what to do always, had tried to not be controlling? Was that what he was saying? And now it was so clear he was mad that he hadn't been, that if I did survive this, he'd probably be worse than ever. I didn't know if I should laugh or cry at the possibilities.

It welled up as a giggle and then broke into a full-out laugh.

He smiled down at me. "What's so funny about that?"

"I don't know. That you tried to not be controlling for maybe the first time in your life? Or that it turned out horribly and the monster you might become because of that? I'm not sure myself what I'm more afraid of right now, the hill or you."

"I'd put your money on me." He smirked.

His eyes grew intent, the hand at my waist pulling me upward.

I knew what was coming, and like clockwork, my spine arched and my lips parted. I opened my eyes again when his lips didn't touch mine.

His gaze was on the back door.

He looked back down at me, dipping his mouth to mine and delivering on what I'd been waiting for until my knees were weak and I was ready to spin up the stairs to his room.

He unwrapped his arm from my waist. "I've got to go handle something. Get some sleep."

24

I grabbed my jacket, trying to ignore all the eyes on me. They were looking at me as if I were some fragile statue that was teetering on the edge of a shelf. The slightest nudge, the smallest draft, I might topple and shatter. I pulled my coat on, steeling myself, trying to give them, and me, a sense of confidence that I didn't feel.

Not long ago, I'd been riding the high of beating immigration. I'd gone up against Dread and come out on top. I'd felt so confident, like I could take on anything or anyone. Now I was afraid to walk across Xest, to a grassy hill, because I might turn into a wallowing mess of need. I might lose myself.

"I'm ready." Hawk met my gaze, and I looked away, remembering the pathetic, needy creature who'd been a bundle of nerves last night.

He tilted his head and then walked into the back room. I followed, a little too eager to hear some sort of reassurance and angry that I was so desperate for it.

He pulled a necklace with a glowing red amulet out of his pocket and went to lift the chain over my head.

"What is that?" I asked, stepping back before he could place it on me.

"It'll block anything that might be there. I made it this morning."

He'd made me a magical security blanket, like I was a scared kid. I didn't know if I should be thankful, insulted, or embarrassed. Probably a bit of everything, but I had too much pride to take it. If I did take it, I wouldn't know how vulnerable I was, and that was crucial going forward. It was one thing to have a weakness and a completely different thing to not know how bad that weakness was.

I shook my head, taking another step back.

"I appreciate that, but I don't want a crutch. I need to face whatever is there and know that it can't get me."

He watched me for a few moments and then tucked it into his back pocket without objecting. He didn't push it any further. He hadn't wanted me to use it either.

We walked back into the office.

"Let's go," Hawk said to Oscar. "Bautere is meeting us there."

We took Hawk's door and were there a few minutes later, Bautere waiting as expected.

Hawk, Oscar, and Bautere spread out slightly, as if trying to each cover a certain area.

"We've all been over this area but haven't picked up anything. What would you normally do?" Hawk said.

My heart began to pound as snow crunched underfoot along the familiar trail, a worn path still there. I stopped as the feeling in the pit in my stomach began to creep into my psyche. A familiar longing reached out, calling me closer. That was when my feet refused to take another step. I wasn't sure if I could move if I wanted to, knowing what lay ahead.

"Whatever it is, it starts here. It'll get stronger as I walk closer to the spot over there." I pointed to the area that no longer had snow cover from me kneeling for so long. "Do you need me to keep going?"

"No, stay right there," Oscar said. He wasn't the strongest in our group, but he was by far the best tracker. He walked over and then knelt beside me, putting his hand on the ground where I stood.

"There's something here for sure." He took another few steps, reaching down again. "Oh yeah, something is definitely off. It's specific to her. I can feel it pulling at her now that she's close."

"Can you pick up a signature?" Hawk asked, walking over.

I stayed right where I was, sorting through the feelings and cravings in me, seeing how far they would push and pull at my psyche.

"No. Whoever or whatever did this was smart about it. It used her magic to cloak any trace of theirs. Hers is too potent to distinguish anything beyond it." Oscar grazed the snow in different spots with his hands.

"Are you saying there's nothing you can pick up?" Bautere asked.

"No." Oscar felt about the area for another few moments before standing, his eyes still on the trail.

"There's nothing?" I asked.

"If you were to think of magic like a perfume or cologne, as it leeched your magic, or perfume, it washed out its own. Yours is so strong that it obliterated any trace of it. I'm sorry, but I just can't tell." Oscar spread his hands.

My magic was perfusing the area instead of pulsing

through my veins. I felt like I'd been robbed, because I had.

"So it might've been anyone?" I asked.

"Not anyone," Oscar said, shaking his head. "This is high-level stuff. Not many witches or warlocks could pull this off, and I know all of the ones that could. None of them would attempt to do this. My guess it was Lou or Xazier or someone associated with them."

"If it was them, they'll be answering for this," Hawk said.

Lou or Xazier. It was as if hearing those names helped break the attraction of what was calling me. It was like having an addiction to sweets but knowing someone was holding out a poisoned candy. The urge to connect was still there, but my desire for vengeance superseded it.

I stepped closer to the area where I'd kneel on the hill. Hawk immediately blocked my path.

"What are you doing?" he asked, even though it was very clear.

"I want to see if I can break it, whatever it is." I looked past him to the spot, refusing to believe I couldn't undo what had been done. If not from magic, then from my will alone. They say adrenaline can make you many more times stronger than you are. Fury was bringing me to a whole new level.

"No." Hawk wasn't budging from his spot in front of me.

I could feel the spell pulsating toward me, urging me forward. All it was doing now was building the anger inside of me. I couldn't let it remain here, whatever it was.

I directed my attention to Hawk. "You don't understand. I need to break it. I *can* do this."

Hawk shot Oscar and Bautere a look.

Bautere left without saying a word.

"I'm going to check out the area over there. I didn't test that spot," Oscar said, walking away.

Hawk dropped his voice to nearly a whisper. "We don't know what happened or what kind of trap was laid. It's too dangerous to play around with. Once we know more, it'll be safer. This isn't the right time." He was standing like an immovable wall in between me and the place I needed to be.

"Whatever spell this spell is, it has to be destroyed. I can't leave this place knowing it exists." I'd thought I could come here and be all right, leave after testing the waters. Turned out I couldn't, but not for the reasons I'd feared.

"It *will* be destroyed." He grasped my shoulders. "But not now."

There was no way I was going to get past him. The man that watched me lure Dread to this same hill, using my very life source as the bait, wouldn't let me get anywhere close enough to test my mettle against this new threat. That was how pathetic I must seem after what happened. He didn't look at me like the woman who could do anything anymore. I was the pathetic girl from Rest who needed protecting.

It felt like the ground had dropped out from underneath me and I was drifting into a chasm of bleakness. I groaned, shaking my head. I would've taken a step back if he didn't have a hold of me.

"You think I'm too weak?" It was a question I already knew the answer to.

"Never weak. Just not ready. First, we get answers. We

question Lou and Xazier, see what Mertie can find out, and then we act."

"I *can* do this."

I looked to the clearing, knowing there was no way I was going to get past him.

25

Breakfast had cleared out but Hawk was lingering, watching me.

"I called for Lou and Xazier to come later on tonight," he said when we were finally alone.

I'd known this was coming. It was a logical step. Now that we knew more, we could push harder. See if one of them cracked or gave up some information. Didn't make me want to see either of them anymore, especially knowing that one of them might be behind it.

"Okay," I said.

"I can handle it alone if you want," he offered, his eyes dropping down to where I'd fisted my hands.

"No. I'll be here," I said, before I walked into the office to work, or do something that didn't include punching random objects. I'd already looked out of my mind enough in the past couple of weeks. I couldn't add beating up a bookcase to my resumé.

Bibbi walked into the office fifteen minutes later. "Sorry! I don't know how I overslept."

I did. I'd heard the noises coming from her room last night. Oscar had gotten back a few minutes before me, and he hadn't wasted his time.

She pulled up a chair by my desk. "Well? How'd it go?"

I was fairly certain she'd gotten all the details already, but I wasn't bringing that up either.

"It was okay. I mean, I felt it, but knowing what would happen, that it was a trap and not something good? It got rid of any urge I had from before."

She let out a long sigh. "What a relief." She tilted her head. "Why don't you look happy?"

"I'm happy that I was able to resist it." That part was true.

"But?" Bibbi rolled a hand in a *go on* motion.

I shook my head. "Nothing." Or nothing I was ready to talk about. As much as I wanted to go back to the hill, wipe out whatever was there, what if Hawk was right? I was too weak to do it, especially now. Maybe if I gave it some time, my magic would regenerate to its former level. I'd get stronger, and it wouldn't matter.

"What is it?" Bibbi asked again.

I drummed my pencil on the surface in front of me, trying to sum up everything. But I didn't know how to sum up all the problems, or what to do about them. Everything I'd thought was the right move had backfired. I dropped the pencil, my beat as off as my decisions lately.

"I don't know what the right thing to do is anymore," I said.

"Then do nothing?" Bibbi cringed, waiting to see if that sounded good to me. Obviously she wasn't too keen on any direction either.

"Yeah, maybe." I shrugged, starting a drumroll again, this one somehow sounding ominous even with a pencil.

"Bibbi, you know where the newsflash papers are?" Zab called from across the room.

"I'll go get them. I wouldn't mind the walk." I tossed the pencil on the desk as I stood up.

Zab froze.

"She's fine, Zab," Bibbi said. "She's got the monkey off her back. No more weird staring, either."

Musso softly laughed on the other side of the room.

I WAS WALKING ACROSS XEST, coming back from getting supplies, when it seemed I was doomed to be stalked by one kind of monkey or another. The No Evils were walking in my direction, dressed like they were a band from the seventies with matching little fur coats and sunglasses.

"Hey, it's Tippi," See No Evil said. "How's it going over at the broker building?"

"Heard we got outta there right in the nick of time," Speak No Evil added, before taking a swig from his tiny flask.

"Word's out the food took a hard nosedive," Hear No Evil said.

"Total wipeout hard. Like, no survivors hard," Speak No Evil said. "Zark has its pitfalls, but he makes a mean buttered bun."

The three of them launched into cackling laughter.

"Well, you heard wrong. The food is great. I can't imagine who you've been listening to." As soon as I got back, I was going to have a long talk with Mertie. It was bad enough how she acted at meals. Did she have to tell all of Xest that Betha's new meals were bombing? How would that help Bertha launch her new business?

"Man, you still can't lie worth a damn. Aren't you practicing?" Speak No Evil said.

"You gotta practice, especially when you're that bad," Hear No Evil said.

"A lot, too. Stand in front of the mirror or something. Everyone needs practice," See No Evil said.

"Well, it was really nice to see you, but I'm running late." I took off before I picked one of them up and squeezed until their little head popped off.

As I walked away, Speak No Evil said, "She's such a mess. I'm glad we broke out on our own. Helping her was a major drain."

I walked into the office a few minutes later like a heat-seeking missile. I located Mertie pouring herself a tea in the back room.

She glanced at me as I headed straight for her.

She went back to stirring her tea as she said, "Why do you look like someone spat on your buttered buns?"

I leaned on the counter so I could get a good look at her face when I asked, "Are you telling people Bertha's new food is bad?"

"I've told several people. Why do you ask?" She looked up at me, clueless as to how that might be an issue. If she wasn't a retired demon, and technically from hell, and I hadn't seen her bad behavior on many occasions, I might not believe her ignorance. But she was a demon, and she was from hell, and she really had no idea.

"You *can't* do that," I said, feeling like I was arguing

with a two-year-old about throwing their food all over the floor, knowing they'd do it again less than a second later.

She squinted as she took a sip of her tea. It took her another few seconds to digest what I was saying. "Why not? It's *really* bad. I'm not talking so-so, either. The worst offenders in hell got better than that fare. Just saying, it feels like I'm being punished at every meal." She took her tea and made her way over to the couch, still nonplussed over anything I was saying.

I followed her. If I fixed nothing else in Xest, I was going to fix this issue.

"For the same reason you can't say it at dinner. It's *mean*."

"You know, I could see that my speaking the truth was bothering you, but I'm still not entirely clear on why it's a problem." She picked up one of the gossip magazines Bibbi kept reading. She pointed to a famous actor on the cover. "Just so you know, sold his soul. I wasn't privy to that deal, but word gets around." She started flipping through it.

"Because it hurts her feelings and it's not nice," I said.

She laid the gossip mag down on her lap and looked at me as if she could barely contain her eyeballs in her head. "It's going to be much more painful when she tries to sell that sawdust and no one wants it. You people all lying and acting like you don't want to vomit after the first bite are the ones screwing her up. I think telling her the truth would be doing her a solid."

I took a deep breath, trying to see a way around her rationale. She did have a solid point.

She was leaning forward with a gotcha look, smiling smugly. "See? You agree. When you think of it, *you're* the one not being nice."

I held out for a couple of seconds before I relented.

"Look, you might have a point that maybe some criticism might not be a bad thing. Perhaps we should say *something*, but there's no reason to tell anyone else in Xest. What happens when she launches her business and it flops?"

"If she keeps cooking like that, it's going to and it'll have nothing to do with me. I'm the one that would've warned her." She threw her hands up.

"That's not the point. Promise me you won't talk to anyone else?"

"You know, for everyone's complaints about hell, it was a lot easier to get along there. You people have a lot of rules about what's right and wrong and nice and nasty. Too many rules by far." She huffed, reopening the magazine and kicking up her hooves onto the coffee table.

For some reason, they always sounded like they weighed more than normal feet. Like when she walked, the floor reverberated with her steps.

"Why did you leave hell anyway?" There must be some story. It wasn't like you saw demons walking around all over the place. It couldn't be that bad of a gig.

"I don't want to talk about it." She buried her nose in the magazine.

"Sorry. I didn't realize it was a touchy subject."

She shook her head briskly but didn't look at me as she said, "It's not."

"Okay, well, if you want to talk about it at some point, I wouldn't judge, not that there's anything to judge."

She stopped flipping her magazine and angled her head partially toward me, but still not looking at me. "There's nothing to talk about."

"Mertie! You working or what?" Zab shouted from the office. "Your ride to go tank the kid's exam is here."

"I'm coming!" she screamed twice as loud as needed. "And tell my ride he's getting paid. If he's got to wait an extra five minutes, he better suck it up."

She dropped the magazine on the table and left without saying goodbye, as she usually did.

26

"Lou's not coming," I said. "He's never late for appointments."

It was an hour past when Lou should've arrived. I sipped on some tea, eyeing up Hawk and Oscar to see if they were going to chime in.

Hawk was standing near the mantel, leaning against it slightly. He was trying to keep his body relaxed, but one look at his eyes and you saw blood.

"You think Xazier is going to show?" Oscar asked, sitting on the opposite couch, looking much less lethal than Hawk.

I shrugged.

Hawk walked over. "If he doesn't, it'll just be more tracking in the morning."

Oscar shook his head. "I can't hop planes."

Hawk glanced at Oscar. "There are other ways."

Oscar's gaze snapped to Hawk like he'd gotten yanked by a bungee cord. "You're not thinking of..."

"It's been done before." Hawk's jaw shifted as a flicker of black hide flashed on his neck.

Oscar got to his feet. "Yeah, but that's..."

Hawk shot Oscar a look that seemed to make him lose his voice completely.

"What are you talking about? Thinking of what?" I asked, not liking the blood lust I saw in Hawk or the edginess of Oscar.

Oscar looked at Hawk then me, and then shook his head.

"Hawk?" I asked.

"Xazier should be here any minute. This isn't the time to explain," he said.

I would've pressed further if not for the sound of the front door opening.

Xazier strolled into the office, smiling like a man who'd just gotten lucky on a date and even luckier that he'd dumped her early. His steps faltered as he looked at me, then Oscar, and then Hawk. His eyes grew smaller as he finished his perusal. He came to a complete standstill.

"Do we have a problem? I thought this was a social call, but I'm getting the sense that something is afoot."

Hawk looked like he was envisioning Xazier gutted on the floor. Being the victim of the spell, being the one who'd been robbed, I was the person with the most to be angry about, and for once I wasn't jumping to any conclusions. That was a lesson learned the hard way and too many times at this point. Things were often not what they seemed, and I wouldn't toss out a possible ally, or pick a fight with someone I didn't need to, without having *some* proof. Although the burden of proof I required was a lot lower than what might hold up in a court of law. There was only so much blood lust of my own I could water down if I smelled guilt on him. This trap had mentally and literally brought me to my knees, and I'd be getting my pound of flesh from someone.

Before I could finish musing on how I'd kill Xazier if he was guilty, Hawk was across the room in a blur. Xazier's jacket was in his fists as he had the demon shoved against the wall, his feet dangling above the floor. Hawk's threshold for evidence was clearly much lower than mine.

"I'd like to remind you that if you kill me, you'll void the act of nonviolence between planes." Xazier's voice came out smooth, if you didn't catch the tremor on that last word.

I made my way closer so I could examine every tiny movement of Xazier's face. If he so much as flicked his glance in a guilty way, I might have to get in on the action. My anger was about to get the best of me.

"You seem to need a reminder on who I am," Hawk growled.

Xazier's eyes went big, and it was pretty clear he didn't need any such reminder.

"Did you set that trap?" Hawk asked, Xazier's feet still dangling.

"What trap?" Xazier asked, his tone a little less smooth this time, like it had gotten run over by a four-wheeler.

Oscar moved to Hawk's other side. "That bullshit isn't going to get you out of this room alive."

It was a good thing Bibbi wasn't here. She would've stabbed Xazier with a butter knife already. Actually, maybe it was unfortunate she was missing this. She really would've enjoyed it. Too bad Hawk had cut everyone else off from this one.

"Don't lie to me," Hawk said, moving his forearm against Xazier's neck.

Could you kill a demon by choking? Didn't seem like a viable plan. Having no previous knowledge of fighting demons, I was going to leave the dirty work to Hawk, who seemed quite at home with it. Xazier didn't seem overly happy, so it had some effect.

Was Xazier lying? I studied his every twitch. It was too hard to tell. If he was a liar, he was the best I'd ever seen.

"Answer me." Hawk shifted his arm higher, forcing Xazier's chin up.

"I knew about it, but it wasn't me," Xazier said, his voice growing raspy. Maybe you *could* choke a demon.

Hawk moved his arm and released Xazier, who dropped to the ground but didn't quite topple to his knees.

"Who set it?" I asked.

Xazier rubbed his neck as he turned to look at me. "Who do you think? It was Lou."

I gave his chest a shove, making him bump into the wall. "You knew this and were waiting for me to get screwed!"

He cringed away from me, but it was probably mostly to do with Hawk looming over my shoulder.

"What did you expect? I wasn't doing it, but there wasn't any downside for me. Either you beat Lou and dragged him into the hill, or Lou sucked you dry and got all your magic. Either way, it wasn't my problem and fixed my issue," Xazier said. He lifted his shoulders, as if I couldn't possibly fault him.

In truth, I didn't. If it had come down to him or me, I would've done the same and not even blinked.

"How do we undo it?" Hawk asked.

"We can't," Xazier said.

"Then we have a problem." Hawk reached out and

grabbed Xazier's jacket, about to hoist him against the wall again.

Xazier tried to pull away. "She might be able to, though."

"How?" I asked, stepping in between Hawk and Xazier. I couldn't let Hawk kill the demon who knew how I could get my magic back.

"The spell pulled at your magic, making you want to give it. All you need to do is pull it back harder and the snare will unravel."

"That's it? Just pull stronger?" I asked, not believing it could be so simple.

"Yes." Xazier stopped trying to smooth the wrinkles out of his jacket and looked straight into my eyes.

"And what if I can't?" What if it was too late? What if I was already too drained?

Xazier looked at me with pity in his expression, as if he knew all of my unanswered questions.

"Then you can't," he said, without any gloating.

He was innocent in this. Of that I was sure.

"Go," I said, wanting him to leave before the violence I could feel coming off Hawk decided Xazier was a good enough target.

Xazier didn't waste any time leaving.

"Lou will not get away with this," Hawk said, before he left as well, Oscar following after him in a little too hurried a manner.

Oscar strolled into the office in the middle of a business day in full swing and headed over to Bibbi. Nothing about that was unusual except the way he scanned the room as he did, and then the way his eyes held for a second on Hawk, and then me, before he went to hang out by Bibbi's table.

Hawk walked out the front door, and Oscar looked at me.

"The job should be done by tomorrow," I informed the client in front of me.

"I always get my work done in a timely fashion, not like you young kids." She skimmed the contract, and I waited, knowing what was coming. "That's absolute robbery. You're taking how much? That's absurd."

She continued, and I let her carry on without comment. Her name was Hildy. She didn't look a day younger than a hundred, and she was particularly good at ruining relationships. The pay she got for her jobs was great because there seemed to be no lack of payment a scorned lover was willing to pay to see their ex miserable.

The big issue was the conversion rate from misery to coin was horrible, so she only saw ten percent per job. There was nothing I could do. No one wanted to hold on to misery.

Oscar was shooting me looks again, then glancing toward the back room, as Bibbi was shifting through her pile.

Hildy finally made her way out the door, giving me a half-hour break before my next client, so whatever Oscar wanted better be fast. In that time span, I was going to eat, fake-bully Mertie into getting me a cocoa, and run upstairs and change my shirt. I'd spilled tea on it an hour ago while pondering what to do about my current predicament.

I headed to the back room, making it easy for Oscar. It took him zero seconds to follow me.

"What is it? Why do you keep giving me looks like the world is ending if we don't speak?" I asked.

"You need to have a talk with Hawk." His voice was urgent but hushed, and he kept an eye on the doors.

Oscar didn't go over Hawk's head and come to me for anything. They had a direct connection. There was never an in-between. If there was, something was very wrong.

"Why? What's the matter?" My stomach plummeted, hit the ground, and bungeed up into my throat, lodging itself there.

"Last night, when he said there were other ways? There aren't. Or not ways that won't put a price on your head. There will be zero chance if he goes ahead with what he wants to do to Lou that I, or anyone in Xest, will be able to save his ass."

I leaned on the counter. "What's he going to do?"

"If you can't get Lou to come here, Hawk's going to go

get him, and not in a good way. It's some real questionable magic, and it's forbidden on every plane of existence."

"Why would he do that?" I asked, shocked I could get enough air into my lungs to speak.

"Because of you. He's protecting you, and you have to stop this." His tone was nearly frantic.

"I'll do whatever I can, but I don't know if Lou will show for me either. He got what he wanted. That's why he hasn't shown." I knew. I was the one who'd handed it to him.

The front door to the office opened, and Oscar tilted his head in that direction. "Just get it done." He walked out without a backward glance.

I turned and laid my hands on the counter, dropping my head and trying to come up with a plan. If I could make Lou do what I wanted, he would've shown up last night. He wouldn't have tricked me. I couldn't control him when I had all my magic, and now that I was at a fraction of what I'd been, how would I ever be able to force him to do anything?

I heard steps approaching and turned, waiting.

"Mute us," I said as Hawk walked into the back room.

He took a look at my face, and the din from the office immediately died. It was a neat trick that I'd always assumed I'd learn one day, when I was bored and things finally settled down. It was the way I'd thought about a lot of spells, until my magic was lost, or mostly. Now muting a room might be beyond my capabilities, and the longer I wondered if it was going to come back, if I'd been robbed permanently of my magic, the more I tossed and turned at night. I realized how comforting it had been to have all the possibilities laid out before me, especially as I stood here now, completely helpless.

"Are you planning on doing something to track Lou?" Subtlety didn't usually work with Hawk. I was hoping there was nothing to tell.

"Perhaps." He turned and moved toward the bookshelves, as if he was either very interested in something else or not at all interested in this discussion.

"What is it?" I stalked him across the room.

"It's better if we don't discuss it. Putting it out into the universe prematurely isn't the best idea."

I leaned both my hands on the back of the couch. It was so bad he didn't want to say it aloud? I stayed that way for a few minutes until he went to leave the room, and it spurred me to action.

I followed him to the door and grabbed his arm. "I don't want you to do it, whatever it is. If it's so bad you can't speak of it, *don't* do it."

"I'm not allowing him to get away with this."

His tone, his stare, even the line of his shoulders— everything about him told me this was a losing argument.

"You didn't want me to go on the hill, and I didn't," I said, refusing to give in.

He didn't say anything. The set of his jaw made me think that the line of reasoning that would make him back down didn't exist.

I shoved away my feelings of loss, my own anger, and looked at the man in front of me. I had to sell him on what I was about to say if I had any chance of saving him.

"I was upset, but the more I think about it, it's better. There's nothing left to fight over. We tell them it's over. We're done. We go on with our lives."

"Nobody is going to take from you and get away with it."

He took a step toward the door, and I got in his way, staring up at him as if I were seeing him for the first time.

He was ready to go down in a blaze of glory because I'd been wronged. If I could watch us from a distance, I was probably looking at him the way that woman outside of the Sweet Shop had been looking at the man who'd handed her a chocolate pastry. What he felt for me wasn't clear. That he'd made mistakes was glaringly obvious, but he was going to ruin his life, risk everything he had, in order to avenge my loss. I'd never had someone do that for me, ever.

I couldn't let it happen. The cost was too high.

"I need the stone," I said, convinced that if I got a hold of it, if even for a second, maybe I could make it shine brighter. It just had to last long enough for him to think I was gaining my magic back.

"It's not available," he said, lying coolly to my face.

"I know you have it, or it's close by." It always was. He owned the stone.

"I have it, but it's not available to you," he clarified.

Nothing about that answer shocked me. "What if I'm getting better on my own and you don't need to do anything? I've always been an Infinite. Maybe it'll right itself." If I wasn't, or I couldn't fake it, what was I going to do?

Things were spiraling fast. Heaven and hell might still be after me because I hadn't given back the magic that I no longer had to give anymore. Hawk was about to do something that would put him in everyone's crosshairs. There was no way to stop him because I was too weak, because I'd been an idiot. This last ploy *had* to work simply because there were very few options left.

He lifted his hand to my neck. I tilted my head back,

giving him access, and then I concentrated harder than I ever had in my life on drumming up some sort of surge. Something that would stop this chain of events.

His hand dropped and so did his expression before he shuttered it.

My shoulders slumped.

He walked out of the room, and there was zero doubt he was harboring as much blood lust as he had when he walked in.

Now what did I do?

28

I was back at my desk with still zero idea of how to fix anything. Oscar had left a couple of hours ago, but not before he told me things were spiraling and I had to fix them. He didn't seem to be absorbing the fact that I didn't know how to fix anything. Hawk had walked out, and I had no idea where to or if it was even too late to fix things. Worse, Mertie was pacing the length of the office for the fiftieth time, as if she had discovered some horrific issue of her own.

Bibbi looked across the expanse toward me, tipping her head toward Mertie. I shrugged. We both looked at Zab. He shook his head.

Musso wasn't around to hazard a guess. He'd taken off, something about Bertha's breakfast not agreeing with him.

"Where's Hawk? Wasn't he here?" Mertie asked as she walked back to the other end of the office—again.

She'd never asked about his location before. Typically, Mertie didn't care what anyone was doing as long as they didn't bother her.

"He stepped out for a couple. I'm sure he'll be back." I should leave it at that. If she was going through something, she was on her own. I had too many issues of my own.

She did another ten laps, and I cracked.

"Is there a problem?" I asked.

"I don't know. Was just wondering. Can't a girl make small talk?"

Bibbi gasped. Zab scowled. I leaned back in my chair, as if I'd been punched. Mertie didn't make small talk. *Ever.* She made snide little remarks for her own amusement, and that was about it.

Mertie walked over to my desk and fussed with my cup of pencils. "Tippi, you got a minute?"

It was the politest thing Mertie had said to me since I'd known her. She knew something and it was bad. Oh no. Was I going to die? Was that what this was? Did heaven and hell know I had only a little magic left and didn't care? They still wanted to kill me because I'd taken it in the first place? Not that I'd meant to, but I wasn't sure there'd be a trial. I had a really bad hunch my day was going to get worse in a few minutes.

"What's up?" I tried to slow my pulse below heart attack range and failed. I might be dead before whatever was coming for me had the chance to do it themselves.

"Uh, nothing much, but maybe we should go in the back room to talk." She crossed her arms in front of her chest, then uncrossed them, before crossing them again.

I was a dead woman.

I rose out of my chair. Bibbi and Zab watched with matching expressions that could only mean they too thought I was going to die.

"We'll be back soon," I said, as Bibbi was about to get up and follow.

I nodded in her direction, patting the air as if to say everything was fine.

When that didn't work, I whispered, "Maybe sit this one out. I think she's got a *thing* going on."

In spite of my soft tone, Mertie heard. Instead of looking offended, she nodded. "Yeah, I got a bad thing. I think I caught it from a guy at the bar the other night." She nodded and made a ghastly face.

That got Bibbi's butt right back in her seat, and Zab's face was glowing red, his nose now an inch from his paperwork.

We walked in the back, and it would've been nice to know the trick Hawk used to mute the room, not that I'd be able to do it now. I was no longer among the witches who could be frivolous with their magic. I might even have to become magically frugal.

"What's wrong?" I asked, keeping my tone low because Zab and Bibbi were probably right around the corner, trying to hear every word. Odds were I'd want to process this alone for a few seconds, before dealing with their input.

"I don't know exactly how to tell you this." Mertie was fidgeting—again.

The back door opened and Hawk walked in, wind-blown and looking as fresh as ever. He paused, as if he immediately sensed an issue.

Mertie let out a sigh as she took in the sight of him. "Thank Satan you're here. I've been waiting hours, and I might need you."

"Why do you need him?" I asked, shifting my attention

back to Mertie. Hawk stood beside me, as if I was the one who'd need assistance.

"In case..." She shook her head. "I don't know... Just in case." She threw up her hands, exasperated, as if I'd told her I wanted her to solve some calculus problem in her head in under two seconds.

She took in a deep breath and then blew it out slower than she'd inhaled. It was a breathing technique meant to calm oneself. It was only calming to her, as I saw steam flow out of her nostrils.

"Mertie, what's the issue?" Hawk asked. His voice had a strange, calming tone to it. The line of her shoulders softened almost immediately.

Had he ever used that on me? I really needed to start paying attention to all his little tricks. He had some good ones, and I'd been a real slacker. I didn't remember hearing that tone before, but maybe when it was used on you, you didn't realize it? Even if I couldn't do his tricks, I'd better know them when I saw them.

Mertie was breathing calmly and leaning against the table, like this was a run-of-the-mill conversation and not some dire information. "You know the message? The one that said relinquish your magic or else, all spooky like? The one that had you running over to the hill and getting drained like a nitwit?"

"Yes," I said. He might've laid that relaxation spell on a little too thick. She was poking in some very sore spots, and I was feeling more like punching her than listening to her.

"Well, you know I've got my sources on the inside. They got themselves some information. What I'm about to tell you might be a rumor, but they've heard it from a couple of demons at this point, enough that they thought it should be passed on. From what they're saying, it's true that the powers that be know of your situation, from the tippy top to lowest low with you having..." She lifted a hand and waved it. "They all know you *used* to have way too much of the Xest start-up magic. They were debating what to do with you as well. That was all confirmed. But that message you got? The ultimatum? It wasn't authorized. My source said it was sent without anyone's knowledge. Lou went rogue to lure you into doing exactly what you did."

"There wasn't a threat from them? They were just aware of an issue?" My voice was a whisper of its normal self, as the shock robbed it of its strength.

"Yep. That's about the long and short of it."

The wind was knocked right out of me. I'd been set up, and so perfectly. If Mertie thought Hawk was supposed to be the calm one, she was wrong. I could feel him vibrating beside me. I took a step away from them, wishing I could have the room to myself to absorb what she'd just said.

"Yeah, so now you know." Mertie stretched out her arms and yawned. "I'm going to go take a nap now. I am wiped out. See you guys for dinner, or not. I might sleep through tonight and fend for myself when I get up. We've already got one man down today. Not sure we can shoulder any more Bertha casualties, if you know what I mean."

I barely listened to her as I walked out of the back room.

The only thought in my head was what an idiot I'd been. So intent on saving everyone, and what did I do? Walked right into a trap.

"We'll fix it," Hawk promised.

"*We* didn't make this mistake. I did." And fixable? I

wasn't going to debate that right now. If it was so fixable, he wouldn't be thinking of drastic measures, and I'd be regaining my magic naturally because I was an Infinite.

"You're not the only one that's made mistakes," he said, watching me as I grabbed my jacket from the coat rack.

"Maybe not, but I'm on a real run lately," I said, walking toward the back door. I almost always used the front, but today, the less people I saw, the better.

"Where are you going?" Hawk asked as I headed out.

"I need to clear my head."

"Don't do anything—"

"Stupid? Don't worry. I've had my fill."

29

I lifted my hand to knock on Hawk's door.

Hawk opened it before I got the chance. He stood there, saying nothing. He probably thought I was here to fight over him doing something or me doing nothing. It was the very last thing I wanted right now, even though fighting might be the easier route to take. Definitely less complicated. But tonight, I needed this. The walk had cleared my head, and I knew what needed to be done. It was now or maybe never.

He took a step back, watching as I squeezed past him into his room. He watched me but made no move toward me.

There were a couple of options. I could tell him why I was here, lay it out raw and bare, and then brace myself to either reap the rewards or rejection. Or maybe I said nothing. I could lay *myself* out raw and bare, knowing he'd more likely take the invite, but the possible rejection would be that much more staggering if it came. It wasn't like he hadn't wanted me in the past. Then there was the other night when he'd kissed me but then left...

I needed to stop thinking immediately or I'd bolt out of this room. Just act. For once in my life, I needed to get out of my head and do it.

I gripped the hem of my shirt, watching his eyes shift to my waist—and then I froze. Was that a look of disgust? Was that interest? I couldn't even tell anymore. I needed to abort immediately. I dropped my shirt and then played with the hem, as if I'd meant to yank it up or something equally idiotic. My face burned as I scrambled for a Plan B. Pick a fight and get the hell out of here.

"You know, you're a hypocrite. You're constantly telling me what to do but don't care when I don't want you to do something."

He raised a brow. "That's why you came here?"

He took a step toward me. I kept my gaze on his shoes. That was the safest place.

"Of course it is. Why else?" I should really look him in the eye. Bluster didn't work well when you didn't have the balls to meet someone's gaze.

He took another step, crowding me, his toes nearly brushing mine.

His hands went to the hem of my shirt.

He knew. That small movement had given me away. I turned to walk away, but he shot his arm out, stopping me and pulling me back in front of him.

"What's wrong? Lost your nerve?" he asked, his voice roughened.

"I didn't lose anything." My mouth grew dry and I swallowed for the fifth time in a minute. His hands grazed underneath my shirt to the flesh of my waist, sizzling where we connected flesh to flesh.

They changed direction, sliding under my waistband. They traveled slowly downward, following the curve of my hips, dragging the soft fabric of my leggings with them until he cupped the curve of my ass. He lifted me upward until I was on tiptoes, pressing me against the hard length of him. I was off my feet, grabbing his shoulders for balance as I wrapped my legs around him.

"What are you doing?"

"Exactly what you came for," he answered, running his fingers over the slick, wet folds of my vagina. "Unless this wasn't what you wanted."

A soft moan escaped me as my head dropped back, only to give him more flesh to ravage. His mouth caressed my throat as he plunged his fingers inside me, pumping slowly while his thumb rubbed at my apex.

"This is why you came, isn't it?" he asked, the low rumble of his voice echoing through me as his fingers paused.

"Yes," I said, knowing I would've told him anything at that point to have him continue.

He plunged back in, hooking and rubbing.

He walked us forward and then dropped me on the bed.

He reached forward, dragging my pants off and then moving quickly to rid me of the rest of my clothes until I was lying bare in front of him. His eyes roved over my body, studying me.

My instincts were to cover up. But what I really wanted was to pull him down to me and strip his clothes from him. I opted for the latter, grabbing a hank of his shirt and pulling him forward.

His chest collided into mine without him losing a grip on my ass. I knew for certain that if I made it past the next couple of days, he would surely be the end of me. But what a way to go.

. . .

"Do you know I waited longer for you than anyone else in my life?" Hawk toyed with a lock of my hair.

"How long do you usually wait?" Hopefully he couldn't hear the smile in my voice. I was glad my face was turned away from him. If he saw me right now, he might see the truth. I was utterly in love with him.

"A day. A couple if I'm particularly interested."

"Hawk? You in there?" Oscar yelled.

Hawk muttered a curse. "I forgot about Oscar. I'll meet you downstairs in five," he yelled.

Hawk stood up, stretching, not an ounce of shame in his nudeness, not that he should. Leonardo couldn't have done a better job sculpting him.

I sat up in bed, looking for my things as well, trying to keep my expression neutral, even as I felt like someone who was leaving a carnival to go straight to a funeral. I might be, too. My own.

Hawk walked over to my side of the bed and leaned down, giving me a kiss that left me breathless and promised a continuation.

"You don't need to get up. I'll leave the door set to open to the building for you. Lie back down. I won't be gone long," he said. He kissed me again before he left.

All I wanted to do was curl up in his bed and wait for him to come back. But the world wasn't going to wait. I wasn't delusional enough to think he wasn't still going after Lou. If he'd been the hurt one, it was what I would've done. It was what I would've done for anyone I loved.

I leaned back against the wall.

He loved me. How had I not seen it? There was nothing

left I had to give him, and yet he was hellbent on avenging me.

I had finally found the man of my dreams, who loved me, and if I didn't do something, he was going to get himself killed. I ran my hands through my hair, feeling certain about what I had to do as I caught sight of my token.

There it was, sitting on top of his chest. In just seconds, I could be at the hill. I'd never been one to believe in fate or karma, but this was a pretty blatant sign. If I'd had any doubts, they were gone. Maybe this was one time I needed to be a believer.

I walked over, picked up the token, and felt its call in my hand. Hawk would be furious. Then again, when wasn't Hawk mad about something I did? When had I ever let that deter me before? And if this worked, I might be able to keep Hawk alive. There was no way I could save him in my current state.

30

I hurried down one set of stairs before racing up another, having no idea how long Hawk would be gone. I did have a strong idea of what would happen if I didn't get out of here before he got back.

The token was in my pocket, but I wasn't sure it was capable of doing what I was planning. There was only one person I could count on, one person who had enough balls to help me, and definitely only one person who might agree to this.

I rapped softly on Bibbi's door.

"Come in."

I opened the door and then stepped over the different piles of yarn, books, and scattered clothing about the floor. I'd thought initially she was just turning into a slob until I caught her reading about rare and unusual creatures. It turned out that dust bunnies' natural habitat was clutter. Bibbi was determined to lure Dusty away from Mertie, his current favorite, and over to her room. I'd told her ten times he was avoiding her because of the bows, but she insisted he didn't mind.

"What's going on?" Bibbi sat up, chucking her book to the floor, adding it to one of the many heaps and motioning to the end of her bed.

"Are you tired? I've got something I need to do, and I could use some help." I stayed on my feet, tracking the minutes in my mind.

I glanced over my shoulder, paranoia making me think Hawk would storm in at any second, as if he knew every thought and plan I hatched.

"Where are we going?" Bibbi was off her bed, grabbing her boots, and almost falling over as she pulled one on and then the other. "Is it dangerous? You know I thrive in danger."

Thankfully, Oscar was out with Hawk because his last warning to me had been *not* to get Bibbi mixed up in my problems. I was pretty sure what I was about to do fell into that category.

"Keep your voice down. This is solely a mission for us." I glanced toward the door again, not sure who might be rushing in next. It might be both of them.

"Oh, covert, too! This is amazing. I usually have to fight to do anything this fun." Bibbi jumped in place, shaking her hands with excitement.

She might not feel so awesome about it after we got there. Once she saw what her part was, there was bound to be disappointment, especially since she was strapping on her glittery dagger holder.

"I'll tell you the rest after we get out of here."

She had her jacket on and was pulling on her hat as we made our way out of her room and to the back alley.

"Okay, give me the lowdown," she said.

I pulled out my token. "We're going to the hill."

She took an immediate step back. "Wait a second. You

said it was dangerous. Not *stupid*. Why the hell would we go to the hill? I thought you were over that craziness? Do you have a problem again?"

She took a step closer, as if getting ready to pin me to the ground if need be. She squinted as she looked into my eyes, like they'd show her something.

"I am, and I need to make sure it doesn't happen again. If I go to the hill and can pull more instead of letting it take, I'll wipe out the spell and undo its influence." I spoke in the most reasonable tone possible, in the hopes the very blandness of my explanation would convince her I hadn't gone off the deep end again.

She didn't look ready to clobber me anymore, but she also didn't seem to be on board. She tugged her hat down a little and then crossed her arms.

"Look, danger could be my middle name. I don't run from a fight, but I'm not looking to watch you die, or worse, get all weird like you were. I'm just not sure it's a good idea."

I grabbed her shoulders, ignoring the Xest ways. "If things don't turn out well tonight, I'll need you to get me help. That's why you're coming. I have to do this and I need you. If I don't get my magic back, Hawk is going to do something very bad. Oscar and I will try to save him and probably die in the process. You'll also probably try to save us, and then die. Do you want us all to die?" There was a time for calmness, but don't let anyone tell you hyperbole doesn't have its uses.

She was shaking her head and sighing, which for Bibbi meant capitulating. "How am I supposed to say no when you put it like that?" she asked. "I don't like it, but I guess I'll do it if that's what you need."

"I do." I'd known Bibbi was my girl. I dug the token

out of my pocket. "Hold on to the other half of it. I'm not sure I made it strong enough to get two people there, but hopefully it will."

If it didn't, we'd be walking, because I wasn't strong enough at this point to make another.

She grabbed the other end. A second later we weren't at the hill, but we weren't terribly far off, either.

"This isn't it," Bibbi said, looking around.

"No, this isn't. We're a bit away. The token wasn't made for more than one person, so it didn't have enough juice." I began to walk in the direction of the hill, hoping this wasn't an omen.

"Maybe this is a bad sign," Bibbi said, walking beside me.

"It's not." Was it? It certainly hadn't been a *good* sign.

"What am I supposed to do, anyway?" She was looking around as if she expected a monster to jump out and eat us.

"If I get stuck, you push me off. Anything else looks weird, you run for help." I held out my coin to her. "Keep that in your pocket. It'll make it faster to get back to the building for help if things go badly."

She took the coin, making a little grunt as she did.

We crossed the last group of trees to the clearing where the hill was. Bautere was standing there.

Bibbi shot me a side glance that pretty much summed up my interpretation of the situation: we were screwed.

"Hey," Bibbi said with fake enthusiasm. "Tippi and I wanted to stretch our legs, and look at this? We run into you!"

I didn't bother holding back the groan. Was this what it sounded like when I lied? I couldn't be quite that bad. It would take practice to be that bad, lots and lots of practice.

"I know why you're here," Bautere said, addressing Bibbi but quickly turning his full attention on me and keeping it there.

He didn't say more, and Bautere might be the hardest person to read I'd ever met. I didn't think I'd ever really know what he was thinking, no matter how long I knew him, unless he spelled it out.

"Are you planning on stopping me?" I asked, cutting to the chase. There was zero chance it hadn't been requested by Hawk.

"No. I'm here to lend help if needed."

"You aren't going to stop me?" Probably not the question to beat to death after I got the answer I wanted. I should've taken the no and run with it, but Bautere made up his own mind. My inquiring as to why was unlikely to sway him once his decision was made.

"It's what I would do. You're facing your weakness. You'll either come out stronger or lose. As long as you've come to terms with that cost and are willing to live with it, it's your cost to bear."

Of all the people I'd expected to understand, I should've known he would. That was how he lived his life. His kind weren't known for being fierce because they backed down. They didn't shirk away from their fears, and neither would I.

"Thank you for understanding."

He turned sideways and took a step back, leaving nothing but the hill looming ahead.

I nodded, glanced at Bibbi, and gave her the most optimistic smile I could before taking a step toward my destination.

"You can back me up, but just so we're clear, I'm lead," Bibbi said to Bautere.

Bautere was silent in reply, but I could just imagine his face. That alone made dragging Bibbi out here priceless, even if Oscar did lose his shit.

I walked up to the spot, feeling a kind of fear I hadn't realized existed. I should've left a note for Hawk. And Zab. And Musso, and...

I should've left notes. What if this killed me? But if I didn't do this, we'd all be dead anyway. The logic I'd used on Bibbi hadn't been pulled out of thin air.

There was no choice. I had to do this, and I might not get another chance.

I dropped to my knees, focusing. The sounds around me dimmed as my head cleared. This might be the most important thing I ever did in my life. I'd never been a selfish person, or a taker. But that was what I needed to be today. I laid my hands on the ground, refusing to let an ounce of magic seep out of me. I dug my fingers in, and all I thought about was taking. Having enough magic to save everyone here. I would save Hawk, everyone at the broker building, everyone in Xest, even Gillian if it came down to it.

The feelings came at me in a rush, and I pulled on them, taking everything there was and more. It felt like I was holding a live wire in my hand, and it took supreme attention not to let go.

Suddenly it was too much and I was thrown off. I landed on my butt a few feet from the spot.

Bibbi ran over, Bautere following, as I got to my feet.

"Well? How do you feel?" Bibbi asked.

I stretched my arms, moving my head back and forth, wanting to let the feeling settle in before I spoke. I'd felt good after I left the hill before, but this was different. After those times, a calmness would settle over me, but also a feeling like I could sleep for a decade. This time I felt like my body was buzzing, near tingling with the energy packed inside.

"I'm guessing she's feeling pretty good," Bautere said.

"I definitely don't feel drained." If anything, I felt more alive than I'd ever felt in my life, if that were possible. "I think I might be back."

"Good, then can we get out of here? I don't like this hill business," Bibbi said.

31

Hawk was waiting when we returned. The cords of Hawk's neck looked taut, and the air felt like it was about to combust. Oscar was there as well, and not looking very happy either.

"You took her with you?" Oscar said, stepping forward and looking like a person I'd never seen. "I told you not to—"

"Bibbi made her own choice. Back off," Hawk said.

Hawk hadn't moved, but it didn't seem to matter. Oscar was still glaring at me, but he didn't say another word. It was a little bit of a relief when he shifted his attention to Bibbi. He shot her a hurt look and then walked out of the room.

Hawk shifted his gaze to Bibbi and tilted his head toward the door. I wasn't stupid enough to think he cared whether she went and calmed Oscar. Hawk didn't want witnesses to the bloodbath and possible murder to come.

Bibbi looked at me.

"He's not going to kill me," I said, hoping I was correct.

"I wouldn't be so confident if I were you," Hawk said as soon as Bibbi went through the door.

"Hawk, you don't understand—"

"Not here," he said, walking out of the back room. I followed him through the office and up the stairs.

His door no longer led to his bedroom but the sitting room I'd been in a handful of times. That was not a good sign.

He followed me in, shutting the door a little harder than needed.

Yeah, I'd gone to the hill without him. Yeah, I knew he'd be angry. But this seemed like a bit of an overreaction considering I was alive, well, and feeling better than ever. I'd won. I'd beaten Lou at his own game. All I wanted to do was talk about it, but Hawk wouldn't calm down long enough to let me.

"You don't need my bed any longer, since you already slept with me for the token. I figured this room might be more appropriate."

I stood there speechless for a minute, watching him walk across the room, as if not trusting himself to get close to me.

"You're saying I slept with you to get my token back?" I asked, repeating his statement because my brain couldn't get past the absurdity of it.

"The timing seems a bit conspicuous." His jaw was hard, his arms folded.

Only a man in love would be that angry over the idea of being used for sex. My desire to fight got eaten alive by the warm, glowing feelings that were growing inside of me. I didn't know how this man had fallen for me, but he had.

Fighting was the last thing I wanted. I took a step toward him.

"I was going with or without the token because I was trying to save you from doing something idiotic." Some of the heat left his eyes, and I took another step in his direction. "I went to your room because I wanted to be with you in case things didn't work out well."

He growled, and I immediately realized that hadn't been the best choice of words.

"You could've died. That spell could've wiped out what magic you had left. Did you think of that for even a second?" he asked.

At least he took a step toward me.

"It occurred to me. That's why Bibbi was there."

He turned away from me, shaking his head. "Bibbi is a Whimsy. Not the best backup."

"She might be a Whimsy, but she's got bigger balls than most of the witches and warlocks in Xest. She'd hit me off the spot with a stick if I had a problem, and keep doing whatever she had to do until it worked."

He took a few steps away, and I followed him tentatively, waiting to see how long it would take him to calm down. He turned and circled around me as I wondered what might get him past this anger. If he'd done this without me, I'd feel the same. I didn't fault him. I just wanted him to get over it so we could move on to more enjoyable things.

Although I could fault him on the token.

"I'd like to mention that you left the token right out in the open. If you really didn't want me to see it, maybe you should've put it under a shirt or a—"

I didn't finish because his lips crashed into mine. He

held me against him as if his existence depended on it, and I reveled in the feel of him, gripping him back harder.

His lips broke from mine. His eyes deepened as he laid his hand upon my throat.

"You feel stronger. A lot stronger. What exactly happened at the hill?" he asked.

"I think I broke the spell. I took my magic back." I smiled, finally having a chance to revel in my victory. It was *almost* as good as having his arms around me, but not quite.

"What exactly did it feel like?"

He dropped his hands as he studied me. His eyes were pensive, but the cords in his neck were no longer on the verge of snapping apart from the tension.

"Hard to put it into words, but I made contact the way I had in the past. This time, though, I was mentally prepared for it to try to pull from me, and I was cautious. I went in with the sole purpose of being the taker, focusing on holding everything close and tight and pulling energy toward me."

"How? Was it a spell?" He rubbed his jaw, watching me.

"No. I was going on instinct," I said, watching him watch me.

"Then what happened?" He kept staring as if he couldn't quite put something together.

"Nothing much. I took it all back. In truth, it must have wanted to come back, because it nearly gushed at me to the point I was startled by how fast it flooded in." I stretched out my arms, taking a deep breath. "I have to say, I feel utterly amazing. I hadn't realized how bad I'd been feeling until now, but I guess that's what happens when something creeps up on you. Now, though, I feel like I'm positively pulsating with life."

He nodded, quiet for a few moments, and then walked closer, staring me in the eyes. "I need to go somewhere. Can you, for once in your life, stay put?"

"I'll make you a deal: I'll stay here until you get back, as long as you promise not to go after Lou until we discuss it."

He paused, as if it were killing him to commit to that.

"I've got my magic back. I think there's some leeway time-wise."

I leaned in closer, brushing my lips over his because he was close and I couldn't not kiss him.

"Okay, until we talk," he said, before upping the tempo of the kiss from slow and leisurely to something that made me want to rip his clothing off.

He pulled away. "I have to go before I can't," he said, then leaned in one last time anyway.

Then he was gone, and all I wanted to do was run laps around Xest. Considering how freaked out he'd gotten, taking it easy for a few hours wasn't the worst thing in the world.

I SKIPPED MY WAY DOWNSTAIRS, so happy to be back to my old self that simply walking wouldn't do.

"I don't know what your problem is," Bibbi said, staring at Oscar.

They both glanced over at me.

"Sorry. I'll just go to the back room." I made my way there, wishing I were invisible.

"No. It's fine. We're done talking," Bibbi said, grabbing

her jacket and heading out, clearly looking for some alone time.

Oscar stared as Bibbi walked out of the room with the hooded gaze of someone who didn't want to get caught watching but couldn't stop themselves in spite of it.

"You're falling hard, aren't you?" I said. I couldn't even be angry at him for his behavior lately, not when he had it this bad for Bibbi.

He jerked his gaze to mine, as if he'd forgotten I was in the room. As if the lights on the place had shut off as soon as Bibbi left the building.

"What are you talking about?" he asked, as if he didn't know exactly what I meant.

"You're falling for her and you don't know what the hell to do about it, do you?" I didn't mean to smile so wide, or want to laugh so hard, but this was Oscar. He'd thought he was untouchable. He'd thought he was in control of the situation, that he could mess around here and there with Bibbi but it wouldn't be that much of a thing. He'd thought wrong.

His only response was a roll of his eyes. He could roll them, huff a bit, add some bluster for good measure. I wasn't buying it.

"I can read it all over you. The second she walked out of the room, you looked like you wanted to chase after her just so you could watch her walk or talk or just stand."

He rolled his head, letting out a huff. The huff turned into a sigh and the roll turned into a shake. Finally, he threw up a hand in surrender.

"I don't know what to do. I don't even know what happened. I thought we were having some fun. For all I know, that's all she's still doing." He ran his hands through his hair. "I don't know how this happened."

As much as I wanted to laugh at his arrogance, he looked a little too desperate.

"It happened because she's amazing," I said.

"She's the most incredible person I've ever met. She's tough and loyal. And holy shit, she rocks my world in bed. I can't get enough of her and"—he waved a hand toward the door—"she flits around like she doesn't care if we end tomorrow."

That wasn't overly apparent to me, but Oscar didn't need to know that. A little humble pie might be the best thing for him right now.

"Have you tried talking to her?"

He walked to the nearest chair and slumped into it, rubbing a jaw that looked a little rougher than usual. "What do I say? I acted like I wasn't looking for anything serious. I thought I was doing the right thing, not filling her head with promises and bullshit. Now look at me."

I perched on the desk near him. "I think you tell her all the amazing things you said to me and see where it goes."

His lips parted with the shocking idea I'd just laid out. "What if she tells me she doesn't want anything more?"

He was frozen in his seat at the idea of it.

"Then you decide how much you care, how long you're willing to wait, and how hard you're willing to fight. Look, you started this like you didn't want anything other than some fun. You might have to suck it up and eat crow for a while. Maybe offer to take her to dinner as a start?"

He nodded at the novel idea of a date. "If she's willing to eat with me, that means something, right?"

"Yes. It's a good start. Maybe surprise her with a little gift, too."

He was nodding again, as if taking mental notes.

"That's a good idea. I gotta go," he said, then got up and headed out. Looked like he planned to take my advice and not waste another moment.

I walked into the back room, grabbed the throw blanket, and settled on the couch. The pitter-patter of little feet made their way across the room and then a nose pressed against my arm. Dusty cuddled onto the blanket next to me. He'd been growing more and more distant the more I'd gone to the hill.

"You feel it too, huh?"

He snuggled deeper into the blanket.

"You cold? Hang on."

It was chilly, and I could do something about it now. There would be no more frugal magic thoughts here. I flicked a wrist toward the fire. It nearly exploded. I waved a hand again, fast, lowering it, but not before it had charred the front of the mantel.

Dusty let out a small chirping sound.

"Yeah, that was a bit strong, huh?"

I'd have to find a spell to fix that tomorrow, but at least now I could. Most important thing was that I was *back*. From the look of that, really back. Maybe back and then some? How much magic had I taken from the hill?

32

I hit the landing and made a right, climbing the stairs to my bedroom. Hawk wasn't back yet, I wasn't tired, but I'd made a promise I'd wait here for him. Although he'd better be back by morning or I might snap.

I stopped suddenly on the stairs, feeling him enter the building. I spun, waiting, not believing that my senses had grown that in tune with his.

A few seconds later, my feeling was proven correct.

Hawk stood on the landing, watching me. "Where do you think you're going?" he asked.

"I was going to bed," I said, not that I'd mind a better invitation.

He reached toward me and grabbed my hand, tugging me back downstairs before pulling me behind him up the other set.

We stopped walking at the same exact moment.

Lou and Xazier were here. It felt as if I sensed their magic as soon as they set foot in Xest, like a jagged splinter in my palm.

Before, my magic had felt like a nagging voice in the

back seat, telling me to pull over or go faster. Now it was as if I were in the back seat, trying to hear over the radio as the car sped in whichever direction it wanted. Or maybe I hadn't gotten more magic. Maybe I'd become unhinged.

He turned, and a look passed between us.

"You felt that?" he asked.

"That wasn't in my head?" I wasn't unhinged. Should I be relieved or scared?

There was a pause, as if he too seemed to be coming to terms with the changes in me.

I was having my own realization about him. As strong as I'd been before, I'd been too ignorant to realize I wasn't on his level. I'd always thought we were equals of a sort, or close. We might be now, but I was no longer delusional about what we'd been. Had he always sensed these things?

"They'll be here soon," he warned me. "You don't need to talk to them if you aren't ready. I can handle it."

Leave him alone with Lou when I'd just pulled this situation back from the brink? Definitely not.

"No. I'm the reason they're here."

He nodded. I headed back downstairs before there could be any more questions about me staying behind.

I made my way into the back room and made tea for no other reason than I wanted to portray calmness, even if I didn't feel it.

"What happened?" Hawk lifted a hand toward the charred wood and stone around the fireplace.

"I think I had a flare-up or something."

He leaned on the back of the couch as I continued to pretend I wasn't nervous.

"What exactly happened at the hill?" His eyebrows were raised as he waited for an answer.

"I told you. I'm not exactly sure." I sipped some tea, giving myself an excuse to not talk, as my mind replayed what happened earlier. I'd leaned down. I'd taken it. I'd left. It had seemed so simple at the time.

"They're here," Hawk said.

I already knew.

Lou walked into the back room. His attention zeroed in on me like a heat-seeking missile. "Do you know what you did? How did you do that?" Lou demanded.

Xazier followed in after him. He dropped onto the couch, looking more like a spectator for an interesting show than an active participant.

Hawk stepped closer. "I suggest you watch how you talk to her. My patience with you has worn dangerously thin."

Hawk was about to rip Lou's head from his shoulders, but I'd already bought us enough trouble.

I discarded my tea. With a hand on Hawk's arm, our eyes met. It took a few seconds, but he eventually granted my request and took an infinitesimal step back. There was no doubt it was borrowed time.

"I know exactly what I did, or you wouldn't be here." Technically, I had the gist of what I did. The finer details were still revealing themselves to me. Even now, I could feel my magic flexing inside of me, pouring through my veins, just looking for an outlet.

"I don't know who you think you are, but you can't do something like this," Lou said.

This didn't seem like a good time to ask for a full explanation of what it was I'd done. But damn if I didn't want to ask.

"Would you care to take a seat?" I waved toward the

couch, hoping to keep this somewhat civil but losing my optimism fast.

Lou took another step in my direction. Hawk moved toward me as well, but I held up my hand.

"I've got this," I said softly.

Hawk tilted his head slightly and then gave a nod, looking interested in what I could do. Him and I both.

"Lou, I think this would be a much more comfortable meeting if you took a seat." I waved toward the couch again.

He opened his mouth, probably to hurl insults my way, but went speechless instead. His body froze up as he tried to fight off the command. Slowly, inch by inch, his feet dragged backward. He dropped onto the seat, and the rage shooting through him was palpable in the air.

That might've slammed the door shut on any hope of civility, but it had been a slim chance anyway. I could see Hawk nodding beside me. Xazier wasn't moving a hair, as if not wanting to draw my attention.

I eased off my control of Lou slowly, knowing he might lunge at me or something worse. There was no back-pedaling from the humiliation I'd just dished out, but there had to be some way to calm this situation down.

The second I released him from my grip, he launched into a tirade.

"You think you're something special? You're just another Xest reject, a peasant in the scheme of things, put here to do my bidding. You haven't seen anything yet," Lou said.

He was leaning forward in his seat, his face nearly as red as Xazier's. His fists were clenched, and if he could, he'd kill me now.

Hawk looked from Lou to me. His arms were crossed

and his muscles tense. I gave him a nod, hoping to buy a little more time to get this back under control.

I took a step toward Lou but then froze. Anything that might appear confrontational, even approaching him with the best intentions, might be a bad idea. "I had to do what I did because you put me in an uncomfortable position. Now, I think we should try to come to some sort of compromise."

It had taken all my restraint to hold out an olive branch, and Lou was sitting there sneering at me. He'd screwed me over any chance he could, and this was what I got? If I didn't have issues with heaven and hell looming, I'd kill him myself—if I could.

"If you think things are going to be copacetic, bygones be bygones, you're delusional, the whole stinking human lot of you. This doesn't end here. You can't have it all. You can't possibly think that this is going to fly with my boss. You'll be dead by the end of the week. Did you really think that you could drain all the magic out of Xest and live?" He was on his feet again.

Wait. What? Drain all of it? Now what did I do? I took it all?

Killing Lou somehow was beginning to look like a real possibility and not just wishful thinking. I'd never have peace with him around. But what kind of a shit show would that bring down on Xest? Did I have a right to take that kind of risk for selfish reasons? Could I have peace even with him dead? Could I put my desires and well-being before everyone here? No. There had to be a way to fix this.

Hawk walked over to Lou, who barely glanced in his direction. Lou wasn't giving heed to him at all, consumed with rage for me. If Lou understood how much power was pulsating through me, how even now it wanted to boil up and obliterate everything he was, he wouldn't be so relaxed and free with his words. I dug my fingers into the arm of the chair and could feel heat surging through me.

The sounds in the room dimmed. My gaze shot to Hawk, who wasn't fully human anymore. His arms had shifted into his beast, black claws out.

I realized what was going to happen, but there wasn't any time to stop it. Hawk was right beside Lou, his hand plunged into his chest. Light exploded like a flash grenade had gone off in the room. I was blinded for a few seconds. As my eyes readjusted, Hawk's hand was no longer in Lou's chest. It was hanging at his side, dripping a strange, clear, gooey substance.

I couldn't speak for a second, as all the possible ramifications tumbled about in my brain at once. What had he done? What did this mean? Was the sky going to part and strike us both down in the next few seconds?

Hawk walked over to the counter, grabbed a rag, and wiped Lou's residue from his now-human hand.

Xazier leaned back in his seat, an eyebrow raised. "We're still good, right?" he asked, looking from Hawk to me.

"I don't know. Are we?" Hawk asked, leaning on the counter and watching him.

"We're good," Xazier said, nodding.

"Did I take it all?" I asked, watching as he edged his way toward the door.

"Seems so," Xazier said, continuing to inch his way out of the room.

Lou was dead. I'd stolen all the magic in Xest. This was definitely turning out to be a bad day.

"I'm just going to..." Xazier nodded toward the door.

"Yeah, sure. Go," I said. Hawk had already killed an emissary from heaven. In my book, that was enough for one day. And if the emissary from hell didn't get out of here, Hawk might want a two-for-one deal—not that things could get much worse, from the way I was looking at it.

Xazier nodded and then paused at the door. "You know, I feel as if I've been typecast this entire time. I *was* always the good one."

"Goodbye, Xazier," I said, hoping he'd hurry it along. The smell of Hawk's blood lust was nearly filling the room, and my own tolerance was fading fast.

I dropped onto the couch, looking at the blob that was once Lou. I wasn't sure if I was more stunned by how easily Hawk had killed him or how plain *bad* this situation was. And there was no way that this wasn't anything but extremely bad. I'd jacked up my magic to try to gain some leverage, but there wasn't enough magic in Xest to fix this.

I looked at the blob in the chair, formerly known as Lou, to the reason we had a blob. He was leaning against the counter still, sipping the tea I'd forgotten about.

I took a couple of deep breaths before I said, "Didn't we agree you wouldn't go after Lou before we discussed it?"

He walked past the blob, sat on the other end of the couch, He kicked his feet up onto the table and rested his arm along the back. "I agreed not to go after him. I didn't. He came here."

"Are you sure that this was the best way forward? Don't you think this could possibly escalate this issue?" He was acting so calm about the matter that screaming "we're screwed" and running around the room didn't seem the thing to do, even if it might be warranted.

"I don't know, but I didn't see another alternative. Lou had to go, and he made it painfully clear tonight. He wasn't going to be happy as long as you existed, and I was tired of his bad behavior. I didn't see a reason to wait."

Didn't see a reason? Really?

I didn't bother arguing with his logic because it was done. Lou was now a blob. I'd already been in hot water. Now I was officially sharing my pot. Didn't Hawk care he was in the pot with me?

There was a magic issue. I couldn't think about Lou, who was now a blob, and the magic, too.

Hawk stood, about to walk out of the room, and nightmares of cleaning the place after he left suddenly plagued me.

"Where are you going? What about...Lou?" I said, pointing at the blob with clothes.

He glanced over. "The cleaning crew will take care of it." He made his way to the door and said, "I'll be back in a little while," before he left.

Bibbi walked in a few minutes later. She threw her jacket on a hook and walked to the couch before stopping short. She stared at the blob for a few minutes.

"What is that? It looks disgusting," she said.

"That"—I stabbed in the direction of the blob—"is Lou. He stopped by tonight, and that's how it went."

IT WAS the wee hours of the night when my door opened. Hawk appeared in the shadows. I'd given up on him coming home. I'd worked it out in my mind as I tossed and turned for the last few hours. He'd go out, clear his head, and realize how badly he'd messed up, and all for me. He'd realize I was too much trouble. After all, according to Lou and Xazier, I'd taken all the magic of Xest. He'd regret killing Lou and putting himself in such a bad spot.

"What are you doing here?" he asked.

My stomach sank. That was it. He'd finally come to his senses. He wanted me to leave for good.

"I'll go," I said, sitting up. I should've known this would happen. How could I have been so stupid? No rational person was going to throw their lives away for me.

He walked forward, picked me up, and walked out of my room. He hit the landing and then started upstairs toward his room.

He dropped me on the bed. He still wanted me? He hadn't come to his senses yet?

I couldn't seem to stop staring at him as he stripped out of his clothes, and it wasn't because of how he looked, or not mostly. Didn't he understand what the ramifications of what he'd done were? No, *I* hadn't told him to do such a foolish thing, but it was because of me that he'd done it. Actually, if I'd known it could be done, and how to do it, I might've done it myself. I was already in the hot seat as far as hell and heaven went. Even if Lou had set me up, I knew there were bigger issues looming in my future. What was there really for me to lose? But Hawk had everything at stake.

"You *killed* Lou." Maybe if he heard it enough times he might begin to understand how much shit was headed our way. Or maybe not.

"Yes. I know. I was there." He spoke as if this were a joke. He moved around the room, as I watched.

"You realize what could come from that?" I asked.

"Why are your clothes still on?" he asked, then walked over and tugged my top off.

Was he delusional? He'd always seemed fairly logical, but unless you crawled into someone's head, it was hard to tell for sure.

"Do you think you can fight off heaven and hell?" Was it possible I'd slept with a madman? Correction, *was* sleeping with. I had every intention of doing it as many more times as I could before we both died some bloody death.

"I'll give it a good shot."

He pushed me onto my back before hooking his fingers into the waist of the shorts I liked to wear to bed.

No. Not delusional, as suspected. But then, why would he do that?

"Were you just overtaken by rage at the moment?" There had to be some logic I wasn't seeing.

He did have a temper, not that I'd ever seen it get away from him—until tonight, that was.

He settled in between my legs, and I put my palms flat on his chest, knowing the minute he kissed me, the discussion would be over. Logic and Hawk didn't seem to mix well for me. He rested his weight on his forearms as he watched me, staring at my lips.

"You want to talk? Fine. I killed Lou because I wanted him dead." He said it like it was so simple.

"I wanted him dead as well, but were you thinking about how that single act could get you killed? Or if you do survive, kill your business and everything you've built? Why would you do that?"

"Because as long as he was alive, he was never going to stop coming for you, and that became very clear today."

He brushed the hair away from my face, his gaze going from my lips to my eyes and then back again.

"Coming for me. Not for you." Did this really need to be pointed out to him? Did he not see the issue?

His gaze hardened. "Coming for you *is* coming for me."

Stupid or not, logical or not, he really did love me. He might never say the words, but I didn't need them when every action he took screamed them so loudly that even I could hear.

And I might've just gotten him killed.

"Except it's not. I'll tell them it was my fault. Maybe I can get Xazier to back up my story if he hasn't said anything." I shimmied up, trying to get a better vantage point. He needed to really hear me.

"You're not doing that." He wrapped an arm around my waist and tugged me back down.

"Why?"

"You're not taking the blame for what I did. I meant to do it, and I'd do it again." He really was insane.

I parted my lips, looking for something I could say that would make him realize how dangerous his actions were.

"Are you done?" he asked.

Were there any words that would get through to him? None I could think of. "I mean...I guess."

"Good, because I've been waiting for this all day," he said, and then kissed me like he really had been.

33

I n my efforts to take back the magic that was mine, had I made everything worse? If having so much magic before was bad, what troubles would it cause now?

I lifted my hand, staring at it and feeling the power that coursed through me. I'd thought it was a high of regaining what was once mine, but now, as I paid closer attention, as it settled in, as it seemed to do so easily, the difference was there. It felt as if a mere flick of my wrist in any direction could start a tornado. I'd had problems before, plenty of them, but this time my cure made it worse.

When I looked up, Hawk was in the room with me. "Don't look like that, as if you're awash in the sea." His voice was gruff.

He wrapped his arm around me, tugging me until I was leaning against him. Instead of fighting or denying that I was wallowing, I sagged into him. I let him anchor me. It seemed like a trend I couldn't break. Whenever I was weak, he seemed to come up and strengthen me. It might be a dangerous habit to form, but right now I wasn't going to worry about it.

"I don't know how to fix the problems that are looming. I didn't mean to take it all, and I don't know how to put the magic back. And the idea of what's in me, I just..." I shuddered at the realization that everything that was in that hill was now part of me. That was why I could hurt people when I'd never been able to before. After I'd trapped Dread in the hill and gotten a surge of magic, things changed. What would I become now with so much more?

"Magic and power isn't good or evil. The people who wield it are. You aren't evil. I've seen evil. There's something wrong with evil people, something that gets warped and bent, misaligned, and everything they do gets shaped by that deformity. Sometimes it's who they were when they were born. Sometimes something deforms them before they're old enough to fight it off. You've already been through trial by fire and come out the other side. You're not evil, and you never will be." He tightened his arms around me, as if he could shield me from myself and the dark thoughts trying to invade.

I shifted in his arms, looking up to see if he really believed what he was saying. There was absolute confidence in his eyes. Hawk didn't speak to flatter, and I hoped he was right.

Mertie groaned from across the room.

"Oh no. First Musso and Bertha, but at least they keep a lid on it somewhat. Then you got Oscar, who's looking like a lost puppy dog. Now you two? Can no one keep their emotions private? Screw on the couch if you must, but please cut it out with the looks unless you're in your own rooms."

She huffed her way over to the counter and began fixing a tea for herself.

"I need you to bring Zurdoch back," I said. "I need to talk to him and see what he knows."

She put the tea kettle down with a bang. "He was furious. If I get him back and you give him a bad potion again, that's it. He'll never talk to me again."

"It's not going to be a problem." Magic was not on my list of issues anymore, that was for sure.

"So it's true? You're back up to snuff? Like full snuff?" She eyed me up and down, as if taking my magical weight with her eyes.

"I'm back." I was something, all right, but I couldn't quite say what.

She leaned on the counter, continuing to size me up. No one could fault her for it. I'd burned her once already.

She tilted her head. "I hear what you're saying, and I see it, can nearly feel it. But if I put myself out there again and you don't come through... I mean, how can I be sure it's not fleeting?"

"Because I went to the hill and took out everything it had." She'd find out anyway. Everyone in Xest would at some point.

Her jaw dropped open and it took her a second to form the word. "All?"

"All." I pushed up my sleeve and held out my wrist to her. It was a vulnerability you'd only let your most loved ones have, but after how I'd put her in a spot with her friend, I owed it to her.

She was looking at my exposed wrist as if I were crazy.

"Do it. She means it," Hawk said, and then gave me a nod before leaving the room.

She lifted her hand but then froze. "You're sure?"

Tired of waiting, I grabbed her hand and wrapped it around my wrist. I felt the jolt of her magic, which was considerably more than I'd thought.

"Not bad," I said.

"Thanks. It's nothing like what you've got cooking," she replied, squinting as she continued to feel the pulse of mine for another few seconds before finally letting go. "That's pretty intense."

"Yeah, tell me about it." If she thought it felt over-whelming secondhand, she should feel it boiling around inside, not knowing if it was good or bad.

I eyed up Mertie, realizing if anyone might be able to tell, I was standing right beside them.

"Not to bring up the subject again, but when you worked in hell, how did you decide who belonged there? Could you just tell they were evil?" I asked, reaching for the tea kettle as I waited to see what she'd say, trying to pretend I was as interested in the answer as I was which brew I'd select.

"I don't know. It's just a thing. You just know." She was back to snapping and giving me weird looks. "You're not going to start asking me questions about hell and good and evil, right? Because I've gotten that my entire life, and I'm so over it."

That had been the plan, but not anymore.

"Why did you leave hell?" Bibbi asked, walking in halfway through Mertie's tirade.

Mertie put her tea down, sloshing it as she did. "Why does everyone ask me about that place?"

Bibbi jerked her head back. "I'm sorry. I didn't think you'd be so sensitive about it."

"I'm not sensitive and I'm not nice," Mertie said.

"No, you're definitely not," I said in a soothing tone,

reaching out to pat her arm. I stopped short, knowing she'd hate it.

"I'm not," Mertie agreed.

Bibbi got one of her *dog with a bone* looks. There was no stopping her from pursuing whatever she'd caught scent of. "Is that what happened? Did you leave because the other demons thought you were too nice?"

Mertie glared her way for a few seconds before she cracked. "If you have to know, I was fired. They said I didn't have it in me to be a good demon.

"Then I went to work at the factory because Marvin thought an ex-demon would be a great employee, but he started catching on. I caught him staring at me when I wasn't mean enough. It was too much. I can't do *all* the bad things. It shouldn't be on me." Mertie bent forward, putting her face in her hands.

Bibbi shot me a wide-eyed stare, jerking her head in Mertie's direction.

I shrugged and threw my hands up.

Bibbi shook her head and then pointed at Mertie's bent form.

Shit. When did I become the soother? When did I become the least awkward person in the room? This was not the role I should be playing. This could only happen in Xest, where things were upside down. Still, I had a Mertie in meltdown mode, and someone had to do something.

"Mertie, I'm sure you did plenty of bad things if you just think about it." It wasn't exactly going out on a limb. It was a guarantee she'd messed up at least a few lives here and there.

She lifted her head and let out a wail that could make your ears bleed.

Musso stuck his head in the back, looked about, and then literally ran. I'd known Musso for a while now and never seen him move quicker than a casual stroll.

Mertie kept on wailing.

"Mertie, I'm sure you did a...really..." Bibbi's voice was barely audible under the wailing.

"Mertie!" I screamed, finally dragging her attention back to me.

She stopped wailing to snap, "What?"

"I've come to know you, and I can say, from the bottom of my heart, that I would trust you to torture someone quite sufficiently."

"I don't believe you," she said, and then continued to watch me, waiting for me to *make* her believe.

This was Mertie. Selling her on how horrible she could be wasn't that hard.

"Okay, well, how about this? When I first started at the factory, I thought you were the most horrid person I'd ever encountered."

She swallowed. "Why did you say when you *first* started? Was I only horrid in the beginning and then you realized I wasn't?"

"Definitely not. In fact, one of the reasons I agreed to let you come here was you were so horrible you would drive out Gillian, or at least make her miserable." Not an outright lie. I had relished in that small victory. "And I love sending you over for cocoa. Highlight of my day." Again, true.

"I do annoy her, don't I?" Her lips tipped up slightly as she fought the urge to smile.

"You're amazing at it."

The smile faltered. "But what about now? You're still letting me stay, and Gillian's gone."

"You've become a fixture in this place, like a bad wart you adjusted to." Again, a thread of truth.

Mertie jerked her head to Bibbi. "What about you?"

Bibbi shrugged. "I would've kicked you out ages ago, but I don't get a say."

That was definitely the truth.

"Okay, that helped," Mertie said.

34

The office was dark as I laid a hand on Helen's beautiful machinery, knowing it was just the bells and whistles that covered the mystic origins of what she truly was.

"I'm so confused, Helen. I thought getting my magic back would save him. There wouldn't be a reason to go after Lou anymore. Now Lou is dead, and I took all the magic. The situation is worse than ever. I feel like every move I make lately is wrong."

Her machinery began to churn, but instead of the grinding wheels and whirly humming that seemed like the sound of machinery for so long, it all made sense. That wasn't just humming. It was her language, and I could suddenly understand.

Some things are destined to play out, she said.

It was like hearing someone speak Latin and understanding it. This wasn't just a hunch of what I'd thought she'd said. I could *understand* her.

I looked for a slip, but there wasn't one. She *knew* I knew.

"What's happening to me?" I asked, not expecting an answer.

She gave me one anyway.

You're part of Xest now, just as I am.

Oh shit. What did that mean, though? I should ask, but for the first time in a while, I was afraid of what she'd say. That she was saying anything at all. What she did say was terrifying. I was part of Xest? I didn't think she meant as part of the community, either.

I grabbed my jacket and headed out, afraid to say anything else.

See you later, Helen said.

I waved in her direction as I hurried out, hoping she'd stop talking so I could try to absorb what was wrong with me.

The streets were empty, which was all the better. Company was the last thing I needed tonight. The wind blew past me, and I tugged up my collar, wishing it would stop.

The wind stopped. The trees were still moving. Snow drifts were gusting around.

Bring it back.

Wind hit me in the face, and I was grateful for the burn. Maybe this walk hadn't been such a good idea. I went to turn around but froze, sensing a presence behind me.

Keeping my breathing even, I didn't need to reach out and feel what was there. I didn't worry that it was going to attack. If it wanted me dead, I'd already be lying on the ground. The power was that immense. I'd thought what I possessed was overwhelming, but it was nothing but a drop in the ocean compared to the energy swirling around me. Even now, it was pulsating, sensing me, tasting my own power. And it wasn't just one. There were several entities behind me. They also hadn't killed me. Did that mean they were harmless? I'd never make the mistake of underestimating a possible enemy again.

I turned, knowing they were waiting.

On an outstretched branch, a blackbird was angling its head, staring back at me. Beside it, a small mouse was standing on its hind legs, sniffing the air. As implausible as it might seem, this was where the power was flowing from, these two small creatures. They were both looking at me and then at each other.

"What do you want?" I asked, splitting my attention between the two.

Neither moved, but I felt them continue to poke at me. As impossible as it seemed, if this was *them*, I might not get another chance of pleading my case. This was it. And worst case, and it wasn't them, what harm would trying do? No one was around to even see me acting crazy.

Did I say something about Hawk killing Lou? No. If by some miracle they didn't know it was him, or they didn't care, bringing it up might make things much worse. I'd stick to my issues.

"I didn't mean to take it." That wasn't exactly true. Not a great way to start off. "Well, I did mean to take some, but only because I thought it would fix things. Then I was going to give it back. If you're who I think you might be, you might know all of this.

"I'll give it back right now if you want." I held out my hands, and the two continued to stare. "I don't know what to do with all of it stuck inside of me anyway. I really don't want to keep it. I don't even feel like me anymore. I feel weird in my skin, if that makes any sense."

Nothing but stares. It wasn't like I expected them to

talk, but couldn't they give me something?

"Look, if you're who I think you are, you know why I did what I did. I would think you would do it too in my position."

Nothing. I couldn't even get a ruffled feather or nose twitch.

I would've kept rattling on, but things were getting weird with no response. I might've been making a worse case for myself. "Look, I don't want a big life. It's not what I've ever wanted. Please believe me when I tell you that even though I botched things, this was not what I was after."

The bird and the mouse might've been the toughest audience I'd ever had. I dropped my head into my hand, wondering if I was losing my mind completely. Maybe Helen hadn't even talked to me tonight. What if this was just a rodent and a crow?

When I looked up, they were both gone. The power I'd sensed was gone with them. Maybe they'd never been there at all. Maybe the magic bubbling up inside of me was twisting my mind.

I headed back to the broker building, but only to make a quick pit stop. I'd never be able to get any sleep until I tried.

◯

"ARE you sure this is a good idea? After all, you aren't in the best situation right now to be losing power. Are you sure you should try to give it back? Just because you think a mouse talked to you?" Bibbi asked as she stood beside me.

"Don't forget the bird," Mertie mumbled.

"I told you, they didn't talk," I said. I should've hiked up here. Then I wouldn't be dealing with this right now. But no, I wanted to get the token and make my life easier.

"I think you should listen to her. She's making a lot of sense, and you really aren't," said Mertie, who'd happened upon us in the alley just as I was pulling out the token.

Now I had both of them, *agreeing.*

"Look, I didn't need you two to come with me, but if you're here, can you try not to distract me?" I asked, leaning over with my hands on the ground.

Mertie walked closer, as if I hadn't said a thing. "This doesn't make sense. Why take it and then give it back?"

I sat back on my heels. "Because I didn't mean to take it all, and now I'm afraid it's leading to worse problems. If I give it back, maybe they'll be so happy they leave things alone."

"The bird and the mouse, you mean?" Mertie said. "Oh, yeah, that'll work."

Mertie looked at Bibbi and rolled her eyes. Bibbi responded with a shrug.

"Can one of you just get a stick in case I get stuck?" I said, wanting them to have something else to do other than hover over me.

"Fine. I'll get a stick," Bibbi said, turning around and looking.

"I'll get a stick as well," Mertie said.

Bibbi stopped. "You don't need a stick. I can handle hitting her off the spot if needed."

"What if you don't hit hard enough?" Mertie said, putting her hands on her hips.

"I can hit plenty hard. Want to see?" Bibbi asked, holding up her fist.

"In about two seconds, I'm going to hit both of you.

Now go get sticks."

I settled my hands on the ground, digging them into the snow until I could feel the solid surface beneath them, ignoring the sting of the cold. If I could connect, they'd warm up fast enough.

~

"Is she stuck?" Mertie asked softly.

"Does she look stuck?" Bibbi asked.

"Who can tell?" Mertie said.

"Look at her face. She doesn't look stuck," Bibbi said.

They were gripping their sticks, as if both wanted to be the one to get me off the hill first. I wanted to rip into them for their constant chatter, but in my gut, I knew that wasn't the problem. The hill didn't want to take the magic back.

I'd been here for an hour and nothing was happening. I pulled my hands out of the holes I'd made in the snow and tucked them under my arms as I stared down at the spot. It was different. Flat, almost. Before, it had always felt like I was connecting to something alive, pulsating beneath me. This place felt like any other hill now. Nothing special.

If the bird and the mouse had been something different, something more than my imagination or a remnant of a dream, they either hadn't cared to take the magic back or had made their decision to kill me already. I didn't know.

"It's gone." Bautere's voice rang out from a short distance away. I wasn't startled, as I'd felt him approaching. Seemed I could feel everything around me now.

He walked closer, closing in on our small circle. "It's

been gone since you took it, and I'm not sure you can put it back in, if that's what you're attempting."

"Do you know why?" If I could take it, logic dictated that I could put it back.

"It no longer exists. It's inside of you now."

"But I need to return it," I said.

He shook his head. "It's like every other thing in Xest. Once the magic is fully gone, it ceases to exist. Whatever was here was so fully drained or transferred that it no longer exists in the form it had. You can't un-kill something." He paused and tilted his head. "Well, sometimes you can, but not if it disappears due to lack of magic. Nothing exists in Xest without some magic to keep it alive."

I straightened to my full height. "You're saying I killed the hill?"

"You absorbed its magic," Bautere offered, not in the least rattled, though I was about to utterly lose my mind.

Mertie leaned closer. "He's trying to be nice, but what he means is you killed it," she said softly.

No—this hill was taking back some of this magic. I didn't need this much, and I wasn't keeping it.

I slammed my hands down on the ground again.

He squatted beside me. "You can beat the ground all day and night for a year. It's not going to work."

I dropped down onto my ass in the snow, not caring about a wet, cold butt.

"Perhaps you were meant to have it? And that's why you can't put it back?" Bibbi said.

"I'm not meant for this. It's too much. This, what I have going on, it's too big for who I am. I'm not supposed to have this." I shook my head, wondering if Bautere was right. Was there really no way to put it back?

"Why do you say that?" Bautere asked, his eyes lit with curiosity.

Didn't he get it? It was so obvious.

"Because I know *me*. I'm Tippi."

He grunted. "I'm not sure *you* know you. I think you have an image of who you were, but that is no longer who you *are*."

"People don't change. I'm not cut out to have this much power. I'll mess it up." If I lived that long. Mertie and Bibbi could think I was crazy, but it wasn't a mouse and a bird. It was them, and they knew it too. I was a fraud. A swindler. I'd stolen all the magic, it wasn't mine to have, and I'd pay for the crime, along with those I loved.

"The people who don't want power are the only ones that are worthy of having it. It's those who thirst for it that should never get it. I think the magic is right where it's supposed to be," Bautere said.

I didn't bother arguing with him. He thought he was right. Mertie and Bibbi thought I was crazy. I was the only one who knew the truth.

"Would you care to come have some bark tea and warm up?" Bautere asked after a few minutes.

I got off my butt so I could resume a kneeling position. "Thanks, but I'm going to give it a few more tries."

"Suit yourself. You know how to get to my place if you change your mind," he said.

Bibbi and Mertie went back to gripping their sticks for dear life, angling for the best position.

I kept trying for another hour, until Hawk walked up between Mertie and Bibbi. He knelt beside me. He took in my position, my bent head and slumped shoulders.

"Are you ready to come home yet?" he asked.

"Yeah. I guess."

35

I was sitting in the back room when Hawk walked in.

"Mertie said Zurdoch is on his way over here."

I glanced at the counter. The vial with the potion I'd made had been sitting there for days, waiting to be claimed.

"I wasn't sure he'd be willing to come back after the last one."

Hawk picked up the vial, tilting it and examining the fluid. "From the looks of this one, he'll be happy he did."

He walked over, putting the vial on the table in between the couches as he took a seat.

"How did you know I couldn't put the magic back yesterday?" I asked. If he'd known there was a chance I could, he would've been at the hill much earlier. That should've been my first hint I was doomed to failure.

"A hunch." He stretched out his legs.

Did the man not have a single nerve in his body? He'd killed an angel. He should be wrapped as tight as a... The only comparison that I could think of was me. He should be as tense as I was.

"Does nothing bother you?" I asked, watching him crack his neck.

"Certain things," he said, and then smirked.

Before I could ferret out what those things were, there was a knock at the back door.

"Come in," Hawk said.

Zurdoch walked in. He shut the door behind him slowly and kept an eye on it even after he did, as if afraid he'd need to make a hasty exit.

Did he think this was a trap of some sort?

I got to my feet but didn't approach him. Instead I moved to Hawk's couch to give Zurdoch space.

"I'm sorry about the initial potion. I hope you believe me when I say it wasn't intentional."

He nodded. "Situations happen. Do you have the replacement?"

I pointed to the vial on the table. "Feel free to sample it."

He uncorked it and took a small sniff. The smell was hard to imitate with anything found naturally in nature. Back in Rest, I would've said it smelled like a strange mix of nail polish remover and floral body wash.

"It smells potent. You must be feeling better," he said, lifting a brow.

He'd clearly heard things, which was exactly what I was hoping for.

"She does," Hawk said.

Zurdoch glanced at Hawk, but his attention reverted to me quickly. He stared a little too hard for me to believe there wasn't talk of what was happening here.

Zurdoch sniffed the potion again before he said, "I have unfortunate news. There's no trace of anything left on the hill, so the options you were exploring there are no longer feasible."

He recorked the potion and placed it back on the table as if it were difficult.

"I know. I asked you here to see if you had other information to trade."

"What kind?"

"You know what happened? What I did?"

He hesitated for a few seconds before briskly nodding, as if averse to admitting he had any knowledge.

"Do you know if there are plans to rectify the situation and how?" I clasped my hands on my lap to stop them from fidgeting.

His eyes flicked from Hawk to me and then around the room before landing back on the vial.

"I've heard murmurs of things, that they aren't sure what they want to do about the situation, but that is all. I can't offer any real information."

I hadn't had much hope for answers, so the disappointment wasn't a huge letdown, and frustration was a feeling I was very familiar with.

"I'll be leaving now," Zurdoch said. He took a long look at the potion on the table before heading to the door.

"Zurdoch, take the potion. I have no use for it," I said.

His lips parted as his gaze returned to the vial. "Are you sure?"

"I am. Consider it a gift." I knew what it was like to want a different life. If I could help him, I would.

"Thank you. I won't forget this." He took the vial, nodding as he backed out of the room, as if I'd become some sort of royalty with that one act.

Hawk was silent.

"What? Do you think that was the wrong thing to do?" I could tell something was bothering him.

"No. I had something else I wanted to tell you." He locked gazes with me. "Have you ever heard of a witch named Giselle?"

"No. I don't think so. Why?"

"I've been tracking down some leads for a while. You need to go and talk to her. She might have some answers on how this all got started, with you having magic from the hill."

I'd watched his every nuance as he answered. He didn't fear heaven or hell, but some witch was making him unsettled?

"Who is she?"

"I have my suspicions, but it's better if you find out from her, because I'm not sure how accurate my information is. I only know that she might have answers for you."

I'd given up on answers about my origins a while ago, telling myself it was better to not know. Now here he was, dangling a carrot of information in front of me. Considering what was going on, my current predicament, could I afford to not go? Even if it was something bad, anything that might help unravel my situation might be good. I couldn't afford to let this opportunity go, even if I didn't want to know.

"I can take you to her or I can tell you how to get to her. It's your choice."

A month ago, it wouldn't have been a question. I would've gone by myself without a thought.

"Do you have the time to come?"

It was a big step, willingly letting him in this much, and each inch was making me edgy, like I shouldn't be doing this at all. I had no idea what this witch might reveal.

He paused, as if he knew exactly what I was offering him.

"I can take you this afternoon."

As soon as he agreed, it was like someone had hit the gas pedal on a straight path to a cliff. My heart kicked into overdrive, my hands grew sweaty, and my chest was tight.

"When we get there, though, what if she... Maybe I should talk to her alone."

"Don't you get it yet? I don't care what she says. It won't matter to me. But if you need more time, I'll wait outside."

I nodded, wanting to believe he wouldn't, and yet...

"Thanks."

36

For the next three hours, all I did was think about what Giselle would say, all the horrible things that might come out, and then imagine Hawk's horrified stare as he heard. No matter how many times I reminded myself that he wouldn't be with me when I spoke to her, it didn't matter.

What if he was close enough to overhear? He'd never want to speak to me again once he realized I was evil. I should've said I'd go alone. Asking now would make it so much worse than if I'd taken the offer in the first place.

Hawk walked through the office and looked my way before heading into the back room.

I got up, grabbing my jacket.

"Good luck," Zab said.

"She doesn't need luck. It'll be fine," Bibbi said.

Musso gave me a grunt. "You are who you are, kid. No one can change that." He went back to work, as if nothing important was about to happen.

Hawk was waiting for me in the back room.

"Are you ready?" he asked.

It would be so easy to say maybe we should wait, and then, in a week, right as he was walking out the door to some other appointment, ask him to scribble down directions. I could conceivably go another few years like that, at least a few months. I'd find out what happened, what kind of monster I was, and no one would be any the wiser but me.

But the truth has a way of working itself into the light of day. Sometimes it does stay hidden for weeks, months, even years, but then it shows its face. Everyone would see me for what I was. No. Whatever horrible things I had in me, I'd rather they come to the surface now.

Plus, I didn't have the time to wait. At any moment, the fruits of my labors at the hill would come back and poison me.

"I'm ready. Let's go." Or as ready as I could be.

The place was a good distance past the outskirts of town, beyond the tree line that would bring you into the mountains but where it was still sparse enough to build a small, cozy house, like the one before us. It made me think of the story of Hansel and Gretel.

Please don't let that be a sign.

"Whatever it is, it will be okay. It doesn't matter, not to me." Hawk gave my hand a squeeze before moving to lean against a large tree, settling in to wait.

I took a step toward the door and stopped. I turned back toward him, not knowing exactly what I was doing other than wanting him there with me. It was the strangest feeling. My entire life, I'd preferred to be alone, to not lean on anyone or anything. A lot had changed.

"I want you to come with me."

"Are you sure?" He straightened off the tree.

"No, but I want you there anyway. Whatever she says, we'll hear it together. I just hope…"

That she doesn't say I'm evil to the bone and run fast and hard away from me. I didn't say any of this, but the way he was looking at me, the way he was walking over slowly, as if I'd run, he must've read it on my face.

"I don't know how many more ways I can say it, but I'll keep on saying it until you believe me. There is nothing that she can tell us that will scare me."

"How can you say that when we don't know what we'll find out?" He couldn't make claims against the unknown, no matter how much I wished they were true.

He cupped my face, forcing me to look at him. "Because how you came to be, where you came from, it doesn't matter to me. It doesn't change anything. There is nothing I can find out from this woman that will make one bit of difference between us."

The door opened, and a woman who looked to be somewhere in her thirties, with jet-black hair and eyes the same shape as mine, stared at me. There was no doubt we were related. A young aunt, perhaps? A cousin?

"Are you two planning on coming in anytime soon or just lurking outside my door indefinitely?" She looked me over slowly, from the tip of my boots to my crazy hair. She nodded. "I've been waiting for you."

She left the door open and took a few steps inside.

Hawk put his hand to the small of my back, not urging me forward or doing anything other than lending me his support. I'd never had anything like what he'd offered in my life. I took a deep breath, mentally clinging to his promise that no matter what was said, it wouldn't change anything.

I glanced back at him again before I took another step.

"You know firsthand how stubborn I am. Do you really think I'll change my mind because of something this one says?" he asked.

That was a good point. He listened to no one.

I walked into the house, knowing who I was, hoping that wouldn't change drastically, that I wouldn't walk out shattered.

"You know who I am?" I asked the woman, who was something of a moving target as she fluttered around the kitchen. I wasn't sure if it was an idleness issue or she was dreading this conversation as much as I was, but I had a feeling it was the latter. That didn't bode well for my afternoon.

"Like I said, I've been waiting for you. I can offer you some tea, but I don't keep much else stocked."

Her lean form attested to the fact she probably didn't eat much.

"That would be nice. Thank you," I said.

Hawk waved off the offer.

We took a seat at her table, herbs hanging from the ceiling and baskets on the mantel filled with other dried plants I didn't recognize. This woman knew her way around potions from the looks of her supplies and the cauldrons lining her shelf. She put a storage store to shame with all the shapes and sizes of vials and containers.

I began to second-guess my acceptance of tea. At least Hawk had declined, so one of us might be able to fight our way out of here if I got poisoned.

"Why have you been waiting?" I asked, watching her lithe movements.

"I figured you would eventually find me and want to

know about your mother." She dropped a few herbs and cursed, her hands not the steadiest.

"You knew her?" I asked, even as I suspected a stronger relationship from the resemblance.

"I should think so, since I gave birth to her."

Birth? The woman didn't look much older than I was.

I shot a look at Hawk. He gave a shrug and a small nod, as if saying it were possible.

"You're my... Are you saying you're..."

She turned, forcing herself to stare at me, even though I had a creeping sensation she didn't want to.

"That's exactly what I'm saying. I gave birth to her. I don't particularly care for aging, and I'm quite handy at spells. Since I'm one of the lucky Infinites, I can do as I please with my magic." She walked over, bringing the pot of tea. "You didn't get everything from that hill. Some of it passed down the old-fashioned way."

I had a grandmother in Xest this entire time, who'd known about me? Why hadn't she come forward? She looked so young. Was she where I got my magic?

"Are you..." Typically you weren't supposed to ask a person how much magic they had. I mean, most people in Xest didn't even touch because it was a private thing. Could a Whimsy be an Infinite? Her presence had a heavier feel than a Whimsy, but could that be because she was an Infinite? How rare of a combination was that?

"I'm a strong Middling, if that's what you're looking to know. It's rare to be an Infinite Middling. Not a common combination," she said as she poured me tea.

I picked the cup up, looking to buy myself an excuse not to drink it, and then paused.

"It's not poisoned," she added, watching me hesitate.

I drank from embarrassment, and she moved back to her fire, placing the kettle back on the hook.

"I'm guessing you want to know about her. What happened? How you came to have the magic you have?" she said, pausing at the fireplace with her back to me.

"If you know, yes." Could it be that easy? After all this time? All I needed to do was come here and the answers would all be laid out?

"I know it all. I know *too* much. It's why I keep to myself and don't bother with people." She glanced my way and said, "Don't need to get that look. I won't hold back. Honestly, I was tired of waiting, knowing this day was going to come."

My intestines felt like they'd been knotted up and then anchored to the bottom of the abyss. I wanted to hurry her up, tell her to spit out all the sordid details. Hawk shifted closer to me, the subtlest of movements, but it helped ease the knotted tension in my gut.

"So, how did I come to have all this magic from the hill? Do you know?" I tracked her around the kitchen.

She was a flurry of motion, touching this and moving that, and then finally she stopped fussing. She stood still for a few seconds before walking over and dropping into the seat across from us.

She rested her hands on the worn wood of the table, running her finger over the ridges as her eyes got a faraway look.

"My Jossie, your mother, she was never..." She shook her head, as if she couldn't find the right word or just didn't want to use the one she'd found. "She was never quite right, if you know what I mean."

I stayed quiet, not sure if she wanted me to agree with her or not. My memories of my mother were clear enough to know exactly what she meant. Hearing it from someone else, it was nearly a relief that it hadn't been a child's delusion.

"As a mother, you always want to make everything right for your child. You want to fix all their problems. But the thing she was missing, I couldn't fix. I tried. In the end, I wasn't able to. I guess that's how all the trouble started in the first place. I've given it a lot of thought over the years, and instead of being straight with her, I kept trying to fix things I couldn't."

With each word, Giselle seemed to slump a little lower, look a little more her age. I was becoming more and more terrified to hear what she'd done to "fix" her daughter.

She took a deep breath, seeming to shake off a little of the trance she'd been falling into, and looked at me. "She was born a Whimsy, you see, and she blamed me. She hated me from the time she was old enough to realize I had more magic than she did. She resented me for having slept with a normal man, which *is* probably why she was born so much weaker. It diluted the blood, the magic. As a high Middling, with infinite magic, I had a lot of options. As a lower Whimsy, she didn't." She looked off into the distance again, and when she continued, it was as if she were talking to herself. "She was right to resent me. It was a stupid mistake on my part."

"You were in love?" I asked.

She scoffed and smiled, but her eyes were endless pools of regret. "No. It was a one-night stand with some lackluster human who wasn't even good in bed. I was drunk and partying in Rest. Back then, it was quite common for a few witches and warlocks to spring break over in Rest. It's frowned upon now, but it was the thing back then. I'd been back in Xest for a couple of months when I realized I was pregnant. I knew enough about potions that I could've done something to end it, but I wanted her and I was arrogant enough to think I had enough magic to make her at least a low-level Middling, even with the insult of regular blood in the mix." She ran her hands over the table again as she got the distant look. "I was wrong. It was quite a disappointment to us both, to be honest. I remember the first time I held her and she had this weak current of magic. I thought maybe it was because she was a baby. The midwife who'd helped me give birth told me that wasn't the case." She shrugged. "I accepted it and loved her anyway. I figured what she wasn't born with, I'd help her overcome with my spells and potions. I had enough for both of us."

Giselle shook her head. "No matter what I did to help her, the older she got, the more and more resentful she became.

"Finally, one day she ran away to the factory. Said she'd rather work to death than be taken care of. She shut me out completely. Wouldn't talk to me or acknowledge me at all."

Giselle stood and began moving about the kitchen again, as if she couldn't tell the story and stay still. She began mixing herbs into a caldron, not saying anything.

I glanced at Hawk, who shook his head, silently agreeing that we'd have to be patient. It was clear why she wouldn't want to talk about any of it.

She moved the caldron to the fireplace, using her spoon to mix the brew. After a few more minutes, she began to speak again. "One day, a couple of years later, she showed up on my doorstep saying I could do something to fix the wrong I'd done to her.

"She'd discovered a hill that gave some of the other Whimsy witches she knew more magic, but it wouldn't work for her. She needed me to help her." She stopped stirring, her head bent. "I would've done anything to help her, so I went there with her and felt the magic in the hill. It took me six moon cycles to come up with a potion that would work, but I finally did it."

She fell silent again, going back to her stirring.

Nothing was adding up. I hadn't remembered my mother doing anything magical.

"Did the potion work for her?"

Giselle turned to me, almost looking resentful that I was sitting there. "It did, but not the way it was supposed to. She was able to leech a lot of magic from the hill—it was *in* her. If I laid a hand on her flesh, I could feel it, that power all building there and boiling in her veins, but she couldn't use it. It was useless. It was like a potion in a vial that couldn't be opened. She was a vessel for it, but that vessel was sealed. It was like pouring gasoline into a container with no way for it to ignite. It didn't want to be in her."

Oh no. And now I knew. I could see the way she was looking at me now, as if she blamed me for robbing it from her daughter. This was why she'd never sought me out. She didn't want to know me.

She fell silent again, but my patience had run thin.

"What happened after that?" I asked, done with the kid gloves. This woman didn't owe me anything, but that didn't stop the burn of knowing that the only relative I had here didn't care about me at all. Had preferred to never know me.

"She was getting crazier by the day, and more and more paranoid that someone would know what she'd done at the hill. The way she was acting, it was probably true. She couldn't jump planes, so I jumped her over to Rest, settled her in a place. Your mother got one thing from me: she liked men a lot. Didn't discriminate at all about who she'd take in her bed. It wasn't a surprise that she got pregnant right away.

She turned, resting her back on her cabinet as she stared straight at me. "She said she was going to have the baby, who probably wouldn't have any magic at all, and that was just fine by her. She was done with witchery. She was going to live out the rest of her life as a normal person in Rest. When your real father didn't want to be bothered with you, she conned another man into believing you were his. They were going to go buy a little house and live happily ever after.

"Then you were born with all the magic she hadn't been able to wield. The magic chose you. Maybe it had always known you were coming. I don't know, but it was the last straw, unhinging her in some way. She blamed me. Said I'd done it somehow. Then she blamed you. Said that you'd stolen it from her and that you were evil. Next time I went to Rest to see her, she was gone. She'd moved you both somewhere." She waved her spoon in my direction. "I thought I'd never see either of you again. Then word spread of a witch from Rest who was more powerful than anyone else in Xest, and I knew it had to be you."

There was absolutely zero joy in that statement. She wished I'd died somewhere.

I stood. Hawk was up right beside me.

"Thank you for your time," I said. Having nothing left to say, I turned and headed for the door, with Hawk right behind me.

"I'll tell you one thing before you go. You'll never have

peace with that magic in you. None. They won't let you be, and you'll destroy everyone around you as you go down," she called out.

I kept walking as her words thudded like a hammer in my head.

37

W e didn't talk on the way back, but Hawk's eyes were on me the entire time. His energy was focused so intently that it was difficult to think beyond it. But I did anyway. I had to.

"She's a sick, unhappy woman. Don't let her get to you," he said as we walked into the back room of the broker building.

Zab and Bibbi were on the couch. Mertie was at the table. None of them asked how things had gone, probably because, from the looks of us, they didn't need to.

"She might be those things, but she also might be right." Giselle had voiced every fear I had. Hawk hadn't wanted to hear it, but he never did. It didn't change the truth.

Hawk looked at our company. "We need the room."

The place emptied in a few seconds. It immediately grew quiet, the din from the office disappearing as he soundproofed us.

Hawk's face was hard, mouth in a straight line. My

heartbeat kicked up, matching the pulsing vein in his neck.

All I wanted to do was wrap my arms around him and never let go. It was the exact reason I should leave. I didn't know what I was now, but I wasn't the same person I'd been. My staying could hurt him, might hurt everyone. Giselle was right. I couldn't take all of the magic from the hill and not face consequences. I was a ticking time bomb about to obliterate everything around me.

"That's it, isn't it? You think you're going to just pack up and leave?" He stared at me as if I were about to slice his heart out of his chest with a butter knife.

"It's not an easy decision." It was the hardest thing I'd contemplated in my life. The idea of him being hurt because of me was unimaginable.

"And where do you plan on going?" he asked, as if there wasn't another single place in Xest I could live that wasn't with him.

"Bautere might have a place he could lend me." Out in the middle of nowhere might be the only safe place for me. There, I'd be isolated. Heaven and hell could do their worst, and hopefully it would only befall me.

"You nearly froze to death in Bautere's place." He shook his head, giving me his back as he took a few steps away.

"I'm not the same person as I was then."

He stopped moving, standing stiller than humanly possible as he warred with our predicament.

I swallowed, forcing the tears not to fall. He'd get past this. I might not, but he would, and he'd be happy. Most importantly, he'd hopefully be alive. I'd find a way to settle the debt that he'd surely incurred killing Lou, and he'd live. That was all I could ask.

"I'm doing what I have to, the way you always do."

I went to leave, and he followed me, getting in my way.

I tried to move around him again, and again he blocked me. "This isn't a game to me."

He shook his head slightly, as if not believing what I was doing or saying. "And you think it is for me? Do you think any part of me takes the sight of you walking out that door as a joke? I've waited a very long time for you, and then wasted more time because I thought I was protecting you. This doesn't end with you walking out that door to protect me. I can protect myself."

He reached out to touch my neck.

I instantly backed up, afraid he'd feel the changes in me and be revolted.

"I don't want you to—"

I was slammed up against his chest, his hand at my throat, my pulse throbbing against his palm.

"You feel exactly the way you always felt to me, like that girl I touched in the shop at Rest that day, the one I took from the factory, the one who lay in my arms and couldn't be touched enough. You feel like perfection. You feel like home."

"You're making it harder for me to do what I know I have to do. You know I'm right."

"Then do what you think you have to." The ice in his voice cut deep.

He dropped the arm holding me to him, and it felt like he'd dropped the only thing holding my heart together. I had no delusions about how hard this would be, and yet I'd still underestimated it somehow.

With no excuse left, I backed away, feeling like every

step ground the shattered pieces of my heart into oblivion.

He was respecting my wishes and letting me leave, and I wasn't too proud to admit how dearly I hated it. I'd have to come back to say my goodbyes to everyone else. I couldn't do it now. I couldn't handle another minute here, or I'd never leave.

I went to the back door as Hawk watched, no longer trying to stop me.

I opened it, for maybe the last time, and then hit an invisible wall. I backed up, looked at the space, and then tried again, hitting it with my shoulder. I turned to where he stood, waiting.

"I thought you said you were letting me go?" I asked.

"I said I was letting you do what you had to do. I am also doing what I have to do." He stepped closer. "Do you want to leave?"

"I have to go." We both knew I didn't.

"That's not what I asked. Do you *want* to leave?"

"Of course not, but it doesn't matter." I threw my hands up. He was making something that felt impossible even worse.

"Then I'm not letting you go," Hawk said.

"If you don't care about yourself, what about them?" I said, pointing toward the office.

"I'll tell them to leave. If they stay, they'll be duly warned, and it's on them."

"You need to let me go. You'll find someone else." I could barely get that sentence out.

"I don't want anyone else." His voice was soft but carried more weight than anything he'd said thus far. I was running out of the strength to fight him.

I shook my head and turned back to the door, fairly

certain I could break through the obstacle he'd put up if I could bring myself to try. I just needed the will to do it. He wrapped his hand around mine, pulling me back to him and putting his hands on my waist to keep me there.

"I want you. If it takes a year before you understand, or a decade, then that's how long I'll fight. Because in the end, it's me and you. You're worth everything I have."

I couldn't fight him anymore. I didn't want to. He must've sensed me weakening, because he pulled me closer and kissed me like he'd never stop.

38

I got up from Hawk's bed, wishing he'd stay asleep. He did. I walked to his door, hoping it would open to the broker building, and it did.

I walked downstairs, and nothing creaked or groaned because I didn't want it to.

This time I couldn't ask for help. I couldn't bring Bibbi. Not even she would back me up with what I was going to do. I wouldn't speak to Helen. I couldn't talk to anyone. This one was all on me. This was my last chance to make things right, to save what I had, or I would have to leave. If I did leave, I'd do it in secrecy. I didn't have the strength to fight Hawk for something I didn't really want.

I walked and kept walking until I hit the edge of town, where the trees grew thick and the magic felt thicker. I pulled out a knife, dragging my coat open and tugging down my shirt. I dragged the blade over my chest, the same way I had the day I drew Dread into a trap.

This time I didn't need a spell. My magic was beyond having to speak the words. The only thing I said was to *them*, and they were listening. Their magic was swelling around me.

"If you want it back, take it. I don't want it. Just leave the people I love alone. Whatever the cost for this, it's on me."

My blood welled red before becoming iridescent and rising from my chest. I stood, letting it flow from me, offering it to them. This wasn't a bluff or a false offering. I'd die on this spot if it would save them, save Xest, save Hawk.

My magic bled out and circled me, creating a wreath, pulsating as if it were a creature of its own. It felt as if the forest and the trees—as if everything around me—were alive and watching.

A bird flapped its wings, coming to sit on an overhanging branch, watching me. A mouse scurried over, sitting at the base of the same tree.

"Take it. I offer it freely in exchange for the safety of the people I care about."

Fear filled me as I stood there, wondering if this was the moment I would die. Determination kept me rooted to the spot. If this bought them, him, a future, then it was worth my life.

My magic stopped flowing but stayed connected to the wreath of glowing energy around me, seeming to pulse with the very force of Xest itself. I lost track of how long I stood there, waiting for something to happen.

The bird flapped its wings, leaving. When I looked down, the mouse was already gone.

"What does this mean? Are you rejecting my offer?" I yelled to everything and nothing.

No one answered, not that I'd expected them to. They'd left. I was alive. Nothing had changed.

I glanced down. The cut on my chest had closed itself even as my magic pulsed in the air. I walked away and watched as it seemed to hover for a moment, before dispersing, almost cloudlike, to the north.

I crawled back into bed with Hawk a little while later, wondering how many more nights with him I'd get. How many I could risk before I'd have to sneak off in the dead of night and not return.

~

WE MUST TALK.

I SPRANG UP IN BED, knowing that I'd just heard Helen talking to me somehow, even though I was sleeping.

"What is it?" Hawk asked.

"I'm not sure. I think Helen is calling me." If this wasn't in my head, and I wasn't crazy, if Helen really wanted to talk, I wouldn't make her wait.

I threw on my sweater and padded barefoot downstairs, Hawk right behind me.

Helen's wheels and gears were grinding as soon as I was in front of her.

They have a message for you, she said, or didn't, really. The only sound was her usual gears.

The raven and the mouse, heaven and hell, God and the devil. This was it.

"What is it?" I asked.

"Do you understand her noises?" Hawk asked, staring at the machine and then me.

"Yes, but I don't know how." Or didn't I? It was the magic. We shared the same magic now. I was a part of Xest the way she was. Even now I could feel Xest's ebb and flow.

Helen's machinery kicked up again and then continued.

"What is she saying?" Hawk asked.

The frustration was written clearly on the lines of his face as he listened to what must sound like gibberish.

I stepped back until my desk was behind me, giving me something to lean on. When you heard something like this, it was a necessity. I gripped the edge as it sank in. Could it be true?

"Tippi, tell me what's going on."

I nodded as I finally let the tears fall.

"They didn't know what to do with me. They weren't sure what would happen if they killed—"

Hawk stepped closer. "Helen, you tell them that I will literally find a way to destroy both—"

"Hawk, they aren't going to kill me." The last thing I needed right now was him picking a fight with heaven and hell.

He turned and took in a deep breath, the cords on his neck strained, and I could feel the amount of control it was taking him to stand down. Hawk was a warrior at heart, and it took every ounce of control to fight the urge to do exactly what he was designed for. Go to war.

"What are they suggesting?"

"They offered a deal. It's over."

The machinery kicked up again as Helen continued talking, laying out all the details. I held up a hand, asking Hawk for a minute as Helen finished.

"They're going to leave me alone, but with a few stipulations. I can't ever leave Xest, not even for a few minutes.

From the way it was just explained, if I did, the magic here might go haywire. If I ever try, it'll be all-out war."

I'd never fit in anywhere else, so that was no loss. I'd miss the opportunity to ever see Rabbit again, but in truth, I had very little back there.

"What else?" he asked, like he expected the other shoe to drop.

"My magic is going to be the ebb and flow of Xest. I'm the new well of magic. Because I'm an Infinite, they think the issue of imbalances will stop. I'm the cure for the problems that were plaguing this place from the beginning."

"Will that hurt you?" he asked.

"No." I knew it, and so did they because of what I'd done last night. My attempt to hand over my magic had eased an area of imbalance. Hawk didn't need to know about that moment, not now, anyway. Maybe someday I'd tell him I tried to bleed out to save him, but we'd been on shaky footing for so long that he wouldn't be able to handle it. For now it would remain between them, Helen, and me.

"It's over. They said that their people will not be a problem, and no one else will be coming. Things will go back to normal. It's done." I slumped, all the tension of the last few months unloading suddenly until I couldn't keep it together anymore.

"Why are you crying?" Hawk asked, his hand on my cheek.

"Because it's over. No one will ever try to get rid of me. I'm home." I'd never have to leave. I'd never be called the nowhere witch, who didn't belong. I was part of this place.

I'd never have to leave Hawk. It was truly over.

"You've been home," he said as he crushed me to him.

39

Hawk leaned on the corner of my desk, watching me as I finished up some notes. When I took too long, he grabbed the book, shut it, and put it to the side. He tugged me up onto my feet and in between his legs, fitting me into his form.

"I really should finish that. I might forget it in the morning." I gave him my best chastising face, not that it ever worked on him.

"I don't think your boss cares," he said, smiling. "Or this boss, anyway."

"You keep forgetting that I work with you, not for you. I also have other employment, so you better be nice to me." Not that keeping Xest balanced had turned out to be much work.

He dipped his head to my neck, running his lips along the tendon. "I'm glad you're not technically my employee. I wouldn't want to be accused of sexual harassment."

"Is that even a thing in Xest?" I asked, arching to give him better access.

"I'm sure you'll make it one. I've heard about the union over at the wish factory."

There was laughter in his voice. Hawk and Marvin had never had any love between them. The worse I made it for Marvin, the more amused Hawk was.

"Someone had to help them." They hadn't even been getting paid before I stepped in. Now he had people actually applying to work there. Marvin might not realize it, but I'd done him a favor.

"What do you want to do for dinner?" Hawk asked, the way he did every night.

I stood, trying not to laugh at where this was going. "You know what I want to do for dinner."

He closed his eyes and then nodded. "If that's what you want, but it's going to cost you."

The shock that he'd stay and eat Bertha's health food line for me was finally wearing off. We were all still waiting for her to give up on the idea, but Bertha was nothing if not tenacious. And to give her credit, she might finally be getting the knack of healthier fare.

"Would it be so horrible if I wanted to take my woman out for dinner away from here for a night?" He brushed a few rainbow strands away from my face and then rubbed the locks between his fingers.

"There's still clients in here," I said softly, knowing we would again be the talk of Xest.

"I thought you'd realized already that I don't care who sees us."

He cupped the back of my head and moved his lips over mine. The same thing happened that always happened. I forgot about the rest of the room.

Someone made gagging noises in the background.

"Ugh. I can't believe you two. Do you never give it a break?" Mertie said, walking through the office.

I broke slightly away from Hawk, laughing.

Hawk didn't bother looking in her direction. "Didn't I see you in the alley with Zab last night, or am I wrong?"

She sucked in a breath. "I'd never..."

Her words trailed off as Hawk glanced over at her with a raised brow.

She stomped off across the room.

"Really?" I whispered.

"Really," he replied. "If you insist we stay, I'm going to go grab a couple of biscuits."

"I do insist."

"Don't forget it's going to cost you later."

It always cost me, and it was a price I was more than willing to pay.

"I'm going to go do my thing, but I'll be back soon."

With a last kiss, Hawk left me. Mertie was standing across the room, and I couldn't stop myself.

"Really? You and Zab?" I asked.

She let some steam out of her nose. "It was just a quick nothing."

"Okay. But if it wasn't, it might be nice for you."

"It was nothing. Where'd your worse half go?"

"To fill up before dinner."

"Smart man. Well, sometimes. Are you ever going to tell him he never actually kept you here? You chose to stay? Because we both know he couldn't stop you at this point." She rolled her eyes as if she couldn't fathom how anyone would think differently.

"Probably, at some point, but I like to let him think he has some control. It makes him feel better to think I can't run out on him at any second."

"Oh, I don't think you're capable of that, no matter how much magic you might have. You're as stuck as he is, the way I see it." The very rare Mertie laugh made its appearance.

Bibbi walked over, leaning on the desk near us, having been listening in. "Oh, maybe worse."

"Well, time to make my rounds," I said, grabbing my jacket.

"Can I come? I've been dying to see how this works."

"Sure, but I told you, it's boring."

She barely heard me in her rush to get her coat.

We headed out the front door, and I stopped to get my bearings, letting the ebb and flow sink in. It didn't take more than a second to feel it. I tilted my head toward the right, and we began walking.

"What do you do, exactly?" Bibbi asked, looking about like some visible miracle was about to take place.

"I'm doing it," I said.

"Right now?" she asked, examining me from boot to hat.

"Yep. There's a patch of magic in this area that's too much. I'm absorbing the excess. Further down the way, someone just got pregnant. As I pass, I'll release magic in that direction. The baby will take what it needs, and then that'll be it for the night."

"So that's it?" She sounded like she'd ordered a caramel latte and gotten a cup of plain black coffee.

"Yeah. I told you it's not that exciting."

When I first started, I'd thought there would be more to it as well. And then I'd realized there was just as much involvement as I wanted. I didn't want to tinker in people's lives or mess with the way Xest was. It was already perfect.

Keeping it that way was the best ability I'd ever been granted.

We continued to walk for a little while, and all the time Bibbi would sneak peeks, as if there had to be something more interesting she was missing.

By the time we were heading back to the broker building, she'd given up, looking like a tired puppy who was ready for a nap.

"So what's going on with you and Oscar? Have you given in yet?" Oscar had been trying to get Bibbi to commit for the last month. We'd all assumed Oscar would break her heart. I'd never thought it would be the other way around, but that was life, I guess. Sometimes the impossible happens.

"No. I'm still thinking about it. I don't feel like I've lived my life enough yet to settle down. In retrospect, I probably wouldn't have gotten involved with him if I knew he was going to get so serious."

We walked back into the office, and my impossibility was standing there. How I'd finagled this man into loving me was beyond comprehension, but I'd stopped doubting it. Now I took everything I could get.

Hawk slung an arm around me, pulling me into his side like it was old hat for us. It didn't matter how often we touched. My heart would still race at his nearness, the heat in his eyes, the warmth of him beside me.

"That was fast." Hawk had a gleam in his eye that matched my own.

"Yes. Everything was pretty much in balance."

"Then we've got a couple of minutes before dinner." He moved toward the stairs, tugging me after him.

"Hang on one second," I said, resisting. I'd never wanted to tinker, except for one rare occasion.

I turned to where Bibbi was tidying up some slips from the workday.

Could I do it? Did I have any maneuverability in that department? No one said I *couldn't*.

I let the tendrils of my magic, the ones that seemed to feel everything alive in Xest, reach out and wrap around Bibbi, giving a slight push in her direction.

She straightened, her eyes narrowing as if she'd felt something but couldn't quite figure out what. She shrugged and went back to getting her table in order.

"What did you just do?" Hawk whispered as I turned back to him.

"Not sure. Maybe something. Maybe nothing."

"Are you done?" He wrapped his arm around me, pulling me up against him.

"With her I am. With you? Never."

"Good thing, because I'm never letting you go."

I laughed softly, deciding this wasn't the right time to break it to him that I *could* leave. Maybe next year. Maybe not.

Use this QR code to sign up for new release notices from Donna Augustine. Don't worry! I won't flood your email box. You're more likely to wonder if you signed up correctly. Two emails in one month is my record.

Or, follow me on one of these platforms:
https://www.facebook.com/groups/223180598486878/
http://www.donnaaugustine.com
https://www.bookbub.com/authors/donna-augustine
https://twitter.com/DonnAugustine

ACKNOWLEDGMENTS

Donna Z., Lisa A., Camilla J., Lori H. and Ashleigh M., it would be impossible to find a better group of people. Instead of enjoying a book, you read my stories with a critical eye that makes the product better for everyone else. You each bring something unique to the table and none of my stories would be the same without you. Thank you for all your hard work!

ALSO BY DONNA AUGUSTINE

Ollie Wit

A Step into the Dark

Walking in the Dark

Kissed by the Dark

The Keepers

The Keepers

Keepers and Killers

Shattered

Redemption

Karma

Karma

Jinxed

Fated

Dead Ink

The Wilds

The Wilds

The Hunt

The Dead

The Magic

Born Wild (Wilds Spinoff)

Wild One

Savage One

Wyrd Blood

Wyrd Blood

Full Blood

Blood Binds